# *Budapest Romance*

## ROZSA GASTON

ISBN: 1480140635
ISBN 13: 9781480140639

Cover photo of decorated arch, Gellért Spa Baths, Budapest, by Kasuba Gyorgy

Back cover photo of Széchenyi Spa Baths, Budapest, by Rozsa Gaston

Praise for
*Budapest Romance*

"*Budapest Romance* is another delicious page turner from the talented Rozsa Gaston. Prepare yourself to be swept away by a romance as heated as the luxurious thermal baths of exotic Budapest."

—Jamie Cat Callan, author of *French Women Don't Sleep Alone, Bonjour Happiness!* and *Ooh La La!*

"A wonderful foreign romance that will stand the test of time."

—InD'tale Magazine

"You will not want Rozsa Gaston's elegant and atmospheric *Budapest Romance* to end. This inspiring journey is a haunting story of true love that is all at once simple, beautiful, universal and loaded with heart. You will fall in love with the characters and get lost in the old time elegance of journeying to the romance of Budapest. As delicate as the snowflakes falling upon the majestic baths of Budapest, the fleeting beauty of *Budapest Romance* is arresting and to be savored."

—Romy Nordlinger, actress, *All My Children, One Life to Live*

"A fascinating excursion to modern Hungary through the eyes of two very appealing characters who meet and fall in love in that famous old city."

—Leslie Ficcaglia, Painter, Leslie's Portraits

For Billy,
the boy I didn't know but would have liked to.
So glad I met the man.

CHAPTER ONE

# HELLO

HOW COULD SHE not notice being noticed? Floating in a thermal bath pool at a spa hotel in Budapest, Kati discreetly eyed the rugged blond man lounging in the next pool.

He had glanced in her direction several times over the past two days.

She was mourning the death of her father the month before, and was in no shape to be looking at the opposite sex. But the man's shaggy, blond hair had caught her eye that first evening in the pools; it had wandered down over his shoulders and powerful chest as well. Béla Dunai would have forgiven her, she knew.

At that moment, the man lifted his head and looked directly at her. Immediately, she pretended to be studying the clock on the wall behind him. She hoped he was too far away to notice the blush that had sprung onto her face. She wanted to pass for a sophisticated European woman while in Hungary. But here she was, blushing like a schoolgirl at a strange man, having forgotten completely about her father's passing for a brief moment.

The next evening at the baths, Kati made a point of keeping a cool expression on her face as she surveyed the room.

The blond man was there again. Careful not to glance in his direction, she obliquely noted he was near a group of men playing chess in the water. He sat at the side of the pool, idly swinging his legs while watching their game. Her eyes flicked over his legs; oak tree trunks came to mind.

Pretending not to have seen him, she stared dreamily in the other direction. Did she sense the blond man's eyes upon her? Arching her neck, she jutted her chin out, hoping it made her look more like her favorite movie actress, Audrey Hepburn.

She wanted to know if he was watching her. Again pretending to look at the clock on the wall behind him, she arched her eyebrows as if realizing she had an important appointment. She didn't.

The man looked directly at her.

Kati completely lost her nerve. Summoning the remains of her composure, she rose slowly from the pool and disappeared into the women's locker room. How could she maintain a dignified mourning posture when she was being distracted by a blond bear of a man?

Upstairs in her room, she felt restless. Her body warmed by the thermal baths, she went out on her balcony where the cold night air pinched her. Something else did too. Her father's spirit nudged her at the railing.

*Who are you kidding, little daughter? You may be mourning my loss, but there's someone with eyes on you now who wants to get to know you. Let him.*

*Dad, I'm here to wrap up your affairs. Not meet a man. It's completely inappropriate.*

*Let life happen to you, Katika. Don't run from it. Once, long ago, I couldn't help noticing your mother. Thanks to her noticing me back, here you are.*

Kati fled inside and got into bed. That night, she dreamt about a golden bear stalking her in the woods. She'd run away from the bear—slowly. Then, she let him catch her. Instead of eating her, he'd kissed her, thoroughly. It was a long dream. When she woke up the next morning, she felt refreshed, with a plan.

On the following evening, Kati eased herself into the middle of the three large pools in the bath hall and closed her eyes. Instantly, her dream of the night before returned. When she opened her eyes, she looked in the direction of the clock. Directly under it the blond stranger caught her gaze.

She gasped. Then she tossed back her hair.

Out of the corner of her eye, she watched as he climbed out of the water and shook himself off like an enormous golden retriever. She turned her head away, unable to keep from smiling at the image.

Next thing she knew, he was at the side of the pool next to her. He crouched, resting muscular arms on well-formed, golden-haired knees.

"Hi. I saw you from the other pool. I'm Jan." He pronounced it 'Yahn.' "From Holland," he added.

She turned to face him. Blue green eyes gazed at her, direct and unwavering. Her body flooded with warmth. She willed herself not to blush.

"Hello," she said guardedly.

"I don't want to bother you, but I couldn't help notice you. Do you speak English?"

"Sometimes," she replied, smiling slyly, but not showing her teeth. Why should she dazzle a total stranger with the wonders of American dentistry?

"Great. What do you speak at other times?" He was quick on the uptake, even if English wasn't his mother tongue.

"It depends. When I'm in the mood, I speak English, when I'm not, I don't speak at all," she said playfully.

"Ahh, you're an American." He beamed, his wide smile revealing equally impressive Dutch dentistry. "From where?"

"I'm from New York," she told him.

"Everyone says New York is wonderful. I've never been there. What brings you to Budapest?"

"That's a long story." She paused. How much to offer, how much to hold back? "What it comes down to is, my father died, and I'm here to wrap up his affairs."

The man's face crinkled. "I'm sorry. What do you mean by wrapping up his affairs?"

"I mean he was Hungarian and I'm here settling his estate."

"You are a good daughter."

"Thank you. I didn't know my father very well; I was raised by my mother's parents." *Why am I mentioning this to a complete stranger?* There was something about the Dutchman's open smile that made her feel safe.

"Was your mother American?" Jan asked.

"Yes. She was *very* American. And my father was *very* Hungarian. I understood my father even less than my mother did and she didn't understand him at all." She could feel the corners of her mouth curve up into a small smile. It was the same one that always formed when she thought of her parents together.

"But she understood enough to fall in love with him." His expression was grave, like a math professor studying an equation.

"How did you know?"

"You look like the daughter of a mother and father who were deeply in love."

"That's an original compliment." She was impressed. The man might look like a bear, but he possessed subtlety. "Thank you, although I have no idea what you mean."

"I'll be honest." The Dutchman's eyes twinkled. "I have no idea what I mean either."

"Thanks for your honesty," she laughed.

"May I ask your name?" he asked.

"Kati," she offered.

"Kati," he repeated after her. "Kati," he said again, looking down at her in the warm pool. "Would you like to—?"

The P.A. system crackled. A booming male voice broke the tranquility of the bathing area. "Kati Dunai, please come to the reception desk. Kati Dunai, come to the reception desk in the hotel lobby now."

She looked at Jan, startled. Very few people knew she was here.

"I have to go," she said.

"Will you be back later?" Jan asked.

"No. I mean, I don't know. Probably not." She hurriedly moved toward the ladder to exit the pool. Why would anyone page her?

"I enjoyed talking with you."

"Me too. I'll see you around, I'm sure," she said distractedly as she climbed the ladder, searching for her robe.

"I'll be here in the pools tomorrow around this time. I hope I'll see you then."

"I have to go now. Goodbye," she threw back over her shoulder as she hurried to the women's locker room.

Upstairs at the hotel reception desk, a clerk handed her an envelope. Tearing it open, she found an urgent message from the only person she knew in Budapest.

Krisztof Nagy had been at Columbia Business School when Kati had been an undergraduate. She had met him at an alumni relations gathering years earlier and stayed loosely in touch via e-mail. They had both recognized the value of having a contact in each other: he for business reasons as at that time she worked for a large Wall Street firm, and she for personal ones, knowing she intended to visit her father's country one day, and knew no one in its capital city.

He was now helping her get through the maze of paperwork and official forms connected with the retrieval of her late father's pension. Krisztof had been a practical source of information for her, as well as an invaluable translator. She, in turn, had provided him with contact information for U.S. private equity and venture capital investors. He was in the midst of buying privatized companies in Hungary which had previously been government-owned.

The message read, "Kati—Call me right away. Plans have changed.—Krisztof."

She hurried to her room and dialed his number.

Krisztof picked up after two rings. "Kati, something has come up. I have to go to Vienna on Thursday on business. We should meet tomorrow instead of later this week, so I can give you the information you need for your Friday appointment at the pension office."

"Thanks for letting me know. I had planned to visit some museums tomorrow, so I'll go later in the week instead. When and where do you want to meet?"

"Can you meet me at Café Gerbeaud around eleven tomorrow morning? I've got your paperwork translated, and I can advise you on where to get it notarized. If I have time, maybe we can go together."

"That's great, where's Café Gerbeaud?" she asked, recognizing the name of Budapest's most elegant café from the tourist guides she'd read. Krisztof had exceptional taste.

"It's on Vorosmarty Ter, in the center of Pest. Take a cab from your hotel. The driver will know where it is. You could walk there too, but it would take you about thirty minutes; you might get lost."

"Thanks, Krisztof. See you tomorrow around eleven." She was fortunate to have her friend's help navigating the maze of her father's affairs. She only wished that Krisztof's own were going so well. He'd told her the evening of her arrival that his wife had divorced him in the past year.

THE NEXT MORNING at quarter to eleven, Kati asked the bellhop to hail her a cab for Vorosmarty Ter. Carrying her red leather Madison Avenue briefcase, she jumped in the taxi and rolled down the window to release the stale cigarette smoke lingering in the back seat.

Hungary was a country with social customs not enjoyed in America, both good and bad. She loved the fact that dogs were allowed just about anywhere—restaurants, airports, cafés, boutiques. A shot of pálinka, Hungary's fiery plum brandy, with your mid-morning coffee? Why not? Cigarette smoking was also allowed almost everywhere, which didn't please her as much.

As she stuck her head out the window to gulp in some fresh air, a tall man with broad shoulders strode along the sidewalk ahead of her. He walked purposefully, a leather backpack on his back. A frisson ran down her arm as she recognized the Dutchman from the night before.

As the cab passed, Kati quickly put her head back inside, but Jan had caught sight of her. His face crinkled into a broad grin and he raised his hand in a wave. She nodded in greeting, then turned, focusing on her meeting with Krisztof.

Within minutes she was at the entrance to Café Gerbeaud, in the heart of Budapest. She entered its gold leaf, double French doors and looked for her friend. Dazzled by the elegant interior, with its Romanesque arches and marble countertops, she finally spotted him, seated by the window at a green marble-topped bistro table, with a sunbeam illuminating his face.

She studied Krisztof for a moment. His brown hair was fashionably cut, his trim figure elegant in a charcoal gray Italian suit. He was a dashingly handsome man of about forty, but somehow the dash had gone out of his dashingness. The sunbeam playing on his face betrayed a tiredness and blankness that seemed out of place for the successful venture capitalist he was.

She shook off her thoughts and hurried toward him.

"Good morning," she greeted him. "I'm glad you chose this place to meet. It's stunning."

"Wait till you try their hot chocolate. You'll forget all about the decor." Krisztof rose, taking her hand and kissing it as she sat down.

She loved the traditional courtliness of many Hungarian customs. Gestures such as hand kissing had caused her Hungarian father to cast a spell on her American mother soon after they had met. Kati could see why.

"I've got the papers here for your Friday meeting at the pension bureau," he continued. "They've all been translated, but you'll need to sign them in front of a special kind of notary for government documents. Here's the name and address of one I know near here."

"Will you come with me?"

"I'm not sure. My office will call in the next twenty minutes to let me know if I have to take a potential investor to lunch. It all depends on whether he's on the eleven A.M. flight from Milan. If not, I can take you. You've got everything you need right here, in any case."

"You've been so helpful. Thank you."

Krisztof had arranged for hours of translation work to be done for her. He'd obtained necessary forms to retrieve her father's pension and had them filled out in Hungarian, none of which she would have been able to do on her own. He was amazing. Why was she not feeling amazed?

Perhaps it was because Krisztof's every move was subjected to the vicissitudes of his business. His clients were wealthy, international people interested in buying newly privatized factories in Hungary. They were making him a rich man. As a result, his every day hinged upon their schedules or whims.

Kati knew plenty about working for the upper one per cent. She had worked as a temp in New York in the private client services division of one of Wall Street's most prestigious firms. Monied people reserved the right to change their minds anytime they felt like it. Anyone who worked for them or handled their assets catered to their whims or risked losing their business.

She wouldn't like being involved with a man who needed to check his voicemail messages or call his office every ten minutes. She bet his ex-wife hadn't liked it either. She watched as Krisztof checked his messages on his cell phone. It should have been exciting to be in the company of an international financier in Budapest's most elegant café. Why then did she feel bored? While he retrieved his messages, her mind wandered.

Jan's face floated before her. Her body tingled as she thought of his promise that he would be at the pool after six that evening. Waiting for her.

She would conclude her business with the notary today, do some shopping to bring back presents to family members and friends who had helped her get through the last year and a half of her father's illness, and then perhaps wander down to the pool around six. Perhaps.

"Kati," Krisztof's voice sliced into her thoughts. "Did you hear me?"

"Sorry. What did you say?"

"I said when they ask you at the pension bureau how you'd like the transaction to be processed, tell them you want an interbank transfer. This means they'll transfer the funds directly into your bank account in New York. You won't have to worry about carrying a lot of cash on you and you'll get a better exchange rate."

"Thanks, Krisztof, I'll do that."

"Now tell me what you were thinking about. Have you met a handsome foreigner here?" He was only teasing, but he could have been psychic at that moment.

"I—I—" Kati tried to hide her blush by taking a sip of the delicious hot chocolate.

Krisztof's cell phone rang. He held up one finger as he reached to answer it.

Kati felt an irrational urge to slap down his hand. "Be here now" had been one of her father's favorite expressions. How right he had been.

"Hello ... Yes, it's me ... He did? ... Where is he now? ... Okay ... Okay ... 12:30 at Gundel's, yes." Kati recognized the name of one of Budapest's finest restaurants. Krisztof had taken her there the night she'd arrived, one week earlier. "Have the reservations been made? ... Good, I'll be there." He ended the call.

Kati had composed herself and was looking out the window. Now she turned to Krisztof, giving him a tight smile. Indeed she had met a handsome foreigner, but she decided not to share this information with her businessman friend at this moment. There was no story to tell, as of yet; what there was she preferred to keep to herself.

"I've got to meet my Milan contact. He's here and I need to close this deal today while I've got his attention. I'm sorry, Kati. Do you think you'll be able to find the notary by yourself?"

"No problem, Krisztof." She shook her head. "I'll be fine. Just draw me a map of how to get there." She handed him a paper napkin.

Krisztof took out an elegant black and gold fountain pen and bent over the napkin.

Kati frowned. Wealthy people seemed more distractible than the rest of the population. They appeared to spend most of their time talking on the phone to their assistants or flying internationally. They were very much in demand. But did it leave them any quality time to spend with those they most cared about? Maybe that was the key. They ended up caring most about business, and after awhile most of their relationships became business ones instead of personal ones.

Krisztof would attract a girlfriend sooner or later, but Kati would not be that woman. She was returning to New York in less than one week and she was focused on retrieving her father's pension and enjoying herself in Budapest while waiting for the process to be completed.

Her mind wandered to the evening before. The Dutchman had gazed at her so intently while they talked about their fathers. She had enjoyed both the conversation and Jan's attentiveness, so different from time spent with the man sitting across from her now.

Krisztof finished his hand-drawn map as Kati took a final sip of hot chocolate.

"You cross Vorosmarty Ter once you leave here, then take a left onto Vaçi Utça, the big shopping street," he explained. "About three blocks down you'll find a small side street that ends in a dead end. It's called Ferenç Marthy Place. When you get to the dead end, you'll see an office plaza. Go into it and walk across the inner courtyard. The notary is in the far corner, diagonal to where you'll enter. Her office sign will say Ungvary Ilona. Remember, surnames come first in Hungary."

"Thank you, Krisztof. Will she speak any English?"

"It depends on her age."

Kati knew that older Hungarians usually spoke German as a second language. Younger ones learned English. Ones in the middle had been required to learn Russian; no one spoke it on principle.

"She may not, so let me write a note so she knows what you need." He scribbled some words on a second napkin, and taking out a business card, handed them both to her. "This explains what you need done. If she has any questions, have her call my assistant Zsuzsanna. She's used her herself, so they know each other."

"You've taken care of everything, Krisztof. Have a good lunch with your client and I hope your deal goes through."

"Thank you. And don't forget one more thing."

"What's that?" she asked.

"Do some shopping on the Vaçi Utça on your way back. It's the best shopping street in Budapest. You'll find things from all over the world."

"What if I want to find Hungarian things?"

Kristztof made a sour face. "If you must, then go to the government tourist store on the corner of Vaçi Utça and Petofi Sandor Square. They've got a bunch of tablecloths and folk items. Don't spend too much time there. It's a big waste of money. Check out the boutiques on the Vaçi Utça to see what young Hungarian designers are making these days." He peered at her slyly, his eyelids lowered. "Plus you might meet a handsome, wealthy man."

She blushed.

"If you haven't already," he added, clearing his throat. They rose from the table and kissing her hand, Krisztof then hurried off to his lunch meeting.

It turned out that Ilona Ungvary spoke English and was very good friends with Krisztof's assistant. Kati got her papers notarized without a hitch and spent the rest of the day shopping on the elegant Vaçi Utça, Budapest's version of Madison Avenue.

BY THE TIME she got back to her hotel it was shortly after six. She had had a full day, but her senses told her the fullest part was about to come. She hurried up to her room where she put on her black bikini, bundled her terrycloth bathrobe around her then headed down to the pools and extensive spa complex one floor below the hotel lobby.

Her time with Krisztof had been fruitful, but his distracted air had left her questioning her own goals. Was it possible that having everything money could buy wasn't exactly what it was cracked up to be? Krisztof was wealthy, successful, good looking and sophisticated. Yet he'd lost his wife somewhere along the way to building his business empire.

Musing over why Krisztof always seemed to be two places at once when they spent time together, she entered the pool area. Slowly, she lowered herself into the warm, bubbling water of the Jacuzzi pool. Part of her friend was in the here and now, and part of him was somewhere else, trying to find something he'd lost. Although he'd done a wealth of favors for her in helping to expedite her father's affairs, she didn't feel fully engaged when she was in his company.

Her father, on the other hand, had always been right there in the moment with her when they spent time together, looking directly into her eyes and appearing deeply interested in whatever she might say. Although they had only shared brief times together, he had given her the framework of what she looked for in a man. It was the ability to give her all of his attention, in a way that made her feel esteemed.

*Look up* an inner voice commanded. She raised her head, keeping her expression blasé, in the best tradition of expectant, attractive women everywhere. As she pretended not to notice, the blond Dutchman strode into the spa area, searching from pool to pool. Was he looking for her, or was he looking for some other pretty foreigner he might have engaged in conversation over the past few days?

In less than a minute, she had her answer. His tall frame towered over her, as he greeted her in the bubbling water.

"Kati, I'm so glad you're here. May I join you?"

"Hello Jan." She gave him a small smile. "I suppose so. Please remember I'm in mourning." She didn't know why the warning had slipped from her lips, but it had to do with reminding herself as much as the man before her of this fact, even though her heart had leapt the instant he appeared.

"I'll remember." Jan didn't take his eyes from her face for a second, despite the mild rebuke. "I'd like to hear more about your father." Easing himself into the Jacuzzi he let out a satisfied sigh that echoed the way she had felt moments before when she had descended into the warm, bubbling waters.

Kati hid her face behind her long hair as she studied him. At that moment, she couldn't think of anything to say. She was glad he'd asked to hear about something other than herself. She couldn't handle the intensity of a strange man asking her personal questions at that moment.

She really was in mourning, although this state was confusing to her with regards to her father. She had not known Béla Dunai well and hardly knew how to assess her feelings about his loss. She had traveled to Budapest for obvious reasons, as she'd stated to Jan. But there were less obvious ones as well.

She wanted to learn more about her father—where he had come from, what kind of culture he had grown up in. She was a woman with half-Hungarian blood running through her veins, but having been raised by New England Congregationalist grandparents, she hadn't a clue as to what this meant. She was here in Budapest partly to find out.

"My father was a Transylvanian poet," she finally said, her voice low.

"Your father was a poet? That is something very special."

"Yes, I've heard from people who read his works that his writing was special. He wrote about Transylvania in particular."

"Have you not read his works yourself?"

"No," she sighed. "I don't speak Hungarian. His books haven't been translated. I've had a few of his poems explained to me; I liked them."

"Tell me about one." The Dutchman seemed genuinely interested.

She was glad he wanted to hear about her father. She wanted to talk about this important man in her life who had largely been an enigma to her. She cleared her throat and gazed into a private space in front of her.

"There's a moth that thinks he's a butterfly," she began. "He's very proud of the way he dances. Every night he dances closer and closer to the electric light bulb on the back porch where he lives. Finally, one night he dances too close to the light and is fatally burned. As he is dying, his body floats slowly to the ground and he thinks, 'I was beautiful and all the other moths enjoyed watching me dance. I have succeeded in my life.' Then he dies, happy."

"Is that a poem about Transylvania or a poem about your father?" Jan asked.

Kati looked at him, bemused. She didn't know enough about either to answer.

"I don't know. But that's a good question." She paused then inspiration struck. "Tell me about your father."

She liked floating in the warm water next to this ruddy blond Dutchman talking about topics that were safe but important. It almost took her mind off the sheer, vital maleness of him.

Almost.

She scolded herself that being in mourning and being attracted to a person she had just met were not appropriate feelings to have at the same time. Then her father's laughing face flashed into her mind.

*Kati, love and death are not incompatible. They're flip sides of the same coin. When you toss the coin, sometimes you get heads, sometimes tails. Flip the coin,* he would have said.

"My father?" Jan looked surprised. "My father died when I was a boy. I don't know much about him. What do you want to know?" His blue green eyes sparked as he studied her.

"What was his favorite color?" she asked.

"You'll be surprised. It was black. My mother used to tease him when he said he liked black best. She said it wasn't really a color."

She laughed softly. "I can't believe your mother said that. I used to tell my father the same thing," she exclaimed. "My father would always agree, but say 'Kati, there is one exception. Black is not a color, unless it's worn by a blonde.'"

They looked at each other's bathing suits. Both wore black.

She had chosen the black bikini in the hotel spa gift shop to observe the mourning period for her father. Or had it been because she knew it would complement her blonde hair and green eyes? She sighed, knowing her father would have not only forgiven her such mixed motives, but highly approved. He was that kind of man.

Apparently the man next to her approved as well. His appreciative smile showed it, his eyes creasing at the corners. Her father would have encouraged her to allow Jan to approach her. She herself would not have been born, if it hadn't been for her mother allowing her father into her life. She closed her eyes and smiled to herself. She had a feeling Jan would invite her out in the next thirty seconds.

It took five.

"Kati, would you join me for dinner? It's getting late. Maybe you're hungry?"

"Umm, thank you, but I've already made plans. Perhaps we'll see each other here tomorrow." She had no dinner plans, but she didn't want to seem too eager.

"Tomorrow I'm visiting the Market Hall." His eyes gleamed as he gazed at her. "It's only open twice a week, and it's really something special. Would you like to come?" He looked out over the pool, scanning the crowd, giving her a moment to herself while she thought.

"Why is it so special?" she asked, her curiosity piqued. She had heard about the Budapest Market Hall, but had hesitated to venture there alone.

"It's special because it's where the local people shop. You won't find tourists there, unless they're like me—or maybe you." He smiled. "It's noisy and crowded. Very colorful. Would you like to see it?"

"It sounds interesting. I need to do some things tomorrow, but ..." She shot him an assessing glance. "What time are you going?"

"How about if I meet you in the hotel lobby at one P.M.?" he suggested.

"I'm not sure." Was it a good idea to spend an afternoon with a total stranger, however attractive, when she knew she was returning to New York in a matter of days? Was it safe?

*What is safe? Is living your life fully safe? Take a chance.* Her father's voice laughed at her again.

No wonder her maternal grandparents hadn't liked Béla Dunai the moment they laid eyes on him.

"Okay, Kati. This is what I'll do. I'll be in the hotel lobby at one. If you're there, you're there. If not, maybe I'll see you in the pool tomorrow evening around this time." If nothing else, Jan was persistent.

She nodded, saying nothing. He'd tossed the ball into her court, where she could decide what to do with it next. It was a clever move.

Kati needed time and space when it came to men. Jan was giving her both. But her plane ticket back to New York in less than a week wasn't. Whatever she chose to do the next day at one, it would be her decision, not his.

Back in her room, Kati opened the door to the balcony and stepped out into the November night. The crisp air stung her face in sharp contrast to the steam and warmth of the past few hours in the pools. Her mood was buoyant. Jan's persistent yet non-insistent approach had piqued her interest further. He had not tried to force an answer from her, but had simply told her where he would be if she wished to join him.

She sighed. There was nothing like an attractive man who knew how to make his interest known to a woman and then step back. Usually, when a man got too close to her, she felt as if she couldn't breathe. All she could do was protect herself and back off. But Jan had stepped back and given her feelings room to flower. He had horse sense, her New England grandmother would have said.

She looked up at the night sky and spoke to her father. *I'm me, Dad, not you. And I'm not just your daughter, I'm mom's daughter too. They called her ancestors Puritans for a reason. I've made up my mind about tomorrow, so be my guardian angel and stop laughing at me every time I hesitate.*

She bid goodnight to the twinkling stars, one of which she knew was her father winking at her, then went back inside and climbed into bed. As she drifted off to sleep her final thought was that she knew where she would be at one o'clock the following day.

CHAPTER TWO

# THE MARKET HALL

JAN WOKE EARLY. Images of the golden skin and expressive mouth of the American woman he had spoken with at the pool for the past two evenings had refreshed his sleep.

It had been three years since his divorce and the face of his ex-wife was beginning to slip away from him. The remote and disappointed expression that had carved itself onto her face after the motorcycle accident five years ago had haunted him long after she'd left him.

She had not been able to forgive her husband for having their son on the back of the bike at the time of the accident. He had begged her forgiveness again and again but she had only turned away in terrible silence. When the time came that she told him she was leaving with their son, his only regret was the loss of Dirk's presence in his house. He had lost his wife's companionship years earlier.

Jan was in Budapest under doctor's orders. Since the accident, he'd suffered minor neck and back pains that benefited from long soaks in the sulfured waters of Hungary's famed thermal baths. Although his job as a social worker in a small town in Holland wasn't high paying, he enjoyed the generous benefits the Dutch government offered its civil servants, including three weeks of treatment at the thermal bath hotel spa he was at now.

That morning Jan felt neither injured not ill, but cracklingly alive. As he swam ten vigorous laps in the pool, images of the golden-haired American woman in a black bikini raced through his mind. With each powerful stroke he willed her to join him later that day. Something strong and confident inside told him she would be there. He felt like the dancing moth in Kati's father's poem.

AT FIVE PAST one, Kati arrived in the lobby. Jan was at the front entrance, in animated conversation with one of the bellhops, who wore a bright red jacket with gold braid. The month of November had ended the day before and Wednesday marked the first day of the Christmas season. Overnight, the hotel lobby and staff had changed their uniforms and were now attired in crimson, green and gold. The festive decor matched her mood.

She did not make her presence known, but studied Jan as she approached him. His dark blond hair was long and curling at the ends. It complemented the red, pink and gold tones of his skin. He wore a red down jacket that looked as if it had come straight from the L.L. Bean catalogue. There really wasn't a world of difference between the way Jan dressed and the way men dressed back in Maine, where Kati had spent childhood summers. He wasn't as nattily attired as Krisztof had been the day before, but he looked vital, huggable—more or less a leaner, handsomer version of Santa Claus.

Kati made eye contact with the bellhop. The man smiled and Jan swung around catching her by the hands.

Quickly she withdrew them, hiding them in her pockets.

"You came, Kati. How are you? Did you sleep well?" Jan asked.

"I slept well, thanks. Let's go see this Market Hall," she replied, curious as to how this would contrast with her shopping expedition along the Vaçi Utça the day before.

The streets of Budapest had been dressed up into holiday, winter wonderlands. The weather was cold, but Jan introduced her to the local antidote—hot mulled wine. *Glühwein*, it was called, from the German for glow-wine. They refreshed themselves from one of the carts of the vendors of this nectar of the gods on their way to the streetcar to the Market Hall.

"With your rosy cheeks you look like a woman from a Rubens painting," Jan teased, as they descended from the streetcar and gazed at the art deco façade of the Market Hall.

"I do? I hope it's not one of those fat women with cherubs shooting arrows into them in parks..." she remarked. Had she gotten her Dutch Masters right?

"You look like a beautiful young mother who only has her son shooting an adoring look into your eyes," Jan gallantly replied.

"Thank you. I hope my looks hold up until something like that happens," she joked. Would such a time come for her? Everyone she knew back in New York City was single and not so young.

The Market Hall experience was everything Jan had hinted at. It was the real, real thing. Kati bought dozens of knick-knacks, only half-understanding what many of them were, but recognizing they were all authentically Hungarian, and couldn't be found on the fashionable Vaçi Utça. Krisztof would have turned up his nose at every one of them.

She bought the humblest of exotic items. She picked up huge strands of dried garlic, bent into different designs. Jan picked out a heart-shaped one, and smiling at her, paid for it and put it into her shopping bag. She bought dozens of large matchboxes of stove-sized matches, illustrated with Hungarian figures in green, white and red folkloric dress.

She also found tablecloths and placemats in bright red, white, and black designs. Some of these purchases required bargaining, at which Jan was good. He didn't speak much Hungarian, but his large frame, expansive hand gestures and broad smile all connected with the vendors in an international language of good will and readiness to do business. At the Market Hall foreigners were few and far between; she and Jan were eyeballed as curiously as they themselves eyeballed the goods and bustling crowds around them.

At last, it was time for a break. Jan steered her to a humble café tucked into a quiet corner of the hall. There they partook of more hot mulled wine, as well as bowls of hearty Hungarian goulash. Why was it that Kati found such simple fare so delicious? She had dined on goose liver and drank champagne with Krisztof the week before and hadn't felt nearly as satisfied. Sitting across from Krisztof, he had looked through her as if she were a ghost, searching for something he had lost and couldn't find again.

Jan sat before her and looked very much as if he'd found something important and wasn't going to lose it. She felt both esteemed and warmed in the bulls eye of his attention.

It was very much the same as sitting across from her father over the years after she had become an adult and gotten to know him on her own terms. They had spent many an evening together in his small New York apartment in Yorkville, the German Hungarian community on the Upper East Side. They would dine on chicken paprikash and drink wine, arguing over Fellini films, why black was really a color, the importance of art and the unimportance of wealth, and most of all—why it was important to live in the present moment.

Béla Dunai had been a sort of antidote to everything her maternal grandparents had stood for. His views had been subversive to many of the values with which she had grown up. She had known this, yet enjoyed their conversations. The blandness of her New England upbringing had left a certain part of her psyche unexplored. The core values she had been raised with were good, but a tiny bit of gypsy spirit roamed around inside her; occasionally it needed to be let loose.

Cocking her head to one side, she squinted at Jan, wondering if he had detected her inner gypsy, and if so, what plans he had to unleash it.

His blue green eyes held her gaze. Then his large hand on the table moved toward and covered hers. She looked down at it, then through her eyelashes up at him like the Cheshire cat in *Alice in Wonderland*. She tapped her forefinger up and down, under his. His forefinger responded, tapping over hers. She tapped again with her thumb. His hand caught her thumb; he raised her hand to his lips then kissed it.

Apparently this Dutchman had picked up a few nuances of Hungarian culture. Kati's father had known how to kiss a woman's hand. He had often kissed hers, as well as her girlfriends.' In fact, her girlfriends had all been delighted by Béla

Dunai, wishing that the men they dated in New York had had one tenth of the manners he had exhibited toward them. Kati's father had known how to make a woman feel special. It had been unfortunate that he had not known also how to bring home the bacon, as her maternal grandparents had frequently reminded her.

"Do you want to tell me anything?" she asked Jan, breaking their spell.

She had no idea where that had come from. It had been some sort of inspiration straight from the gypsy inside her.

"I want you to know that I'd like to get to know you more."

"How can that happen when I return to New York in less than one week?" she asked.

"Let's not be apart until you leave," Jan responded.

"I'd like to get to know you more too," she choked out. "But I'm the kind of person who needs to take a long time to get to know someone, and to let them get to know me. A week isn't enough."

"You're right. One week isn't enough to get to know someone like you. But let me try."

"That sounds like a line." She laughed. "I don't want to lead you on. I can't get involved with you for only one week. It would be too sad. I wish you lived in New York, and then we could take all the time we need to get to know each other."

"I live in Holland, you live in New York. But we're here in Budapest, together, now. Let me get to know you over the time we have left."

"I can only go at my own pace, and it's probably a lot slower than yours. You could find someone else to match your pace if you wanted to."

"That's not the point." Jan looked frustrated. He cradled her forearm in his large hand. "The point is that I want to get to know *you*. I'm not a nineteen-year-old boy, Kati. I can wait. If you need to go at your own pace, I'll match it. Will you let me spend time with you over this next week?"

She nodded slightly, smiling. The cornflower blue of his eyes momentarily turned green and hungry, then became blue again. She wanted to get to know Jan every bit as completely as he wanted to get to know her. But she wanted him to really get to know her, not someone she was pretending to be, due to circumstances that rushed them unnaturally into something she wasn't ready for.

"Show me more of Budapest." She stood from the table.

"Agreed." He rose and helped her put on her coat. "Let's take a walk."

Exiting the Market Hall, Jan steered them over the nineteenth century Szabadság or Freedom Bridge connecting Pest to Buda. On the less commercial, more elegant and residential Buda side they began to climb a hill. Between breaths he told her there was a lookout point that afforded a view of the entire city at the top.

Kati hiked alongside him, noting that spending time with Jan included getting a workout. Their breathing became short with exertion as they climbed. Finally, they reached the summit, where several couples leaned over an ancient stone wall.

The city of Pest lay spread out before them, with the steel gray Danube in the foreground. Within less than a minute, a cold drizzle began to fall and Jan pointed to a nearby café which looked like an old hunting lodge. They hurried toward it.

"How did you know about this place, Jan? It's extraordinary." She looked around, taking in the roaring fire in the hunting lodge's large hearth.

"I found it last year when I walked up this hill for the first time. It was raining then too, so I came in here to dry off. Not too many people know about it; it's an old hunter's hangout from the eighteenth century.

"Did you come here by yourself?" she asked, the question escaping her lips before she could think twice about how silly she must sound. He had a perfect right to have come here with anyone, including an attractive woman he might have recently met.

"No, I was alone." Jan chuckled and met her eyes. The blue had flashed to a hungry, hunter's green again. "Last year I wasn't ready to be with anyone, so I spent time by myself for the most part."

"What do you mean you weren't ready to be with anyone?"

Jan looked away then back at her. His face had tightened. "I mean my wife had left me the year before, and my son went with her. I was still trying to forgive myself for the accident."

"What accident?"

"Motorcycle. It's why I'm here, taking the waters." He rubbed his neck. "Neck injury."

"Not your fault, was it?" Kati probed gently. She knew enough people who had been in motorcycle accidents to know it was almost always the fault of the other driver.

"The accident wasn't my fault, but something worse was." Jan stopped abruptly and looked away.

Immediately the thought crossed her mind that perhaps Jan had cheated on his wife. But what did that have to do with a motorcycle accident?

"You'd better tell me, before I imagine the worst." She smiled, although Jan's mood had become serious.

"It won't be worse than what happened," Jan quietly replied. "My boy was on back of the bike when we were hit by a truck. We were both thrown off, but he landed close to the bike and it rolled over on him. His legs were crushed."

"Ohh." She tried not to gasp. "Do you mean his legs are—are—"

"I mean his legs are there, but they don't work. He's been in a wheelchair for four years now."

"I'm so sorry. But why do you blame yourself so badly? It could have happened to anyone," she said.

"Yes, but I'd promised my wife one month before it happened that I wouldn't take our boy on the back of the bike with me on the main roads. We were only supposed to drive around our property, but then he asked me if we could go down to the bakery in town and get some apple tarts. It was entirely my fault. I shouldn't have had him on the back of the bike. He lives with my mistake now for the rest of his life." He looked away, his face stony.

"Does your son hate you?"

"No, but my ex-wife does."

"Do you think your son loves you?"

"Yes, my son and I are close." For the first time in minutes, Jan's confidence seemed to return. "It's just that his mother took him to another town to live, and I don't see him very much anymore. I miss him." Again, he glanced away.

"It's a tough story." She put her hand on top of his big, warm one. "Thank you for telling me. What's your son's name?"

"Dirk. It's Dirk. He's a devil of a boy. An angel and a devil," His face lit up, rearranged from the moment before.

"Dirk," she repeated. "Here's to Dirk," she said, raising her mug of hot chocolate and clinking Jan's.

"To Dirk," his voice rang out.

The beam on Jan's face made Kati's heart dance. She hoped Dirk's heart danced too, at times, even if his legs couldn't. He had fallen to Earth and hadn't been able to get back up again.

His father had fallen too. His body had gotten back up, but had his mind?

They made their way back to the hotel. They were both ready to soak their tired limbs in the warm Jacuzzi jets of the pools, after all the walking they'd done. She was looking forward to more quiet conversation with Jan, now that he had told her a bit more of his own story. She shivered under her jacket, thinking of how hard his life must have become in the recent past. She couldn't begin to imagine how his son's life had changed.

As they hurried toward the warmth and light of the hotel entrance, a car door opened.

"Kati," a man called out.

It was Krisztof. He stepped out of a black Mercedes sedan and strode toward them. Quickly he assessed Jan beside her, who was doing the same.

"Kati, could I speak with you a minute?" Krisztof asked, stepping into the light, a worried expression tightening his face.

"Will you excuse me a moment?" she asked, turning to Jan.

"Will you be okay?" Jan looked at her, ignoring Krisztof.

"I'll be fine. Jan, this is Krisztof Nagy, a friend of mine from grad school back in New York." She prayed that the connotation for "friend" for a Dutchman was not the same as it was in German. When the Germans said "my friend" it could mean anything from a casual acquaintance to a long standing lover.

"Nice to meet you," Jan said to Krisztof, not looking as if he meant it. "I'll be in the lobby, Kati."

"I'll be there in a minute," she answered as she tried not to blush. Why was she blushing? Krisztof was just a friend, in the

American sense of the word, and what was he doing here in any case? She moved away from the light, turning to him anxiously.

"Krisztof, are you okay? I didn't expect to see you today."

"I'm not great. I called but they said you'd gone out. I was driving around, so I thought I'd stop and see if I could catch you on your return. I'm sorry, I didn't realize you had plans." He gestured vaguely toward the hotel entrance, indicating Jan.

"Uh—I don't actually have plans. Jan and I just spent the afternoon at the Market Hall."

"If you're sure you don't have plans—could I ask you a favor?"

"Of course." How could she refuse Krisztof a favor, when he had already helped her in sorting out the details of her father's legacy? "What can I do for you?"

"I have to attend an art opening tonight. My ex-wife will be there, with her new husband. I don't feel like going alone. I could have called one of my friends—but they all know her and most of them know him too. Budapest is a small world. Would you care to join me?"

"Tonight? Krisztof, I could, but look at me—I've been hiking up and down hills in the rain. I'm a mess."

"If you're too tired, I understand. But if you're not, I think you'll enjoy it. A lot of business and cultural leaders in Budapest will be there. I'll be happy to wait for you here in the lobby while you go change. Take all the time you need."

She thought quickly. She had had a delightful afternoon with Jan, which she would very much have liked to continue on into the evening. However, she was also scared to death of continuing to spend time with him now that it was clear that their interest in each other was mutual. As usual, with men, she needed time to savor each step, to reflect, before taking the next one.

Also, she owed Krisztof a favor, and would need to ask him for a few more before she had concluded her father's business. The last thing she wanted to do right now was to get all dressed up and attend a fancy social function, but she could hardly say no. Jan would have to understand. She went into the hotel to look for him.

He stood just inside the lobby, waiting for her.

"Jan, I had a wonderful time this afternoon. I want to thank you."

"You're thanking me by now going out with another man for the evening?" he responded wryly, sizing up the situation accurately.

"I—I *have* got plans for this evening. I'm not going out with him personally, I'm just accompanying him to an opening."

"I see. How long do you think you'll be gone?" Storm clouds scuttled across his face.

"I'll probably be gone for the evening, Jan. I'm sorry. This was—unexpected. I need to help my friend."

"How much help does your friend need? He isn't going to need your help overnight, is he?" he devilishly inquired.

"Definitely not." Kati looked directly into Jan's eyes, willing him to trust her. "I'll be back later. But it will be late. How about if we see each other tomorrow?"

"How about if you give me a call when you get back so we can discuss our plans for tomorrow?" he countered.

"I—uh—how do I connect to your room?"

"Ask for Jan Klassen. Or my room number, 107."

"Okay, I'll call you. Even if I drank half a magnum of champagne, I'll call you as soon as I'm back," she teased, hoping to lighten his mood.

"Fine. Talking with a drunk you will be better than not talking to you at all tonight. Have fun, and behave yourself." His eyes flashed green as they bored into hers.

"I will. Talk to you later." She gave him a special smile that let him know she remembered all they had exchanged, both spoken and unspoken, earlier that day. Then she turned and walked quickly to the elevator banks trying to remember what she had brought with her from New York that would announce her as a Manhattan sophisticate this evening in the eyes of Budapest's glitterati.

WATCHING KATI'S BACK glide gracefully toward the elevator banks, Jan wondered who this friend of hers really was. What did he know about American women? Did they sleep with their 'friends'? Jan knew plenty of Dutch women who did. But something about the way Kati held herself back told him she was a conservative woman in her heart of hearts.

He was disappointed that the evening had suddenly shifted direction in an unexpected way. He wanted to get to know this woman better. He could spend the next few hours getting to know some other woman or two at the hotel lobby bar, but he wasn't interested.

Instead, he thought he would check out this 'friend' of hers and give him a not too subtle warning to keep his hands off the beautiful woman from New York who was beginning to occupy a room in his heart.

Turning toward Krisztof, he gave him a significant stare. The well dressed businessman met his gaze. Then Jan walked over to the Hungarian man, who looked somehow forlorn, for reasons he didn't know but could understand as a man, having been there recently himself.

"Have a drink?" he asked.

Krisztof paused for a second, his shoulders stiff, then shrugged. "Sure, why not?"

They walked together to the lobby bar where Jan signaled the bartender, who came over, looking as if he were wondering whether these two men were both after the affections of the attractive, foreign blonde woman who had just exited the lobby.

They ordered beers, then turned to take each other's measure as they drank off the foam from their drafts. Jan wondered what Kati saw in this dapper, slightly effete looking man of about his age. Whatever it was, it wasn't what she was looking at in him. They were polar opposites in body type and fashion sense. Jan wouldn't be caught dead admitting to having any fashion sense at all, frankly.

Krisztof was compactly built and fastidiously dressed. Jan was a large bear of a man. He wondered if Kati found Krisztof attractive and reasoned that she must, to some extent—otherwise, why would she now be readying herself to spend an evening out with him? Was he rich?

Jan had a weak spot in his generous nature. His ex-wife had not just left. She had left him for a doctor. They had had myriad problems, all of which contributed toward the break-up, but Jan couldn't help but wonder if his ex-wife had ultimately chosen a higher earning partner over himself. As a result, he felt a certain amount of bitterness when he evaluated male peers in higher paying professions than his own. Jan was well-educated and naturally intelligent. He had too much life experience not to have noticed that women frequently chose higher earning, but less worthy male specimens over lower income men who were more attractive in every way.

He tried not to think about it, but it bothered him. Were women really that superficial? Or did how much money a man makes really matter that much in the natural selection order? He wondered where Kati's values lay in regard to this particular question. He knew women went out in girl groups and sat around drinking and talking the evening away discussing these types of issues. Where did a guy like him rate on their scale of who constituted a good catch? Was there anything such as true love out there for a man like himself? He thought he'd found it once; he'd been wrong.

Taking a long swig of beer, he eyeballed Krisztof. Why was it this rich looking guy somehow looked as if he'd lost something? Jan made a note to ask Kati later about her friend's status. Had his wife left him? He looked like she had. Jan realized this was exactly his own situation, but he wasn't feeling nearly as bad about it as the man sitting next to him appeared to be. If that was indeed his story.

"Have you known Kati for a long time?" Jan asked Krisztof.

"About two years. We met at an alumni event in New York."

Jan had no idea what an alumni event was. But his senses told him they hadn't been a couple.

"What about you? Have you known Kati Dunai long?" Krisztof asked, his tone formal.

"No, but I'd like to." Jan gave him a meaningful stare.

"Sorry I'm getting in your way tonight. She's really helping me out," Krisztof replied, without giving any clue as to exactly how she was doing that.

"Great. I hope she doesn't help you out too much. Understand me, friend?"

Krisztof stared at Jan, his lips a thin line that finally curved upward at both ends into the smallest hint of a smile.

"Perfectly."

They both turned back to their beers.

Despite the fact that Kati had dumped him for the evening to spend it with this guy, Jan's instincts told him she'd be thinking about him while she was at this party. He sensed she liked him. Every blood vessel of his body told him so when they were together. He thought about earlier that afternoon, when she'd taken his hand. Her own hand had been small, warm and firm, just like Kati herself. She and he had begun a dance that would not be interrupted by one brief evening away from each other. He wondered how it was that he knew this so surely. Yet he did. He was the moth dancing close to the flame. But he had already been zapped. Surely he couldn't get zapped again.

EXITING THE ELEVATOR in the lobby, Kati looked for Krisztof. He was at the hotel bar, having a drink with—Jan.

Willing her cheeks not to flame red, she walked regally toward the two men—one blond, one dark-haired; both looking directly at her. It was all she could do to keep her wits about her. What was Jan doing there, talking with Krisztof? What had he told him about her? Krisztof probably knew more about their relationship right now than even she did.

"Help me, grandma," she whispered to herself, thinking of her grandmother's former modeling days. She had coached Kati to carry herself well by making her walk across her bedroom with a heavy telephone directory on her head.

"Good evening, gentlemen," Kati greeted them with a tight smile, meeting first Jan's gaze, then Krisztof's.

"Good evening," they chorused together.

Krisztof rose then went to pick up his coat and briefcase.

Kati looked at Jan, hoping he would see in her eyes everything that had transpired between them that afternoon.

"I have one question for you, Kati Dunai," Jan began.

So he had learned her last name. What else he had found out about her in his conversation with Krisztof?

"How friendly are you with your 'friend?'" he asked pointedly.

She laughed. "You have nothing to worry about." She gave him an impish smile then turned to exit the hotel with

Krisztof, fully aware of Jan's eyes most likely boring holes into her back every step of the way. She tried not to sway her hips even slightly, yet they swayed regardless of her brain's commands. Her father's voice chuckled inside her—*Kati, you may have delayed getting to know this man better tonight, but you will not be able to delay seizing your life by the horns for too much longer. You are my daughter, after all.*

CHAPTER THREE

# THE ART OPENING

It took Kati and Krisztof a quick fifteen minutes to drive over the Margit Bridge to Buda and pull up in front of a large art deco townhouse nestled in the hills, overlooking the Danube. Krisztof came around to open her car door and, taking her arm, he hung onto it as they walked into the house. The party was already in full swing, and the host came over to greet them while an attendant took their coats.

"Krisztof, you devil. Where have you been hiding this beautiful creature? Is this the one you mentioned from New York? Hello, darling. My name is Ferencs Szabo. Delighted to meet you." The elegantly dressed gentleman bent low over Kati's hand and kissed it. He had known Krisztof since they had attended high school together and was now a successful art dealer who frequently sold paintings to Krisztof's clients.

He also threw excellent parties, to which Krisztof enjoyed bringing his clients when they visited Budapest.

Feeling like Eliza Doolittle in *My Fair Lady*, Kati looked to Krisztof for cues. It was evident she was on exhibit this evening, as Krisztof's escort. Straightening her back, she lifted her chin as she surveyed the well-dressed crowd. Europeans tended to be intrigued by New York City. She would represent Manhattan this evening as well as its reputation deserved.

"Yes, this is my colleague from New York, Kati Dunai," Krisztof told Ferencs. "I'm enjoying showing her around Budapest, so behave yourself. I want her to get a good impression."

"Welcome to Budapest, Kati." Ferencs laughed and signaled a server to come over. Taking two champagne flutes off a silver tray, he handed them to her and Krisztof. "I've heard you don't speak a word of Hungarian and I'm relieved to hear it." Never taking his eyes off her, he murmured something in Hungarian to the other man.

Krisztof snorted into his glass.

Kati wasn't sure of what to make of their exchange, so she decided to greet the party on her own terms. Turning away from them, she walked slowly into the main room, her back ramrod straight. It was a trick her grandmother had taught her for navigating high society functions. This was undoubtedly one.

There looked to be seventy five or so people there already. The women were as chic as Kati had already noted the women of Budapest to be. No traces of the last half century's Communist regime lingered anywhere the eye rested.

This was the glittering atmosphere of the Austro-Hungarian Empire of the Habsburg family that had ruled from 1867 until the end of the first world war in 1918. Many of the men wore avant-garde eyeglasses, looking as if they'd joined the party straight from New York's Soho. She stepped closer to the wall to examine the artwork, while the women around her shot glances her way. Apparently the artist whose work was being shown was interested in the relationship between very young females and very old males. She studied a painting depicting a young girl wearing minimal clothing on the lap of a man who looked to be about sixty.

"Hmm." She tried not to wrinkle up her New England nose, as she recalled her father's comments on the rule of the Habsburgs—"glittering and decadent," the latter of which had led to their demise with the start of the First World War.

"Enjoying the paintings?" a voice next to her inquired.

She turned to face a small, gnome-like man with a goatee, who looked to be the age of the male figure in the painting.

"I'm enjoying the party. Are you?" she deflected the question, as she hadn't really thought highly of the artwork on the walls, but for all she knew, this was the artist himself standing before her.

"I am. Do I guess correctly that you are American?" the man asked.

"Yes, from New York," she informed him.

"Ahh, the center of the art world. Wonderful. What brings you to Budapest?" he asked.

"Umm, I'm wrapping up some business matters," she coyly responded.

"And what brings you here, tonight?" he pressed.

"My friend, Krisztof Nagy. Do you know him?" she asked.

"Of course. Krisztof is one of Budapest's brightest businessmen. I didn't know he had such good taste in women as well."

Kati was beginning to feel like a fine cigar or a bottle of vintage wine being ogled at this party. She turned to locate

Krisztof, and instead found herself gazing directly into the eyes
of a woman of about her age with ash blonde hair and hazel
eyes. She was elegantly dressed in a grey suit that was exquisitely tailored to fit an expectant mother of her slim size. Kati
guessed she might be about six months along.

She gave her a cool smile. The woman returned it with equal
coolness, and turned back to her companion, a tall, auburn-
haired man wearing a cravat with his suit.

Soon Krisztof appeared. He took Kati's arm and steered her
away from the gnome-like man, who was now sizing up an even
younger woman standing in a group on his other side.

"Having fun?" he asked.

"More importantly, are *you* having fun?" She looked at
Krisztof closely.

"I'm okay. Who've you met thus far?" he asked, looking
more relaxed than he had seemed back at the hotel.

"Well, no one really, except for that short, older man who
just abandoned me for a younger woman he spotted. I'm getting some interesting looks from some corners."

"Really? From who?" Krisztof asked, as he accepted a caviar
blini from a waiter.

"Well, a woman who looked like she might be expecting
seemed to be staring at me. She's standing behind you to the
left," she told him.

"Expecting? What is she expecting?" Krisztof asked, then
brushed a speck of dust from his left shoulder so that he could
see who was behind him.

"She's expecting a baby," Kati explained.

Krisztof turned back to her, his face as gray as the blonde
woman's maternity suit.

"That's her," he murmured. He looked as if blood drained
from his veins as he spoke.

"What do you mean, that's her? That's who?" Kati whispered back.

"Let's get some fresh air," Krisztof took her arm and steered her out onto the balcony, where he leaned heavily on the balustrade.

"That's my ex," he breathed out.

"Ohh. I see. When's the last time you saw her?"

"A few months ago, in the summertime." Krisztof paused. "I didn't know she was pregnant."

"Was that her new husband next to her?"

"Yes." Krisztof looked as if he didn't want to talk about it any longer, so Kati followed suit. Apparently, it was taking him more time to get over his ex than it had taken his ex to get over him.

"Krisztof," she said after a moment of silence, "someone once told me 'face your demons.' Do you know what I mean by that?"

"I don't really want to face anymore demons tonight," he said dully. "I think I've already faced enough for one evening."

"If I were you, I'd go back into that room, make your way over to your ex-wife and her new husband and give them your warmest congratulations on their expected baby. That's what I mean by facing your demons."

Krisztof stared at her then nodded. "Will you come with me?"

"I'll come with you. I know how you must feel. But you'll feel better if you do the right thing." He had related to her a few details of his divorce, namely the mismatch of his lifestyle of constant travel and his former wife's desire to lead a more settled existence. He had described it as a civilized parting, as if love had quietly packed its bags and checked out. It had seemed too sad for words to Kati.

"Come." Krisztof straightened up his suit and took her arm.

They re-entered the reception room, and made their way over to his ex-wife and her new husband.

"Anne-Marie, it's wonderful to see you again. Hello, Stefan. May I introduce my friend from New York, Kati Dunai?"

"Hello, Krisztof," Anne-Marie greeted her former husband politely and shook hands with Kati. Her husband, Stefan, reached out his hand to her as well.

"It looks like congratulations are in order. I'm very happy for you both," Krisztof bowed his head slightly and looked into his ex-wife's eyes.

Anne-Marie gave him a level look back that seemed to indicate he had done the right thing and now it was time to go.

"Thank you, we're very happy," Stefan replied.

Kati smiled then turned to Krisztof, whose gaze was locked onto Stefan's face. Krisztof had asked her here tonight to help him get through this moment. Now was her chance.

"Krisztof," she asked, taking his arm, "did you say the artist himself is here somewhere? I'd like to meet him."

Krisztof's gaze broke from Stefan's and Kati quickly steered her friend away.

"Do you really want to meet the artist?" he asked as he placed his glass on a nearby silver tray and took two more champagne flutes, handing one to her.

"No. I really want to congratulate you for having done what you needed to do," Kati told him. "Let's go toast to your future."

"Good idea. Let's toast to yours as well."

They touched glasses, both lost in private thoughts.

The rest of the evening passed in light banter and witty conversation. Every now and again, Kati would note a sad tone creep into Krisztof's voice, but she told herself her friend would move ahead with his life now, as there was no possibility of moving back. What was done was done.

She sighed. What a monumental sea change the arrival of a child brought. Would her own life include such a life changing transition to motherhood?

By eleven the party was breaking up, and Kati and Krisztof said their goodbyes. In the car on the way back to the hotel, Krisztof seemed pensive.

"Would you like to come over for a nightcap?" he asked in a quiet voice.

"No thanks." She looked at him warmly, but sternly. "I'm proud of you for facing your demons at the party tonight. Now you have to go home and face your demons alone. I can't help you with that. You have to do it by yourself, and when you're ready, I know you're going to meet someone perfect for you, and you will be perfect for her because you'll have learned something from the mistakes you made in your first marriage."

"What have I learned?" His laugh was brittle.

"I'm guessing, but maybe you've learned that for a marriage to work, both people need to be in the same place at the same time at least most of the time."

"You're right, Kati," he said sadly, "If there's ever a next time, I'm going to be home more often." He sighed as he steered the car over the Margit Bridge, resplendent in holiday lights.

Only a few hours before she had walked over the glittering span with Jan. At that time, it had been less glittery, but she had enjoyed it more. Tingling, she thought of the call she would make to him when she got back to her room.

Krisztof pulled up in the hotel driveway. He kissed her on the cheek. "Thank you for coming with me tonight. And also for all your good advice. I'll go home and have a nightcap with those demons now. See you when I get back from Vienna."

"Don't fight those demons all the way to the bottom of a bottle," Kati warned with a laugh. "Remember, Krisztof, tomorrow is the first day of the rest of your life."

She thought about what that might mean for herself and Jan, her step quickening as she hurried up to her room. She could hardly wait to find out what plans the Dutchman had in mind for them for the following day.

BACK IN HER room, she stepped out of her high heels and unzipped her dress. Then she took a moment to lounge on her bed before picking up the hotel room phone. Electricity rippled through her as she asked the hotel operator to connect her to room 107.

Jan answered after a single ring.

"So—you're back. How was your evening?"

"Well, it was fun, but a little sad too," she admitted.

"What do you mean?"

"It's a bit complicated, and I'd rather tell you when I see you in person."

"How about if I come to your room and you can tell me now?" he suggested, his tone warm, immediate.

"No, Jan. Remember what I told you earlier today about needing to go at my own pace? I want to spend time with you this week, but coming to my room at midnight is moving too fast for me. Do you understand?"

"I understand, little Kati." He laughed rakishly. "So what about tomorrow afternoon? I thought I would take you to Budapest's largest public bath house, the *Széchenyi Fürdo*. It's where the local people go to enjoy the waters. They have pools indoors and outdoors, all of them heated. Are you interested?"

This time Kati didn't hesitate. "Yes. What time should I meet you?"

"Meet me in the lobby at half past two and don't forget to bring your black bikini."

Kati laughed and bade him goodnight. Rising from her bed, she then stepped out onto her balcony and thought about the two sides of Budapest she had seen that day. Were they also reflective of the two men she knew in this city? She had enjoyed both, but the time she had spent with Jan had resonated with her both emotionally and physically. Knowing that it was within her power for something substantial to pass between them or not, she shivered.

Her evening with Krisztof had been entertaining, but there was nothing adventurous or unknown about spending time with him. Without a doubt he was still mourning the failure of his marriage, going through the motions of putting on a good face as he led a glamorous and outwardly successful life. She had helped him to put on a good face in front of his friends this evening, but it was only a role she had played, and life, after all, was not a game. If she treated it as such, perhaps it would become one; she wanted the real thing.

Jan too had recently experienced the failure of his marriage, but he appeared to be farther along the healing curve than Krisztof. Jan's attention was firmly focused on her when they spent time together. He had been frank with her and told her he had spent a lonely time the year before. This year, it would seem, he was ready to engage in life around him.

She could hardly wait to see what might happen in the sweet web of potentiality they were now spinning around themselves.

# CHAPTER FOUR

# THE SZÉCHENYI BATHS

KATI MET JAN in the hotel lobby at half past two the following afternoon. She noted his rugged style in a plaid shirt with jeans and work boots; it suited him. As he zipped up his red down jacket he looked to her like an impish male Rubens, all in reds and golds.

They took a series of streetcars and buses. Each involved a great deal of jostling and crowding together. Jan's arm reached around to grab Kati's waist every time she lost her balance; she didn't mind.

Tendrils of desire were beginning to curl around something deep in her gut. Her senses hummed at the adventure of being in new territory—it made her more reliant upon the man standing next to her. His eyes told her he enjoyed this, as his arm protectively caught her again and again.

Finally they stood in front of the centuries' old bath-house known as the *Széchenyi Fürdo*, located in one of Budapest's largest parks. It was a vast and magnificent pale yellow palace that took Kati's breath away. She had never visited a public bathhouse that resembled the palace of Versailles. Its bright façade contrasted richly with the raw, gray day. It looked as if it might snow.

Proceeding into separate entrances, one for the men, and one for the women, they changed into swimsuits and showered. Kati noticed that Hungarian women did not appear to have cellulite, even when they were not thin, and she wondered if this was due to diet, or perhaps to the strenuous anti-cellulite massages that are a specialty of Hungarian and Romanian masseurs. She had been the recipient of a few anti-cellulite massages back at the hotel, from which she had barely been able to drag herself to the pool area after finally recovering sensation in her thighs and backside. These massages were not for the faint-hearted.

She met Jan at the entrance to the indoor pool halls. The interior of the bath house was marble and mosaic, most definitely Turkish-influenced. Despite conventional thinking about the Turks' contributions to Western culture or lack thereof, the Turks were responsible for many wonderful architectural styles and culinary dishes in Hungary and Romania. The bath house experience was one of them.

They eased themselves into the first pool, where they admired the intricately designed mosaic tiles covering the walls. The water was warm and the atmosphere friendly. She began to observe the local people around them. This wasn't at all like the thermal baths back at their hotel, where most of the clientele were foreign. Here were the local Budapesters, who paid the equivalent of two dollars to come here and lounge for a few hours, instead of the twelve dollar daily entrance fee to the baths back at her hotel spa.

What she really liked about Hungarians was that they were so different from people back in Connecticut, where she had grown up. Hungarians appeared to be the least puritanical of all ethnic groups she had observed thus far, with the possible exception of Brazilians. Bathers in the pool lounged, talked, and embraced, apparently giving themselves over to guilt-free sensual delight in plain sight of everyone else.

Couples everywhere held each other in the warm water, wives leaning on their husbands' shoulders, quietly talking and bobbing up and down while sodium, calcium and sulfur-laden water polished their skin and healed their internal organs. Kati guessed these were married couples, as most of them were not young and all of them looked completely indifferent either to their own appearance or to their partner's. They touched, groomed, and leaned on each other as if one partner was an extension of the other partner's body.

Jan and Kati progressed through a series of three interior pools until they arrived at the *pièce de resistance*—the outdoor pool. She eased into the water, her body warm and toasty as the frosty evening air stung her face. Reveling in the contrast of hot and cold, she drank in the magnificent backdrop of Austro-Hungarian architecture surrounding them on three sides. Her mind as well as her body felt alight with fire.

After a few moments, it began to snow. The combination of the snow coming down, and the steam coming up off the water created a mystical fairyland in which languorous bathers lounged dreamily.

Slowly, they made their way to the furthest end of the outdoor thermal pool. The fresh, cold air bit into their faces while warm, sulfated water enveloped their bodies. Her thoughts were beginning to turn to the closeness of Jan beside her. She glanced sidelong at the Dutchman, her eyes flickering over the large expanse of blond hair on his chest.

"Are you comfortable?" he asked.

"More than comfortable," she replied, sighing.

"Me too," he agreed.

His left arm along the pool ledge inched closer toward her. She pretended not to notice. Soon his hand rested lightly on her left shoulder. His fingers were large and muscular, the nails well-trimmed. She willed her chest not to heave; it did, regardless. Her entire body was rising up in insurrection against her brain, which the warm water had apparently lulled to sleep.

Then Jan's fingers pressed into her shoulder, turning her to face him. Taking her other arm, he pulled her slowly toward him. She could have stopped him.

Instead, she floated straight into his arms.

"Hello, Kati," he said in a low voice.

"Hello, Jan," she replied, reaching up to rest her hands on the shoulders she had been admiring for days. Inhaling his scent, it was all she could do to resist burying her face in his broad, golden-haired chest. Then, her hands found their way to either side of his neck.

They spent the next few minutes in a *pas de deux* of sensual exploration. He supported the small of her back while she floated, the icy caress of snowflakes falling onto her face. He brushed them off her cheek, then massaged the back of her neck with strong fingers.

Each time she opened her mouth to say something, she lost her train of thought as his hands found their way to another part of her body. They introduced themselves to her upper arms, then forearms; her hands, then her back. Finally they encircled her waist.

Suddenly, she was staring directly up into his blue green eyes. Their faces moved slowly toward each other until mouth met mouth and they kissed.

After an eternity of several more minutes, Kati pulled her mouth from his, but kept her eyes on him to reassure him.

Jan's smile was catlike, dreamy. He was a golden lion with snowflakes adorning his mane.

She looked around. No one else was there. It was closing hour. Moving together in a dream, they got out of the pool, dried off, dressed and exited the bath house. Snow silently fell around them as they walked through the large park. She was walking away from a moment in time that would never recur but she would always remember—that first kiss between a man and a woman. Poignancy mixed with hot electricity stabbed at her, as she thought of what had just passed between them and what might come—if she wanted it to.

If only she didn't have to return to New York in less than a week. At that moment the new job waiting for her back home seemed far less exciting than the touch of Jan's large, warm hand, which had slipped into hers. They strode side by side in the snow, back to their hotel, as the velvety November evening wrapped itself around them.

Once they got inside, Jan invited her to dinner. This time she accepted. Their growing friendship had accelerated rapidly in the past day and a half. Milestones had been passed. More loomed ahead, beckoning to her like an enchanted forest.

Instead of dining in the hotel, they agreed to change their clothes and meet in the lobby. This time, she didn't wear her black dress. She put on black brushed velvet jeans and a simple black and gold combed cotton shirt she had bought on the Vaçi Utça, two days earlier. She had told herself at the time it would be for a special occasion. The gold design on the shirt was a

Székely one; it was the Hungarian ethnic group tribe to which her father's people belonged.

There were eight Hungarian tribes, the most well known of which were the Magyars. However, her father had hailed from Transylvania, deep in Romania and southeast of the present borders of Hungary. It was there that the Székely Hungarians had settled in the twelfth century, emigrating on horseback from the plains of Central Asia. An interesting feature of the Székely written alphabet was its resemblance to Sumerian Sanskrit; trying to understand her father had been a bit like trying to understand Sanskrit.

When she sat down in the dark, wood-paneled restaurant near the hotel Jan had steered them to, his sharp intake of breath as he helped her take off her coat told her she had made the right choice of what to wear.

"You look beautiful, Kati," he said, his eyes riveted on her. He sat down quickly burying his face in the wine list.

"Have you tried Bull's Blood yet?" he asked, his eyes wandering down over her black and gold top then back to her face.

"No, but once in the south of France I ate another part of a bull's body" she responded teasingly, remembering a surprisingly tasty dish she had eaten in the Camargue. Bulls' testicles were a local specialty there; they were served especially on wedding nights.

"It's not bull's blood, it's the name of Hungary's most popular red wine. Here it's called *Egri Bikavér*, very robust. Like to try it?"

"Yes, I'm curious." About so many things.

He ordered a bottle from the waiter.

The week before Krisztof had introduced her to another Hungarian wine called Tokai, which European kings had drank on their deathbeds in order to give them a foretaste of heaven, so they would not be afraid to die. Krisztof had described Tokai wine as one of Hungary's most exclusive exports. It was made from grapes made incredibly sweet by mold growing on the bottom of the clusters, giving it the nickname of "noble rot."

She drank a glass the first night she'd arrived in Budapest, when Krisztof had escorted her to dinner, and had woken up with a crushing headache the next day. Apparently those dying kings had not woken up at all the following day, so had not had to worry about hangovers.

Would the difference between the wine Jan was introducing her to and the one Krisztof had offered reflect the differences in the two men? After the waiter had presented the bottle and opened it, Jan took it from him and filled Kati's glass. They held their glasses up to the light, and admired the richness of the deep red color.

"To us," he said, touching her glass with his.

In that moment Kati knew he was fully ready to move on from the sadness of his last few years to the joy of the present moment. So was she. She drank, feeling the fiery red wine pass down her throat, warming her instantly at the pit of her stomach.

They ordered venison with forest berry relish, a classic Hungarian dish called *ôzgerinc erdei ízesítéssel*. Neither of them had the faintest idea how to pronounce this in Hungarian, so Jan simply pointed to where it was written on the menu. In the far corner of the restaurant a violinist began to play what sounded like folkloric tunes. The violin's tone was so sweet and sharp that they both took note.

"Only in Hungary can you hear a violin played like that," Jan remarked.

"I heard a violin played like that once in a Hungarian restaurant in New York," she said, thinking back to her father's funeral reception at The Red Tulip restaurant in the Yorkville neighborhood on the Upper East Side of Manhattan where he had lived. "We're somewhere exotic for both of us."

"When we get to know each other more, will you be more exotic to me or less?" asked Jan. His eyes sparked like the flame from the candle on their table.

Kati liked both his question and the spark in his eyes. Was this moth dancing close to the flame? His eyes told her he was only too happy to do so. "I have not only Hungarian blood mixed with my Puritan half, but my father was a Hungarian from Transylvania. Does that answer your question?" she teased.

"I knew your answer would be yes," Jan said in a throaty voice. "You're exotic even to yourself."

"You're right," she replied, bemused. "How did you know that?"

"Because you're a beautiful mix of opposites."

"Who says?"

"I say."

"You say what?"

"I say opposites attract and both parts of you are definitely attracting me."

"Don't dance too close to the flame, you might get burned," she warned.

"You're already making me burn, Kati." His eyes flickered green in the dim candlelight.

She drew back in her seat and examined his face under cover of the shadows. He wasn't handsome so much as he was all male. There was no hint of distraction in his demeanor, every inch of him focused on her at that moment.

"Pretend that this is me." She leaned forward, putting her right elbow on the table. She cocked her forefinger at Jan. "Only my forefinger. Right here." She waved her forefinger casually at him. "Now say hello."

His eyes slit into twinkling orbs and he leaned in, putting one immense elbow on the table and cocking his forefinger at hers.

"Hello." His finger danced around hers.

She retreated a step or two. His finger retreated a step as well. Her finger moved forward again and waved at his. He slowly walked his finger over to hers and stroked its side, then retreated.

Her finger trembled, but she willed it to be still. She moved her finger toward his and gave it a slow, light stroke along the side. He curled his finger around hers but didn't try to capture her hand. They looked at each other motionless, until she became aware of the waiter standing before them holding two steaming hot plates.

"If I may serve you now..." the man said, smiling discreetly.

Kati leaned back and tried not to giggle while the waiter served their meal.

"Kati, you like to play games," Jan observed.

"Sometimes," she agreed. "Do you?"

"I like to play games only with someone I'm not playing games with. Do you know what I mean?"

"I do." Inside, she smiled. "And I am."

"Yes you are."

They attacked their meal. The waiter had apparently tipped off the violinist that a couple with romance on their minds was seated in the corner, because the music came nearer, until finally the violinist stood at their table and asked if they had a request.

"Play something that tells me my future," Kati said. She didn't know where she got such ideas at times. Her inner gypsy was fully activated, her fortune for the night as yet untold.

The violinist thought about her request for a moment, then bowed. He began to play something plaintive and tender with an unimaginable sweetness. After several minutes, the tempo picked up, and the tender tones turned into a wild gypsy dance. Then the final movement came, both regal and sweet, with a gorgeous ending. They applauded loudly along with the other patrons, and gave the violinist some *forints*. He had been magnificent.

"Come, let's take a walk." Jan signaled to the waiter who brought over their bill. Kati fished in her handbag for her wallet, but Jan took her wrist and pulled her hand away. "I invited you."

"Thank you." She imagined that Jan didn't have much money, but he was generous with what he had. They had no need to go to fancy places to have a magical time in each other's company. It was as if the simpler the backdrop, the less it distracted from the lush complexity of what was happening between them.

They went out onto the street and crossed over to the river. A thick stone railing bordered the side of the road that paralleled the Danube from the east to the west of Budapest. Leaning against the stonework, they stared into the dark swirls of the river, the cold night air stinging their cheeks. Jan put his arm around her shoulders. They turned to each other, and his mouth found its way to hers. They kissed for a long time, while the late night traffic hurried by, taking people home to their waiting beds.

Kati was already warm and cozy, snug in Jan's arms, but her thoughts had turned to bed. *What should I do?* Would she listen to her father's voice, with his wild and crazy urgings to let herself go, or should she listen to her grandparents' sage advice to be careful and proceed cautiously? She could only do what she felt most comfortable with. She had to be herself.

After a time they turned and strode silently back to the hotel. Jan walked her to her room door.

She paused, her hand on the doorknob to her room.

He looked at her.

"Do you remember what I told you yesterday at the Market Hall about needing to go at my own pace?" she asked.

"Yes. Do you remember what I told you about wanting to spend as much time as possible with you before you return home?"

"Yes. I want to spend as much time as possible with you too."

"Then let's spend tonight together." Jan's fingers closed around her wrist.

"I'm not ready to become lovers, Jan." She gave him a warning look. Do you think it's a good idea to spend the night together if you know that's how I feel? If you convince me to change my mind by morning, I may have a smile on my face, but part of me deep inside will be angry at you and angry at myself. Don't you think it would be wiser for us to say goodnight now and see each other tomorrow?"

"That's a good question." He thought for a moment. "Let's go inside and talk about this out on your balcony. You have a balcony, don't you?"

How cleverly he had refocused the conversation. She didn't want to say goodbye just yet and it would probably be wiser to discuss matters of love and lovemaking in private, rather than in the hotel hallway. They had already given the waiter in the restaurant something to think about with their hand dance earlier that evening.

She opened her door and let Jan in. He went straight to the French doors and opened them, stepping out onto the balcony.

She joined him, and they turned to face each other in the bracing, cold night air.

"I want to match your pace," he began, putting his arms on her shoulders.

"I want to spend as much time with you as possible until I leave Budapest," she murmured, putting her arms on his chest.

"I want to make love with you," Jan whispered back.

"I want to be the same person here that I am back in New York," she told him. "Otherwise, I'll get lost."

"What can we do together that's good for both of us?" he asked.

"I'm not sure. If you stay here tonight, will you think that I didn't really mean what I said about not being ready to become lovers?"

"I'll remember what you said. But what if our bodies ignore us?" he asked, hugging her tighter.

"Our bodies are already ignoring what our minds are telling them. Which do you want to be your master? Your body or your mind?"

"My mind. And my mind agrees with my body that it's a good idea to stay here with you tonight."

"Jan." She put her head next to his chest. His heartbeat was fast and loud. "I'll let you decide, based on what I've already told you. If you choose to ignore my rules, no matter what my body says to yours in the middle of the night, you won't get to know me further, I promise you. I may look like I'm still here in the morning, but part of me will have gone into hiding, because you'll have stolen something from me."

"I assume you're not talking about your virginity," he noted, his tone neutral.

"No, but I am talking about my virtue. It's something important, and if I lose it, I lose myself. I'm afraid to trust you to stay here tonight, if you don't promise me you'll help me keep my promise to myself."

"You're a challenging woman, Kati." He put a hand on either side of her face, stroking her temples. Restraint tempered his caress. "I want to be with you. Let me stay and by morning you'll know what kind of man I am."

HOW FULL OF surprises she was. She clearly held the conservative values of her New England background, but every so often some sort of cocky, inner gypsy put in an appearance. The contrast of personalities dueling it out inside her intrigued him. He was not entirely sure of who Kati was, but he wanted to proceed carefully so that she would continue to unfold herself to him in her own way.

During the night he learned many more subtleties about her. New landscapes were explored, but Kati's boundaries were left intact. By morning he had proven to be the man he said he was. When he awoke, the smile she gave him was radiant, a different smile than one that might have followed a more obvious outcome. Jan felt as if he had passed some sort of test. It was a good feeling, after spending so long feeling as if he had failed so many others.

Would she continue on the path of discovery with him? They kissed and agreed to meet later that day.

BACK IN HIS own room Jan thought about Kati's subtlety as he shaved. Her restraint opened his senses to new pleasures. Never would he have expected an American woman to teach him, a European, how to slow down and smell the roses. Imagining Kati was there beside him, he inhaled deeply. Then he splashed on some aftershave.

# CHAPTER FIVE

# SHOPPING ON THE VAÇI UTÇA

TODAY WAS THE day Kati was to pick up the final amount of her father's pension. Jumping into her jeans, she hurried to the drab government office on a side street near the main shopping district, and joined a long line of Budapesters of all ages. She smiled at toddlers and petted the dogs who accompanied their owners in the queue. It was as if she had just fallen in love with the entire world.

Although the line moved slowly and the final paperwork was tedious, everything she did that morning seemed special and magical. She was reaping what she had sown. Her father was able to help her in death in a way he had not been able to in life.

The night before Jan had respected her boundaries. He had shown her how strong his feelings were for her by controlling them—not an easy thing to do for a man. Perhaps it was the mark of a real man. By showing restraint in his behavior of the night before, Jan had proven that if he could control his feelings with her, he would also be able to control his urges if apart from her. Could they continue to develop their relationship even on different sides of the Atlantic, once she returned to New York?

At that moment, she couldn't think of anything other than how much more she wanted to get to know Jan Klassen. She couldn't imagine leaving Budapest in four days' time and never seeing him again.

Finally, the last bit of paperwork was completed. In her hand she held the receipt for the transfer of her father's modest pension from the Hungarian government to her bank account in New York. On her way home, she decided to further explore the Vaçi Utça.

In the first days of December, the Vaçi Utça was newly decorated in holiday garb and traversed mostly by locals. She had a feeling that Jan was not the kind of man who'd enjoy visiting frilly boutiques, so she decided to do some serious Christmas shopping on her own before their pre-arranged meeting at four that afternoon.

She bought a Christmas present for every member of her family, as well as for every friend who had helped her through her father's final illness and death. Every time she bought a present for someone, she bought one for herself too. She imagined it was her father buying it for her, and asked herself each time, "Is this something Dad would have liked to see me wear?" or "Is this something Dad would have liked to get for me?"

The number of times she had felt thoroughly spoiled in her New England childhood had been so few, that she knew her father would have approved of her spending this one day of total indulgence due to the windfall he had left her. If Kati ever had her own daughter, she would tell her about this particular shopping trip and indulge her at least once in a similar experience when she was old enough to appreciate it.

She bought wineglasses for her cousins, gorgeous burgundy and gold goblets with stems as thin as pencils, packed carefully in a green felt satin-lined box. For herself, she bought a long, gray, winter coat with a lambswool collar that looked as if it came straight out of the Prussian Officers Corps. She picked out crystal earrings for her sister and girlfriends in the outdoor marketplace. Finally she indulged herself in a soft lilac-colored knit dress, thinking of her meeting with Jan back at the hotel later.

She was happy that she had spent so much time swimming in the thermal pools over the past ten days; now he would have the opportunity to admire her well-toned figure in the snugly fitting, soft knit dress. Her stomach muscles contracted as she imagined his large golden-haired arms encircling her later, crushing the fine fabric to her ribs.

The Budapesters on the Vaçi Utça were no fashion slouches, especially not the women. The females on the streets and in the shops looked chic and sexy—not in the least affected by a half century of Communism. Post-Communist Budapest appeared to be in the midst of a fashion backlash. While she strolled down the wide avenue of the Vaçi Utça, she studied the women to figure out what they were doing that she should be doing too.

With Hungarian blood running through her veins, she wanted to represent her ethnic background well, even if she couldn't speak more than five words of her father's native tongue. Since she had inherited Béla Dunai's slanting green eyes and high cheekbones she thought she might try to act Hungarian, at least in front of the opposite sex. These Budapest women looked like they knew a thing or two about attracting men.

The men who had been in Kati's life, including Jan, had usually told her sooner or later that there was something exotic about her. She had always taken this to mean that they noticed her Hungarian-ness, although she had very little idea what that might mean. She was beginning to see that, at least for the women, this meant being highly fashionable as well as flagrantly feminine in a devil-may-care way sort of way that the French summed up so nicely with the term "gamine."

Kati wanted to learn more about how these Budapest women achieved this effect. It might be a useful skill to apply back in New York. Or on Jan that evening. The gypsy in her was wrestling with the Puritan-backgrounded New Englander; on that day the gypsy was winning the tussle. She would definitely have to put the brakes on the gypsy before the evening was over, but she had no idea how she would do this. Just thinking about sleeping in the Dutchman's arms the night before, with her head on his golden chest was enough to cause her Puritan side to beg for a scarlet letter.

Exiting yet another fashionable boutique, she passed a men's clothing store. She backed up and studied the window displays carefully. Jan was definitely not among the avant garde in his sartorial sensibilities. However, she was taking him on an adventure at this moment, so she decided a slight fashion upgrade was in order.

She entered the store.

The sales staff sprang to attention. She guessed they recognized a promising customer, courtesy of her half dozen shopping bags along with her exuberant mood.

A handsome male clerk asked in English if he could help her. What was it about her that tipped off the Budapesters that she was a foreigner? Was it her clothes or her air?

Looking down at her shopping bags, all from high-end boutiques, she realized that only the tiniest handful of Budapesters, perhaps those among Krisztof's circle of friends, would have shopped in all of these places on the same day. She was clearly a foreign woman on a mission, with plentiful resources, all noted instantly by shopkeepers up and down the Vaçi Utça. While the good looking male clerk asked how he could help, a second clerk stepped forward and took her bags from her hands, putting them carefully in a corner. A third clerk asked if she would like something to drink.

About to automatically decline, she caught herself. Why not go the total nine yards of shopping nirvana? This was likely to be one of the few days in her life when she would go on a mad shopping spree free of guilt and loaded with resources. Was it not a moment to savor?

"All right," she told the clerk. "What do you suggest?"

"Anything, Madame. An espresso or cappuccino? A Coca Cola? A glass of wine, perhaps?"

"A cappuccino would be perfect," she replied, looking around at the fine wool and flannel trousers and tailored shirts, neither of which she could imagine Jan wearing at any point ever. Did they have anything slightly more casual in this store? She didn't want to add to his collection of plaid lumberjack shirts, but perhaps there was something in between the two extremes of the fashion spectrum for men that Jan would feel comfortable in.

"What kind of man are you shopping for?" the handsome salesclerk asked.

Kati raised an eyebrow. What did he mean? The possibilities were endless. She was shopping for a brand new man in her life. A man who might one day be her lover. A man who already made her feel as if he were her lover. A man who was still a mystery to her, but with whom she felt completely comfortable as well as electrified. What kind of response could she possibly make to such a complex question?

"A very special one." She met the clerk's eyes. "Tall, blond and very interested in me." She paused, noting the clerk's sharp intake of breath. "I'm looking for something not too formal. For casual wear," she continued. Jan was anything but casual. He was a deliberate sort of man. She liked that. A deliberate man who dressed casually was far preferable to a casual man who dressed deliberately.

Krisztof's image popped into her head. Had he taken his wife's feelings a bit too casually, assuming she would always be there for him, no matter what country he was living in or traveling to on business? Then one day Anne-Marie had no longer been there for him. Krisztof was most likely now re-examining aspects of his life he had taken too casually in the years of building his business.

"Tall, blond and with very good taste," the clerk commented, looking at Kati with admiration. "Is he also American?"

"No, Dutch."

The second clerk handed her a steaming cup of cappuccino on a delicate china saucer that had just been brought in the door on a silver tray by a waiter from the café across the street. Shopping, Budapest style, was agreeing with Kati.

"Very good, Madame."

Was he referring to her taste in men or just her taste in general? Already, she was feeling like a fashion forward Budapest woman. Except that she was a New Yorker. She sucked in her breath and straightened her posture. She would give these Budapest clerks a taste of Manhattan style before she left their shop.

"Let me pick out some things while you enjoy your coffee. Please sit here," the clerk added.

Kati lowered herself onto an elegant salmon-colored love seat. The Ralph Lauren boutique on Madison Avenue could not have done better. She sipped her cappuccino. Delicious. Everything seemed deliriously delicious to her today. Was it because her body remembered the touch of Jan's body next to hers throughout the night before, or because her mind was perfectly at ease, knowing she was ardently desired by someone who had also respected her values? She felt both enveloped in the love of her father and the regard of the new man in her life. It was a good moment.

The clerk reappeared with an armful of sweaters, button-down and casual knit shirts. He held them up, one by one.

Shopping for Jan was proving harder than she had expected. She didn't know him well enough to know what the limits were of his willingness to be upgraded. Did most men like to be upgraded?

"Yes," she told herself emphatically, especially when they were in the hands of a woman whose esteem they wished to win and hold. Wouldn't Jan be receptive to anything she gifted him with? But she herself wanted to guess correctly what he might really like and feel comfortable in.

*What would he like, Dad?* she asked her father's spirit.

The clerk held up a lemon yellow button-down oxford. It was attractive, but had a logo over the breast pocket. She had a feeling Jan would not go in for obvious status symbols. And what if her status symbols weren't his? Maybe someone's polo player was someone else's pig? What if an alligator in America meant a lizard in Hungary and a pretentious status symbol in Holland? Her gut told her the Dutch didn't go in for designer logos. At least not Jan.

She shook her head at the clerk.

He held up a navy blue and white striped V-necked sweater in the softest wool imaginable. She stroked the fabric briefly.

What if Jan didn't like V-necks? Men could be very fussy about the shape of their sweaters' necklines.

"Show me more," she told the clerk.

He pulled out a brown knit shirt in a richly textured nubby pattern with three buttons at the collar.

She felt the material. How nice it would be to feel the muscles of Jan's broad chest underneath it. It wasn't a New England sort of shirt at all, but more of a New York style. She could see Italian-American guys with tasseled loafers wearing a shirt like this one. She put it down.

Jan was no preppie and neither was he a tasseled loafers type. The man from Holland could use a little work in the fashion arena, so she thought about how she might expand the horizons of this particular male from the land of windmills and dikes.

The clerk showed her a chocolate brown leather jacket with the texture of butter. The leather was so soft it rippled when touched. Kati took the jacket and held it up to her face. It smelled manly, like Jan.

She imagined how expensive it must be. Her eyes flicked over the price tag. Indeed it was.

She looked at the jacket and then back at the navy blue and white sweater. She knew Jan would love the jacket. But what would he think of her making such an extravagant gesture? Would he be offended? Perhaps it was a bit too much. But her feelings for this man were intense. *What should I do, Dad?*

Inspiration hit. She would get the leather jacket for Jan, but she wouldn't give it to him until the moment she left. That way, she wouldn't be there to see his reaction to her gift. She would be safely on the plane, flying back to New York. Maybe he would be thrilled, maybe abashed. She wouldn't embarrass him or herself by standing there in front of him when he opened it.

"I'll take the jacket," she told the clerk.

He smiled approvingly. Not only had she chosen the best selection, but it was the most expensive item he had shown her.

Kati sighed, thinking of how over the top her New England grandparents would find this purchase. But her father would have approved. In fact, he himself would have looked spectacular in a chocolate brown leather jacket such as this one.

Kati's mother had shown her some photos of her father from when she had first met him. He had been a good looking man. He too had had dark blond hair and blue green eyes, something Kati hadn't thought about until that moment. But Béla Dunai had been of medium height and build, whereas Jan Klassen was a big bear of a guy. She eyeballed the jacket again.

"Could you just try it on, so I can make sure the shoulders are broad enough?" she asked.

The clerk put on the jacket; he appeared to be swimming in it.

"Perfect," she told him.

He smiled straight into her eyes with a look that told her he thought she was close to perfect too.

After saying goodbye to all three of the salespeople who had attended her, Kati waltzed out of the store with an enormous black, glossy shopping bag with something incomprehensible in Hungarian embossed in gold on the side. She hoped Jan would not be in the lobby upon her return to the hotel, because if he was, he would not be able to miss this bag with the words "Men's Boutique" in English below the Hungarian name of the shop.

She hailed a cab, feeling like Sarah Jessica Parker in *Sex and the City* on the ride back. It was one of the best days of her life and she was enjoying her moment. To top it all off, the anticipation of meeting Jan in the lobby at four that afternoon was almost too wonderful. What should she wear? What would he say when he saw her? What would he suggest they do? What would happen after they did some more sightseeing together? Life overflowed with limitless possibilities, every one of them including being together with a man who knew how to focus his attention without crowding her.

Arriving at the hotel, she hurried up to her room. There the message light on her phone blinked at her in red. Who had called? She hoped madly it wasn't Krisztof needing another favor, as he was supposed to be in Vienna. She didn't want to waste another minute away from Jan.

Jan Klassen was giving her something most men she'd dated thus far didn't understand she needed—time and space. As a result, her heart rushed toward him. It was a much more enjoyable feeling than trying to escape from a man moving too fast in her direction. How did he know so well how to approach her? Was it because he was older and wiser, or was it, quite simply, because he was exactly right for her?

Kati was somewhere she'd never been before. It wasn't just Budapest, either.

CHAPTER SIX

# TAKING THE PLUNGE

JAN HAD SPENT the day swimming, working out in the hotel gym
and taking a run along the banks of the Danube. His confused
thoughts had been consumed by the woman with whom he'd
spent the night before.

He'd never been with anyone as attractive as Kati, a woman
who had forced him to slow down and smell the roses along
the path of a relationship. As he jogged along the greenish
grey waters of the Danube, he considered what they might do
together that afternoon. He enjoyed offering new adventures to
her each day. Now he realized it was she who was offering him
new adventures together at night. Who would have thought
that he'd enjoy time in bed with a woman who wouldn't let
him make love to her? Before last night, he would have laughed
at such a notion.

After his run, he returned to his hotel room to shower and make some phone calls. He had an idea to surprise her, and after making the necessary arrangements he called her room. Getting her voicemail, he left a message.

"Hi, Kati. I was looking for you, but apparently you're still out. I'm going to a very special place, and I'd like you to meet me there at four if you can. I'll be at the Hotel Gellért at the entrance to the spa baths. Wear casual clothes and bring your bathing suit. We're going to do something new together."

After hanging up, he wondered if he'd left the wrong impression with his message. Would she think he'd booked a hotel room for them at the Gellért? That he was assuming since they'd spent the night together, she was ready to rush full speed ahead to becoming lovers? He cursed himself for not having thought first before leaving the message. He wished he could erase it and rephrase himself, but it was too late. Dressing quickly, he decided to walk to the Gellért to blow off some steam.

An hour later Kati returned to her room and retrieved the message. Something very enjoyable together? One thing was on her mind, and it was precisely what she had told Jan she was not yet ready for. Whatever else could he mean? She glanced at her watch. Knowing the Hotel Gellért was Budapest's most historically significant hotel, she quickly changed into the lilac-colored dress she had bought earlier that day, tossing her black bikini into her handbag.

Rushing down to the lobby, she hopped in a cab and told the driver to take her to the Hotel Gellért. After a few minutes, the cab pulled up in front of the gorgeous Art Deco front entrance of the Gellért. A doorman stepped forward to open the passenger door.

Suddenly, she was back in the era of pre-World War I, when the Habsburg monarch Franz Joseph ruled the Austro-Hungarian Empire. She straightened her back and walked regally into the main lobby. Somehow, she couldn't envision Jan in this atmosphere, with his red down jacket and hiking boots. Where was the entrance to the Gellért spa baths? She asked at the concierge desk and was directed to a side entrance. Exiting the grand lobby, she made her way down a side path to a very different kind of atmosphere.

At the end of a long path leading to the back of the hotel, she saw an elegant art deco sign announcing Gellért Spa Bath in gold letters over enormous double doors. She opened the doors and immediately felt fragrant steam hit her in the face, swathing her in warmth and humidity. She swung open a second set of doors and entered a world of exotic beauty.

The sheer size of the pool halls was staggering. The ceiling was at least forty feet high and supported by pink marble pillars that looked as if they had come from the Parthenon in Athens. An enormous skylight was overhead, letting in the sun's final rays from the December afternoon. Gorgeous and intricate mosaic tiles covered the walls, blending the best of both Austro-Hungarian Art Deco styling and Turkish influence. The one hundred foot long main pool was breathtaking. Stained glass windows on the far wall let in the last of the afternoon light, which played upon the bathers.

After her eyes had feasted on everything, she became aware of Jan at her side. He had appeared from nowhere, dressed only in his black swim briefs. She greeted him warmly, trying to kiss him on the cheek. He turned his face and met her mouth with his instead.

"Get changed," he said softly. "I want to introduce you to the pools of Budapest's most famous hotel."

"Jan, this place is beautiful."

"I'll meet you here in ten minutes. You have a lot to see. There are eight separate pools."

She couldn't believe it. What a lifestyle this city offered! How did any Budapester ever get anything done in business or at home with this kind of luxury available? And this was only the off season. She hurried into the women's locker room, and changed into her black bikini.

She met Jan poolside, where she found him already in the water. Sliding into the pool, she felt his arm slip around her waist under the warm, bubbling water. After so many hours of shopping, every bone and muscle in her body responded to the energizing waters as well as to the man next to her.

"How did I do last night?" he asked, his eyes locking onto hers.

"You were amazing." She sighed happily. "I know it was hard, but you did the right thing for me."

"For us," he corrected her.

"For us," she joyfully agreed.

He lifted her hand and kissed it. There had not been a single day thus far in her life anywhere near as perfect as this one. She leaned her head back against Jan's shoulder and closed her eyes. The evening ahead would be even better.

Over the next hour, they paddled and floated in half a dozen of the eight different pools comprising the Gellért Baths. Jan explained that the thermal waters of the pools came from deep within Gellért Hill directly behind them. The waters left a slightly chalky coating replete with many minerals on one's body.

"What's the difference between these waters and the ones on the other side of the Danube at the Széchenyi Baths?" she asked.

"I don't really know, but this pool spa has a few different features from the Széchenyi Baths. Have you ever taken a plunge bath?"

She shook her head.

"Then you're taking the plunge today."

"What is it?" She loved the fact that Jan was so full of surprises.

"This will be my turn to find out if I can trust you. The plunge baths are located in the men's and women's locker rooms. I can't go in yours with you, but I'll know if you did it or not when you come out."

"How will you know?" she asked, baffled.

"Let's just say, I'll hear about it one way or another."

"What does it do for you?" she probed.

"It revs up your circulation and makes every cell in your body come alive. You can't do anything better for your skin or circulation." His eyes danced. "Well, maybe you can do one thing that would have the same benefit, but in your case, this is a way to experience heaven and maintain your virtue at the same time."

"Hmmm," she hesitated. "How long will it take?"

"A matter of seconds. No one stays in a plunge pool for longer than the time it takes a rocket to shoot off a launch pad."

"What if I don't want to do it?" she asked, her curiosity piqued.

"I want you to do it, so you know what it feels like. And I want to know if you're brave enough to do it. Your skin will tingle and glow for hours afterwards. I promise you."

"All right," she said, more than ready. "Where do I go, and where do I meet you afterwards?

"There's the entrance to the women's locker room. Tell the attendant you want to use the plunge bath. She speaks English;

she'll show you what to do. It'll all be over in less than five minutes, then I'll meet you right over there in the Jacuzzi pool. You'll need some Jacuzzi jets to take the edge off once you're done."

"And my reward for this?" She gave him a saucy look.

"You'll find out when you're done." His eyes narrowed, but gleamed. "And don't cheat. I'll know if you didn't go in."

She got out of the main pool and sauntered over to the women's locker room, tossing an impish grin back at him. She wasn't sure of what was going to happen, but after the night before, she was ready to trust him. Her time in Budapest was turning out to be the adventure of a lifetime.

As she entered the women's locker room, an attendant in a white coat greeted her in English.

"Could you tell me where the plunge bath is?" Kati nervously asked.

"Have you taken a plunge bath before?" the woman asked, pointing toward an inner room.

Kati shook her head.

The attendant smile broadly and handed her a large towel. "First, take off everything and go into the steam room for a few minutes. When you've had enough, come out and I'll take you into the plunge room.

Kati undid her bikini and wrapped herself in the plush towel. Once inside the steam room, she reclined on the upper ledge and laid on her back with her feet up against the wall. In moments the steam began to open her pores, bathing her in hot moisture. She anticipated the plunge bath to be some similarly agreeable sensation.

Eager to report back to Jan, she hurried out of the steam room, where the attendant led her through another door into a small room. She was the only one there. In front of her was a circular opening in the tile floor with a ladder leading down to a small body of water.

"What do I do now?" Kati asked the attendant.

"That depends on how brave you are," the attendant replied. "If you are very brave, you jump into the water. If you are not so brave, use the ladder, but in either case, go all the way in and make sure you put your head underwater. Otherwise, you won't get the full benefit."

"How long should I stay in?" Kati asked.

"Your body will let you know. But remember to go all the way in. Immersing your head is an important part of the treatment."

What an odd ritual. She desperately wanted to run back into the locker room, pull on her bikini and go find Jan. But he had made it clear he would know if she hadn't taken the plunge. She couldn't lie to him; even if she could, she didn't want to.

Eyeballing the ladder, she moved slowly toward it. If she eased herself into the cylinder of water, she would have time to back out. She didn't want to chicken out; jumping in was the only alternative.

"I'll jump. Just tell me one thing. Has anyone ever died from jumping into this tank?" Of course she sounded ridiculous, but she had no idea what she was getting into.

"No, darling," the attendant chuckled. "No one has died. Many have screamed, but no one has died. Go ahead, you'll feel wonderful afterwards."

Kati liked the way Hungarians called each other "darling." It suited their warm, interactive culture. Encouraged by the attendant, she shuffled to the edge of the tank, crossed herself, tightly closed her eyes, and jumped.

It was as if she'd leapt into the Antarctic Ocean. Shooting up to the surface, she screamed loudly as she scrambled up the ladder out of the tank. Her entire body felt as if it were being stabbed by tiny ice shards.

"Aarghh!" she screamed again.

"You are brave, Madame." The attendant beamed approvingly. "Not many jump. You will feel the reward for the rest of the day." The woman opened the door to the locker room, where some of the female guests looked at Kati and smiled or laughed. Apparently, the walls of the plunge room weren't soundproof.

Kati wanted to kill Jan. Putting on her bikini in what seemed like less than half a second, she marched out the women's locker room exit. She felt as if she had just been plugged into a wall socket and was glowing like a lamp.

In the Jacuzzi pool, lounging, Jan looked up at her, his expression wry.

"I had no idea you could scream so loudly." He chuckled.

Her face flamed. Wading into the Jacuzzi pool, she paddled over to him and splashed a large wave of water straight into his face.

"How dare you do that to me?" she hissed at him.

Other bathers looked on amusedly. The plunge bath was an exciting introduction to spa therapy for many foreigners who visited the Gellért Spa Baths.

Still chuckling, Jan grabbed her arms. Smart move or she would have surely slapped him.

"Do you have any idea how good that was for your skin?" he asked her.

"Do you have any idea what I'm going to do to you later in revenge for this?" she fumed.

"Do you have any idea how beautiful you are right now?"

"Shut up. I'll never listen to another one of your ideas again. Someone get me a fire extinguisher."

The contrast of the icy cold plunge bath of a moment before and the warm Jacuzzi jets on her muscles right now was having its effect. Like silly putty, her body went limp in Jan's arms. It wasn't a bad way to feel. Instead of slapping him, she gave him as vicious a pinch as she could manage on one of his cheeks. She could kill him, but she was starting to feel like a million dollars.

"A little pain, a lot of gain..." he philosophized.

She sighed. Life was good.

After another quarter hour or so of quiet relaxation, he gave her a squeeze. "I have another surprise for you," he whispered in her ear.

"I don't think I can survive another surprise like the last one." She moaned.

"This won't be like the plunge bath," he reassured her. "I have a friend who works here. He's going to give you a treatment."

"A treatment?" Her eyebrows shot up. "What kind of treatment? Is he going to submerge me in an ice cube bath? Forget it."

"No, darling, he's going to do something very gentle and relaxing that will not compromise your virtue in any way." Jan gave her a wicked look. "I'll be there too, making sure you're enjoying yourself."

She liked the way Jan had referred to her as "'darling." It was a different sort of "darling" than the Hungarians' way of addressing each other as "darling," which was more or less akin to a waitress back in New York asking, "More coffee, honey?"

"Which part of my body will be engaged so as not to compromise my virtue?" she asked, savoring the fact that Jan enjoyed teasing her about her virtue, but at the same time understood this was something serious for her. It was wonderful to laugh and be serious at the same time; sort of like playing games with someone she was not playing games with.

"It will be a part at one end of you," he offered.

Kati rolled her eyes and tried not to laugh. Everything she did with Jan made her want to laugh, if it didn't make her want to melt. He was a very merry man to spend time with. And he liked to play games in the same way she did. Safe games that were fun and didn't hurt anyone. But games, all the same. She couldn't remember ever feeling this playful back in New York, where everything was business all the time, even the business of dating.

"Is he a hair stylist?"

"No."

"Thanks for the big clue."

They climbed out of the Jacuzzi and headed for the locker rooms.

"Just put on a robe, and meet me at the exit. Trust me. Have I let you down thus far?" He chuckled again and looked down at her.

She made a face and turned on her heel, then marched off to the women's locker room. Jan Klassen was too exciting not to take up on a challenge. The plunge bath had been a shock, but she would never have done it if he hadn't dared her to. And now she was proud of herself that she'd jumped in. Her entire body still tingled. Wait until she told her friends back in New York about this.

They met at the locker room exits wearing white, terrycloth bathrobes and took off for the treatment area. Walking through wide double doors, they entered a part of the baths that looked more like a hospital. Therapists and patients were walking around, the former in white jackets, the latter in white bathrobes and slippers. A man of about fifty in a white jacket came up to Jan, greeting him warmly.

"Sandor, may I introduce you to Kati Dunai from New York? Kati, this is my friend Sandor Toklas, who works here. He helped me with my neck last year, when I really needed it."

"Hello, Kati. Are you ready for a foot massage?" Sandor asked, smiling at her.

"A foot massage?" She breathed a sigh of relief. It sounded divine, and a lot less shocking than the last surprise Jan had had for her. "Yes, I'm ready."

They entered a treatment room and drew the white curtains that served as a door. She lay down on the massage table and Jan settled himself next to her in an armchair. Sandor began to spread lotion on her legs, ankles and feet.

"Don't talk, just close your eyes and relax," Jan ordered her.

She nodded in agreement, happy to comply. How was she ever going to go back to her life in New York after experiencing all this? Was it possible she was going to be punished sometime soon for having had such a pleasurable time in Budapest? In her mind her father's voice laughed at her: *Kati, my little Puritan, life is for enjoying, not suffering. Taste, drink and touch everything it offers, my daughter. Remember, you are a Hungarian woman as well as a New England one. Don't hesitate, jump.*

Closing her eyes, she imagined once again jumping into the plunge bath. Instantly, she fell into a deep sleep.

When she woke up, Jan and Sandor were conversing softly in what sounded like Dutch. She could pick out words that sounded like their English equivalent here and there, and heard the name "Dirk" several times. As they spoke, Sandor massaged her left ankle in a slow circular motion.

She watched them from under her eyelashes, noting the seriousness of Jan's tone as well as his strong broad back. Whatever Sandor was doing to her ankle and foot was having its effect on other parts of her body. Had Jan tried different types of massage on Dirk? If so, to what effect? She had heard damaged or severed nerve endings could grow back with the right therapy and stimulation. Could Jan's son's condition improve one day to the point where he might walk again?

"Hello, gentlemen," she said to let them know she was awake.

Jan turned. His expression was calm, but serious.

Kati studied the two vertical lines that had appeared on either side of his nose to mouth. Was it possible to change the lines in someone's face by falling in love and growing old together? She pushed the thought out of her mind.

"Were you talking about Dirk?" she asked.

Jan nodded, his face sober. "Sandor spent five years in my country working at a sports injury clinic there. His Dutch is very good. We'll switch into English now that you're awake."

"Sandor, have you met Dirk? Is there anything that could be done for him using massage therapies?" She hoped she wasn't being too forward, asking about Jan's son in front of him. She wanted to know everything about him, not just the fun side of him she had met on vacation.

"I met Dirk in Holland a few years ago, but I didn't have a chance to work on him. I think there are some modalities that might benefit him. There are some massage techniques that promote healing for nerve damage."

"I have an idea," she continued. "Show Jan some techniques he can use on Dirk back home. Pretend I'm Dirk."

She longed to help Jan forgive himself for having caused his son's accident. One spill off a motorbike had altered the landscape of an entire family's future. She couldn't fathom it, but she knew Jan needed to work his way through it, if he was ever to heal on the inside the way he had on the outside.

Jan looked at her, his face guarded. She had the sense he had been down this road many times before, with limited success. Finally, he nodded his head at Sandor to signal agreement.

"I can show you a few things to try with Dirk," Sandor said. "But my Dutch is better than my English. Do you mind if I speak in Dutch when I can't explain something in English?"

"Not at all," she replied. "Go right ahead."

"I'll explain it to Kati in English if you need to tell me something in Dutch. What do I do first?"

"Take her left foot and we'll get started."

Sandor gave Jan some lengthy instructions in Dutch while she closed her eyes and began to drift. She would like to help Jan's son to walk again one day. If it were not possible, so be it, but why not use whatever resources fate put in their path that could be harnessed to help the boy? Before another thought floated into her brain, she fell asleep.

Sandor woke her a moment later, signaling to her to sit up. He touched the back of her head lightly while holding the base of her skull. She felt nothing. He moved his fingers subtly all around the back of her head near the mid-line. Very faintly, a sensation stirred in her left calf, then her right one.

"I feel something in my legs" she exclaimed.

Sandor looked pleased that his technique had had an effect. Then she had another idea.

"Why don't we put you on the table and try this on you?" she suggested turning to Jan. "Then you'll know what you're aiming for when you try it on your son."

"Why not?" He shrugged.

They exchanged places. Sandor's technique was subtle; for several minutes nothing much seemed to be happening. Jan closed his eyes and Kati watched his face for any signs of reaction, as she steadied his shoulders with her hands. After a moment, he grunted pleasurably and said something in Dutch to Sandor.

"Translation, please," she ordered.

Sandor chuckled. "Your man told me that my damn massage is doing nothing for him, but it's very pleasurable the way you're leaning on him, so keep doing it."

Kati liked the way Sandor had referred to Jan as "your man." It was probably just an accidental way of phrasing things that a Hungarian saying something in Dutch would translate into English. Yet the way it came out fired her thoughts as well as her heart.

They continued on for another ten minutes, then it was time for Sandor's next appointment. She and Jan thanked him warmly and made their way back to the locker rooms from the treatment area. They parted ways and agreed to meet at the Gellért Baths exit in ten minutes.

In the locker room, Kati glanced into the mirror. Her face glowed back at her. The plunge bath had had its effect, as well as all the other ministrations of the last few days. She would not be returning to New York the same as she had been before. Spending time with Jan in Budapest had transformed her into a woman who knew how to enjoy herself and not feel a moment of guilt about it. She was already anticipating with relish the feel of Jan's hand on her back as he discovered the lines of her body under her clothes. Pleasure was her new close friend. It fit her as well as the soft lilac-colored dress she now slipped on.

# CHAPTER SEVEN

# AN UNEXPECTED EVENING

EXITING THE GELLÉRT Baths, Kati and Jan stepped out into a clear, starry night. The fog and drizzle of the past two days had cleared up and the brisk cold air caused Kati to inhale sharply, filling her lungs after the warmth and steam of the last few hours in the baths.

They walked toward the front of the hotel. Taxis, Mercedes-Benz's and BMWs were pulling up to the Gellért's majestic entrance.

"Would you like to take a cab back to the hotel?" Jan asked.

"Let's walk for awhile," she said with a shake of her head. "It's fresh out here. Do you think it's safe to walk along the river?"

"When I'm with you, you're safe. Let's go."

Did he have any idea how nice his words sounded? He didn't seem to even realize how some of the things he said made her heart melt.

They crossed the street and began strolling on the promenade along the Danube. It was bracingly cold and neither had worn gloves. He took her hand after a moment. His was warm, dry and muscular. She liked the way his fingers closed authoritatively around hers. Their bodies seemed to have a rapport with each other all their own; if passersby saw them they might think they were a newly married couple.

At the head of the bridge to Budapest's Margit Island, he steered her to the stone parapet. Putting one hand on each side of her waist, he lifted her onto the broad stone wall, then stood in front of her. Reaching inside her coat, he encircled her with his arms, looking up at her face, his eyes green and wolf-like.

She put her hands on his shoulders, squeezing them. He groaned with pleasure. Reaching up to her, he pulled her face toward his and kissed her. She allowed him to explore her mouth then kissed him back. He pulled her body closer to his. Her legs came up to hug each side of his waist. She tried not to think of how perfectly they might lock together if only time and circumstance would allow them more of a chance to get to know each other.

Staying like that for several minutes, she played lion tamer, Jan her large, golden lion. At last, he released her and lifted her down off the stone wall.

HIS ATTRACTION TO Kati was more than skin deep. Jan wanted her desperately, but also wanted to prove to her he was someone she could trust. At first, he wasn't sure why he had told her about Dirk's situation. But then she had asked to learn more about his son. Another woman might not have wanted the details of his less than fortunate home life. It was easy enough to have fun with a wonderful woman for a few days on holiday in Budapest. It was not so easy to go back home and face the reality of perhaps never seeing his son walk again.

Every time Dirk smiled at him, the thought stabbed his heart that his son was smiling at the man who was responsible for him being crippled. Sometimes Jan couldn't stand himself.

Suddenly, the thud of a body hitting the pavement hit his ears. He knew the sound from times when Dirk slipped out of his wheelchair. Several yards ahead, a man rolled on the ground, jerking convulsively.

"Stay there," Jan shouted to Kati as he ran ahead. Upon reaching the fallen stranger, he knelt on the sidewalk and pinned the man's arms to his sides.

"Kati, come help me. Hold his arms, so I can grab his tongue."

She ran up alongside them, and kneeling down, put one knee directly on the man's arm, so he couldn't move. She leaned over and pushed down the other arm with both of hers. As she struggled to hold him still, Jan pulled the man's jaw open with both hands, then reached in to grab his tongue.

The man twitched wildly and reflexively snapped his jaw shut on Jan's hand. Jan shouted in pain, snatching his hand away. The man appeared to be choking now. Foam and saliva were coming out of his mouth and his eyes had rolled back into his head, so that only the whites showed.

"Help me turn him over," Jan yelled. Together they pushed the man's body so that he rolled over on one side. With this motion, his jaw fell open, and Jan quickly reached in again and pulled out the tongue, clearing the airway. The man began to sputter and cough.

Meanwhile, a group of teenagers had come up behind them and were staring at the scene.

"Get help," Kati yelled to them. "Call an ambulance. He needs to go to a hospital. Please get help right away."

The teenagers ran across the street.

The sound of a siren a minute later announced they had understood. A police car pulled up and two Budapest officers jumped out, addressing Jan in Hungarian, while assessing the prostrate man, who was still unconscious but breathing.

"I'm from Holland on vacation here," Jan told the officers. "He had a seizure. We were walking behind him and he fell down in a fit. We don't know who he is."

Two of the teenage boys had returned and began translating Jan's words into Hungarian for the police officers. Apparently the younger generation of Hungarians had had much more exposure to English than those who had been educated before the fall of the Communist regime in 1990.

The policemen reached into the man's trouser pockets, retrieving his wallet. One officer pulled out a notepad, while the other read the man's name aloud. To Kati's ears, it sounded like "Kovach Lazar."

The teenagers repeated the man's name, whispering amongst themselves in Hungarian. No one knew who he was. He looked to be in his late fifties and was well dressed, in a thick, wool overcoat. One of the officers radioed to headquarters and soon the wail of an approaching ambulance siren filled the night air.

Meanwhile, Jan's hand was bleeding. The policemen pulled a first aid kit out of their patrol car and wrapped his hand in gauze. He grimaced while they worked. The man's teeth had broken the skin, sinking deeply into his right hand. One of the officers said something in Hungarian, which one of the teenagers translated.

"You will go to the hospital. The police will take you and your wife."

"I'll be fine. Tell him I don't need to go to the hospital. It's just a small cut."

The policeman responded, telling the teenager to tell Jan he must wait for the ambulance to arrive, so the attendant could look at his hand. Meanwhile blood was seeping through the gauze bandage, and Kati took his hand in hers, so as not to stain his jacket.

She smiled up at him. Had she noticed the policeman had called her his wife? He liked the sound of it. Then he remembered. He had had a wife and he had let her down.

The ambulance pulled up and a flurry of attendants jumped out to attend to the man lying on the sidewalk. They brought a stretcher alongside him, gently lifting him onto it. Then one of the attendants addressed the police officers, who pointed to Jan's hand. Taking his hand, the attendant unwrapped the gauze. Pulling back the skin of the wound, he shook his head and said something to the policemen in Hungarian. Jan grimaced in pain as the other attendant wrapped his hand up again in a new bandage.

"He says you will need stitches," the teenage boy addressed Jan. "You have to go to Telki Hospital where there are English speaking doctors. The police will take you."

"I don't think I really need to go to a hospital," Jan protested, turning to Kati.

"You need to have a doctor look at your hand, so you have to go." She took his hand gently and looked at him firmly. "I'm coming with you." She turned to the police officers, saying,

"Thank you for offering to take us to the hospital. We're tourists here and have no idea where it is."

The teenage boy began to translate, but the officer cut him off. "I understand. Please come with us. We'll take you to Telki Hospital directly."

As the man with the name of Kovach Lazar was wheeled into the back of the ambulance, Jan glanced at Kati.

"I hope he'll recover," she said.

"He'll be okay," he replied, loving this gentle caring side of her. "The only danger from having an epileptic fit is if the person hurts himself when he falls or swallows his tongue and chokes to death."

They got into the back of the police car and drove off into the night. The two officers were friendly, offering him some bottled water.

"We will take your name and address for our report," one of the officers declared. "You are a good man to help him. Maybe you save his life."

"Thank you," Jan said. He was unable to use his right hand to write down his name and address, so he motioned for Kati to pull out his wallet and give them the requested information.

KATI SCANNED JAN'S driver's license, taking in all the information she read as she wrote it down. Jan Klassen lived at Schalterdalweg 16 in Beekbergen, Holland. His birth date was October 12, and he was six years older than her. She busied herself putting all the information in the correct spaces while the police car stopped at red lights. Soon they pulled up in front of a modern glass-paneled building with *Telki Kurhaz* lettered in front. She surmised that might mean "Telki Hospital" or "Cure House" in Hungarian.

The police got out and spoke for a few minutes with the administrative staff inside. A form was given to Jan which he handed to her to fill in for him. At the bottom of the registration document, some Hungarian words had been scribbled.

"What does this say?" She pointed to the words.

"Bill to be paid by Budapest Police Department." The clerk smiled. "Are you in pain, sir?"

Jan shook his head.

"Please take a seat and a nurse will be out soon."

They sat down in the waiting room, which was empty except for an elderly woman sleeping in her chair.

"Does it hurt?" Kati whispered to Jan.

"It doesn't hurt as much as it will saying goodbye to you next week." He winked at her then winced.

"How did you know what to do when he fell down?" she asked, taking his bandaged hand in both of hers and giving him a tender look.

"I didn't really, but as soon as I reached him, I saw he was having a fit. I work with kids and old people in my job, and I've seen people have epileptic attacks before. The most important thing is to make sure they don't hurt themselves or swallow their tongue while having the seizure. The seizure itself is something you can't do anything about. It's something mysterious going on inside the brain. All you can do is keep the person out of trouble until it's over."

Jan had so many practical skills. The one she liked best was his ability to look directly into her eyes and not allow anything to distract him. He was doing this now, while she stroked the fingers peeking out of his bandaged right hand.

"We're having a lot of adventures together," she whispered.

"It's because you're an adventurer," Jan whispered back. "When we spend time together something exciting always happens. It's because you get us into trouble." His eyes twinkled as he bent down and kissed her on the cheek.

"You have no idea what kind of trouble we could really get into. You haven't seen anything yet," she teased, wondering how such words could have escaped her lips.

"I'm ready for many more adventures with you, little one. You know how to match me, and that makes me want to match you."

"I know what you mean," she whispered, kissing him on the cheek. He turned his head and caught her mouth with his.

"Good evening, could you come this way please?" a heavily accented female voice spoke above them.

Kati looked up. An attractive middle-aged nurse smiled, beckoning them through the glass door to the triage area. She must have seen them kissing, because her eyes twinkled when Kati passed by her, evidently in silent approval of the tall, attractive man at her side.

Jan sat down in the triage area. "What happened?" the nurse asked, unwrapping his hand.

Jan quickly explained about the unknown man having a seizure.

"Did you succeed in helping him?" the nurse asked.

"Yes, he did," Kati cut in. "The man was choking, but Jan turned him on his side and got his tongue away from the back of his throat. He had stabilized by the time we left and they took him away in an ambulance."

"You did the right thing," the nurse said, with a kind glance at Jan, then Kati. "We'll have the doctor look at this and decide if you need a stitch or two. Meanwhile, I'll get you some pain reliever. Are you allergic to aspirin?"

"No, neither to brandy." Jan replied, teasingly.

"I was going to recommend that for right before going to bed tonight. Your wife will remember to dose you with a small glass, no?" The nurse turned to her playfully.

Kati was enjoying all these mistaken assumptions about her relationship to Jan. Did they look like a couple? Apparently so, to everyone around them. She beamed.

"I'll give him his dose, and one for myself too," she replied.

Why were they having so much fun when Jan was injured and they were in a hospital instead of her hotel room after such a full day? She couldn't believe how good she felt, with the residual tingle of the plunge bath on her skin, and Jan's recent kiss on her mouth making her heart beat faster. She would have to get a grip on herself if she was to be a good nurse to him that night.

"Is there any risk of infection?" she asked the nurse.

"Most likely not, but we'll give him a short course of antibiotics just to be safe." The nurse's coy smile to Kati seemed once again to indicate she approved of her taste in men.

A doctor entered the room.

"Let's see what we've got here," the physician said, washing his hands then taking Jan's right hand and twisting it lightly.

When he winced, Kati winced with him.

"We're going to give you a stitch or two, and a prescription for antibiotics. You'll be fine in a few days. The stitches will dissolve within a week, and you'll have a small scar." Turning to the nurse, he said, "Put him in treatment room three and prepare the set-up. I'll be there in a few minutes."

They moved to the interior of the hospital, walking past an elderly man on a stretcher in the hallway, then a young couple with a small child on her father's lap. The child was crying, but when Jan passed by, she pointed and said excitedly, *"Mikulás bácsi!"*

Jan made a funny face at the little girl, then boomed out, "Ho ho ho!" in a loud voice.

The child squealed with delight.

"She thinks your husband is Santa Claus," the nurse chuckled to Kati.

Kati found it amusing that Jan would come across as Santa Claus to the young girl. He was a kind of Santa Claus to her too, but more in terms of the multitude of intangible gifts he showered on her. There was his total attention to her when they were together. There was his willingness to match her pace in the development of their physical intimacy. Then there were his ideas about where to go and what to do that were off the beaten track. He'd offered her substance, with a lot of humor and adventure mixed in. All were proving to be satisfying gifts, the memory of which would linger long after the Christmas gift-giving season had passed.

She turned to Jan. "How did you know she was saying Santa Claus?"

"It's not the first time I've been called *Mikulás bácsi* here. He's the Hungarian Santa. Last November, I had a five-year-old girl following me around the hotel trying to give me her Christmas list."

Kati studied Jan for a moment. He didn't have a beard, but he was tall, broad and had on a red jacket. She could vaguely see a resemblance.

She helped him take off his jacket in the treatment room. She wasn't looking forward to seeing the stitches put in, but she would stay.

"I'm going to give you a local anesthesia to make you more comfortable when the doctor begins," the nurse said as she removed the gauze pad then ripped open an alcohol swab packet and dabbed the inside of his wrist above the wounded hand.

"You're giving me a shot?" he looked worried.

"Yes." The nurse, with her back to Jan, rolled her eyes at Kati. "It'll be over before you know it," she said over her shoulder. Then she instructed Kati. "Hold his arm steady, while I take care of this."

Kati tried to stifle a giggle. It appeared that Jan didn't like needles. Here he was, a man well over six feet tall who had just put his hand in the mouth of a convulsing man, yet he was turning white at the thought of a tiny needle about to be stuck in his arm.

"Would you like me to sing you a song right now?" she asked.

"A song? Yes. What song?" He looked surprised.

"Well, I usually sing the Barney Song when I'm babysitting my friends' children and they get a boo boo and are crying. But that song might not be appropriate for you. What about a song that Fats Waller made famous?"

"Sure," he said, his face lighting up.

She cleared her throat. "Okay, here goes." She counted off and launched into it. "Uh-one-uh-two-uh-one-two-three.... You're mean to me, why must you be mean to me? Gee honey, it seems to me... you like to see me crying, well I don't know why.... I stay home, each night when you say you'll phone—you don't and I'm left all alone singing the blues and sighing..." She hit some high notes. "You treat me coldly each day of the year..."

Just at that moment the nurse pricked Jan with the needle. He flinched slightly but didn't take his eyes off Kati's face.

"You always scold me," Kati continued to sing, making a face at him. "Whenever somebody comes near—dear—It must be great fun to be mean to me, You shouldn't for can't you see what you mean to me..." There she ended the first verse of the 1928 Fred Ahlert and Roy Turk song *Mean to Me.*

The doctor entered the room, and both he and the nurse applauded.

"*Brava*, that's a wonderful American song. Like from an old movie," the doctor exclaimed.

Jan looked as if he had forgotten he was in a hospital emergency room.

"Encore, encore," the doctor and nurse both pleaded.

Kati was pleased. Gazing at Jan, she asked, "Okay, what would you like me to sing while you get your stitches?"

"Sing another one by Fats," he told her. "I liked that song. It was so American."

"*Mean to Me* wasn't written by Fats Waller, it was just made famous by him. But here's one that he wrote himself. It's called *Squeeze Me*."

"I like it already," Jan approved.

"I thought you might." She counted off and launched into a slower, bluesy number. "Oh Daddy squeeze me and squeeze me again," she sang. "Oh Daddy don't stop till I tell you when..." she continued, as she wandered through the first verse of Fats Waller's 1923 song *Squeeze Me*.

At that point, a group of hospital personnel had gathered by the door. The doctor began to sew, but Jan barely noticed, his eyes riveted on Kati's hips swaying in time to the beat of the song.

Applause echoed up and down the hospital corridor when she ended the tune. Jan couldn't clap, so he whistled admiringly.

"I wish your husband had a more serious injury so we could hear more." The doctor walked to the door. "But I'm all done with him. Take him home and sing him to sleep."

"Will do," She had enjoyed playing Mrs. Jan Klassen for the evening.

"Sounds like a good plan, Doctor. Thanks," Jan echoed.

"We'll give you your first dose here, then you should get this filled tomorrow morning." The nurse handed him a piece of paper with a prescription for antibiotics on it and then a cup with a pill in it. "Take one pill twice a day, morning and evening for the next four days. Take it with food."

Kati picked up Jan's jacket as the nurse wrapped his hand.

"The stitches will dissolve within a week, so you don't need to come back unless you're feeling pain," the woman explained. You should keep the bandage on for the next week, and change it every day. Here's some extra gauze to take with you."

"Thank you, Madame. You've been very kind." Jan gallantly took the nurse's hand with his left one and kissed it. The best Austro-Hungarian customs had not gone unnoticed by him.

"Thank you." She turned to Kati. "I wish you were here all the time. We would all have a much more enjoyable time with you singing songs to our patients. They would recover sooner too."

"Thank you, *köszönöm*." Kati used one of the only words she knew in Hungarian to say thank you.

"*Köszönöm és jó éjszakát!*"

"You too," she responded, asking Jan quietly, "What did she say?"

"*Jó éjszakát!*" he called back to the nurse. "It means good night, little Puritan with the Hungarian face," he whispered to Kati. "Promise to sing *Squeeze Me* when you put me to bed tonight. Doctor's orders, remember?" His face was stern, but his eyes twinkled as he waved the forefinger of his bandaged hand at her.

"I've got another Fats Waller song in mind for you later. It's called *Ain't Misbehavin*."

Jan rolled his eyes at her. "I like the *Squeeze Me* song better."

"Sorry, that song is retired for this evening. Maybe if you're a very good patient, I'll sing it to you again tomorrow."

"You Americans really have a way with words when you set them to music," he said.

"Yes, you Europeans have over one thousand years of culture and we Americans have Fats Waller and baseball, among other significant contributions."

"Americans know how to have fun. I like that."

"Thanks. I'll remember that."

"You don't need to. You *are* fun, Kati." He squeezed her arm, above the elbow. "You don't need to think about it, because you *are* it."

"Well, I like that. But you've had enough fun for today. Let's go home and put you to bed."

She was talking to Jan as if he were her longstanding boyfriend. The events of the evening had thrown them so closely together it was as if they'd dated each other for years instead of days. Was this what having an affair in a foreign country did to someone? They hadn't even gotten to the "affair" stage yet, but already it felt like much more.

At the hospital entrance they hailed a cab, then rode back to the hotel in companionable silence. It was late. Jan's hand was still anesthetized and he silently cursed fate that it was his dominant hand that had been injured. This would make it easy to follow Kati's guidelines on maintaining her virtue throughout the night. He prayed that his nurse would attend to him until morning. Wasn't there a risk of him developing an infection and getting feverish in the middle of the night? She couldn't desert him in his hour of need.

They reached the hotel and Kati helped him into the elevator.

"What floor number should I press?" she asked.

"Yours."

"Are you sure?"

"Don't you remember doctor's orders? You have to sing me to sleep. And what if I develop a fever during the night?" he badgered her. "Wouldn't you feel bad if I were dead in the morning, all because you hadn't looked after me?"

"I want to take care of you. But don't try to take advantage of being injured, okay? My guidelines still stand."

"At this point, I'm not in a position to take advantage of anything. You have no idea how clumsy I am with my left hand." He shook his head, trying but not succeeding in looking sad.

"Fine. You need to rest. We can resume this conversation in the morning, but promise me you'll behave yourself as well as you did last night, if you're going to stay."

"Promise. The fates have given me no choice, so I'll be your hero once again tonight. Just remember, I'm not your brother."

"I've noticed." She reached up and kissed him on the mouth. Then she opened the door to her room.

She went into the bathroom to undress, while Jan found some drinks for them in the mini-bar. When she came out, she wore a paisley silk dressing gown in deep shades of blue, green, and purple. It made her look like a queen. What was under the dressing gown? God, he should stop thinking about such things if he didn't want to alarm her with the swell of parts of his body other than his injured hand.

Finding soda water in the mini-refrigerator, he went out into the hallway to fill the ice bucket. He thought it might be a good idea to hold the ice bucket against his lower torso on his way back from the ice machine, both to cool down and hide parts of his physique. Kati had a way of heating him up, even when she was lecturing him on the virtues of maintaining her guidelines.

Returning to the room, he mixed their drinks and they toasted each other.

"Here's to you being Kovach Lazar's hero today," she said.

"Here's to being your hero tonight," he replied, thinking somewhat ruefully that he'd never found himself in such a situation before with a woman he liked so much.

They clinked glasses and laughed. Suddenly they were starving. Kati pulled out the room service menu, handing it to him.

"Pick something enormous for one, because I don't want to order for two. Foreign women staying alone at hotels shouldn't be entertaining men in their rooms."

He sighed. Women had a lot more social conventions to think about than men, but she was right. He wanted to protect her as well as make love to her. It was confusing. Even more confusing was the fact that he didn't mind feeling this confused about a woman. It was a first for him.

"Okay, how about the cheese and salami platter and a big bowl of goulash with lots of bread? Get a half carafe of red wine too."

"Works for me," she agreed. She picked up the phone to call room service. After placing the order, she warned him that he would need to step into the bathroom when room service arrived.

He made a face at her.

She got up to move her chair closer to his, but instead he grabbed her arm with his left hand and pulled her onto his lap. He was doing a poor job of keeping his vital parts cooled, but couldn't help himself. He needed his private nurse near.

She sighed and reached over him, flicking off the lamp.

Suddenly, the room was bathed in moonlight. They both looked out the French doors to her balcony, while their eyes adjusted to the night, making out the stars and a full moon high in the December sky.

"I've got you right where I want you," he said, hugging her to him with his left arm.

"Funny, I was thinking the same thing," she agreed, adjusting her position against him.

"Nurse, I need you to kiss me." Kati's nearness was making his internal temperature soar.

"I'm in charge here and I'll decide if you need a kiss or not." She turned around and leaned into his face. Tracing the corners of his mouth with her fingers, she brushed her lips against his, tickling him.

He followed her motion and their noses brushed against each other, back and forth. He nuzzled her cheek with his mouth, then her ear. Then he lightly bit her earlobe.

At that moment a knock at the door announced room service had arrived.

Scrambling out of his lap, Kati rushed to the bathroom door and opened it, shooing Jan in. Then she adjusted her paisley robe, and opened the door an inch with the security latch still on.

Meanwhile, Jan studied the items on Kati's bathroom sink counter. Bottles, jars, compacts and mysterious items were scattered everywhere. What did women do with all this stuff? No wonder it took them forever to get ready to go out. He picked up a flat round object and opened it. Something red and powdery was inside. He dusted it on his cheeks. Opening a smaller compact, he found four shades of purple and blue powder, all of which he rubbed on his eyelids. Studying himself critically in the mirror, he realized something was missing— lipstick. Picking up a gold tube, he uncovered something flesh colored, clearly not lipstick. "Under eye concealer" was written on the bottom. He tried a few other tubes until he found what he wanted. Applying deep red lipstick, he realized he was supposed to do something with a Kleenex to finish it all off. He'd seen it done on TV. He took a Kleenex and blotted his mouth. Done.

"JUST A MINUTE," Kati called to whoever waited in the corridor, sweeping the room with her eye. Jan's jacket was thrown over a chair. She tossed it in the closet, then made sure her robe was closed up to her neck. Taking off the security latch, she opened the door. A Hungarian youth wheeled the cart into the room. In a moment he was done setting up and on his way out.

Closing the door behind him, she turned as Jan stepped out of the bathroom. She frowned. Then switching on the light, she laughed.

"You've got nice coloring without makeup, Jan. I don't think you really need it."

"I don't think you really need it either, but since you wear it, I thought I'd see what it could do for me."

"Jan, I like you all pink and gold the way you are. Too much rouge makes you look cheap."

"Are you saying you prefer me in my natural Santa Claus state?"

"Yes. And I like all the presents you've been giving me."

"I noticed. To be continued after dinner."

They took their seats and feasted hungrily upon the simple, delicious fare. Room service had included a tapered white candle on the cart, which they lit, switching off the room lights.

"What day are you leaving?" he asked.

"My flight leaves Monday at one in the afternoon."

"How're you getting to the airport?"

"Um, taxi I suppose."

"I'll come with you," he told her.

"I'd like that. When are you leaving Budapest?"

"Wednesday. I fly to Shiphol," he said, referring to Amsterdam's international airport, "then drive back to Beekbergen. It'll take less than an hour."

"Are you going to get into trouble on Tuesday without me?" she asked sternly.

"I promise I'll only look at blondes who remind me of you."

"Just looking is fine. Make sure you spend the day crying because I'm gone."

"How about if I spend the day shopping for a Christmas present from Budapest for you?"

"I guess that means I'll have to give you my address in New York to send it to," she said, looking down to hide the blush she felt reddening her cheeks as she thought of the leather jacket she'd gotten for Jan, now hidden in her closet.

"I guess so. You already have my address, since you rifled through my wallet when I was busy having my hand bandaged."

"Yup. Got to see your birth date too. You're a Libra."

"I am? What are you?"

"I'm an Aquarius, born in February."

"How do Libra and Aquarius get along?"

"You'll have to do some research and find out." She had read that Libra was Aquarius's ideal marriage partner; she wouldn't share that with him just yet.

"Okay, but I need to know your exact birthday."

"February 10th."

"What year?"

"What cheek," she slapped him down.

"What do you mean, 'cheek'?"

"I mean it's none of your business what year I was born." She tossed her hair, giving him a sphinx-like look.

"It's not?" Smiling he grabbed her hand with his left one. "Why isn't it my business? Don't you like me finding out your details? Isn't it my business then to know you like having your earlobe bitten?" He reached over and kissed her ear, then tugged gently at the earlobe with his teeth.

She shivered.

"Let's talk about my earlobe, not my birth date," she murmured.

"Let's not talk at all," he whispered, pulling her next to him and nibbling up and down the perimeter of her ear. Soon he moved on to her neck. He pulled her hair up into a high pony-tail and kissed her skin at the base of it. Then he gently bit.

With a gasp, Kati shot straight up into the air. When she came back down she was on Jan's lap. He had discovered the hottest of her hot spots outside of classified zones. If she let proceedings go farther, those zones were in danger of becoming declassified. She needed to put the brakes on right away, and she would—in just a minute ... or two. How could he have possibly known that the area hiding under her hair on her neck was the one public spot on her entire body that was cataclysmically erogenous? She had always thought those male vampires had known what they were doing, when they mingled love with death. At least their female victims had died in a state of ecstasy.

"You're one hellcat of a Puritan, darling." His laughter rumbled as he buried his face in her hair. "I think your body and mind are at war with each other."

"That's the human condition, friend," she parlayed, then whispered, "Do it again."

He bit her neck again, less gently this time. She shot out of his lap and rested her face against a cool pane of one of the French doors. He stood and came up close behind her, pressing her into the glass. They both stared out at the full moon, panting like wolves in heat.

"It looks like one of those full moon kinds of nights, little girl."

"Remember you have an injured paw, Tiger Boy." She didn't know where some of her remarks came from. Her inner gypsy had escaped and was on the rampage. Again, she felt like Hester Prynne the night she earned her scarlet letter.

With Jan pinning her to the glass door with his body, she slipped her hand onto the door latch and managed to open it. They tumbled out onto the balcony into the stinging cold of the night air.

She leaned on the railing, gasping. Her body was a runaway train, about to go off track. She needed to find the brakes fast.

Jan took her in his arms and kissed her mouth deeply. She put her hand between them to push him away. Instead, the part of his body she brushed against came alive beneath her touch.

Recoiling as if she'd touched a hot burner on the stove, her hand shot into the air. She was making all the wrong moves to protect her virtue, yet every one of them felt so right. Where would this lead? Thank God, his right hand was out of commission.

They clung to each other, their bodies as warm as they had been in the waters of the Széchenyi Baths. They had shared their first kiss there two days earlier. Had it really only been forty-eight hours since they'd first given into their passion for each other?

At that moment, time, space and reality had come to a complete stop. There was nothing more beyond Jan's hands on her body, the endless night sky and the pounding of her wild heart. Was this what it was to exist entirely in the present moment? She wished she could stay forever.

# CHAPTER EIGHT

# LAST WEEKEND TOGETHER

THE NEXT MORNING Kati and Jan awoke, wrapped in each other's arms. Jan had managed to observe her guidelines, but if he hadn't been hindered by the enormous bandage swathing his right hand she suspected it might not have been that easy—for either one of them.

It was all about going slowly. Maybe this wasn't altogether slow, but it was slow enough that he had spent an exquisitely long amount of time exploring her earlobes and neck. If she'd allowed him to explore other areas...?

She smiled slyly to herself. Perhaps there were reasons for restraint that had as much to do with increasing a woman's pleasure, as they did with maintaining her virtue. Her father had sometimes said that when it came to what went on between men and women, being a bit confused wasn't so bad. She was beginning to understand what he had meant.

She stretched slowly then got out of bed. The day was overcast, with no traces of the clear sky of the night before. Padding to the door, she slipped it open, retrieving the *International Herald Tribune* on her doorstep. She flipped to the page with weather forecasts for all major international cities.

Snow was expected in Budapest. It would be a cozy day to spend together with Jan. Looking at her watch, she opened the door again. Her morning coffee and continental breakfast were due to arrive any minute. She put a note outside saying "Please leave breakfast tray outside door" so she wouldn't need to hustle Jan into the bathroom when it came.

Looking down at the sleeping man before her, she drank in what she saw. He was a study in red, pink and gold—his large well-muscled chest and arms wrapped around a pillow, which he had substituted for her the minute she had left the bed. He looked like a man comfortable with having a partner.

Leaning over him, she kissed his nose. He opened his eyes and pulled her down on top of him.

"Good morning, Nurse."

"Good morning, my patient."

"How'd I do last night?"

"You were very good. How'd I do?"

"You were very naughty. I now know all your secrets."

"Not all of them, but enough to be dangerous. I'll have to keep you tied up for the rest of the weekend," she teased.

"Oh good, I love being tied up by a beautiful blonde."

"What do you mean—a beautiful blonde?" She pushed him back onto the bed. "Am I just another beautiful blonde to you?"

"No, you're *my* beautiful blonde. At least, for two more days."

"If you send me the right Christmas present, maybe I'll be yours a while longer," she challenged him.

"Thanks. That was my plan for something to do after you've left."

They hugged, shoved, tussled with and kissed each other until the aroma of coffee wafted from under the door.

"Breakfast," she called cheerfully as she went to retrieve the tray.

Bundling up their terrycloth robes around them, they stepped out onto the balcony with steaming mugs of coffee. Life was delicious.

"I smell snow in the air," he said.

"What're we doing today after we get your prescription filled?" she asked.

"I need to buy a present for my boy and don't have any idea what to get. Will you help me?"

"I'd love to." She beamed. She liked shopping for presents and she wasn't surprised that Jan needed help. The complementarity of the sexes made men and women indispensable to each other in many ways. It felt good to be needed; it pleased her that Jan liked it too. Neither one was afraid to show they needed the other—a good sign for the future.

She frowned. What future? The logistics seemed so daunting.

Finishing their coffee and croissants, they agreed to meet in the lobby in forty-five minutes. After Jan set off for his room, she fished in her closet for something casual yet special to wear on this penultimate day together with the man who had now taken up residence in her heart. She pulled out a periwinkle blue sweater with a scoop neckline and put it on along with her jeans.

They set off for a pharmacy to get Jan's antibiotics. The hotel concierge had given them the name of an "apotheke" in the direction of the Vaçi Utça, after Kati had asked him for some suggestions on where to shop for an eleven-year-old boy.

The sky was laden with unburst snow clouds, the air bracing, expectant. Kati liked the way she always ended up doing something physical with Jan. It was a refreshing change from the wining and dining she had done with Krisztof the week before. There was only so much champagne she could drink in one lifetime; she was beginning to think she'd had her fill.

After twenty minutes they reached the Vaçi Utça. Kati decided not to point out all the boutiques she'd visited the day before, especially the one where she'd bought the leather jacket she planned to give him, now hidden in her hotel room closet. As they strolled by, the female salesclerk of the day before was setting up a display in the window. Kati pretended not to notice, but out of the corner of her eye observed the woman taking a long, lingering look at Jan as they passed. She made a silent prayer that the pretty salesgirl would find a man like Jan to fill her days and nights sometime very soon.

They continued on down the street and found the address the concierge had given them. An enormous glass window revealed pale yellow walls inside, with chandeliers hanging from high ceilings. A balcony with delicate latticework on the back wall faced them. It was filled with boxes of medications—sure enough, this was the "apotheke." Jan swung open the double doors and ushered Kati into the most elegant pharmacy she had ever seen.

Walking over to a display counter, Jan gave his prescription to an attractive female clerk who motioned them to some chairs where they could wait.

The beautiful upholstered armchairs available for customers were red with yellow striped seats. The magnificence of the Austro-Hungarian period in Hungary's history appeared to be making a resurgence in Budapest's post-Communist era.

Tourists from all over the world would enjoy getting their prescriptions filled in a pharmacy such as this one, Kati thought. It was enough to make a visitor want to come down with a mild travel bug while in Budapest.

Instead of sitting down, they wandered up and down the aisles admiring the goods for sale in elegant display cases. Everything was well-appointed, but she couldn't imagine a single item in what she pictured Jan's home to be like in Holland. He didn't seem the type to have a designer soap collection for guests or monogrammed hand towels in his bathrooms. Would she ever find out?

The clerk called to them, and they returned to the pharmacy counter to retrieve the prescription. "Take these with food, once in the morning and once in the evening for the next four days." She rang up the purchase and they exited the shop.

Now it was time to find something for Dirk.

"What does he like?" Kati asked.

"He likes to read, especially books on design and architecture." Jan stroked his chin. "We also build models together."

"Do you think Budapest has a Museum of Architecture or Design?" she mused.

"There's the Museum of Fine Arts, but that's mostly paintings and sculptures. Let's go have a coffee so I can take my pills and check the guidebook." He pulled out his tourist guide.

"Want to go somewhere special for a coffee?" she suggested. "My treat." The Café Gerbeaud was just around the corner. It would be fun to compare experiencing it with him with the visit she had made last week with Krisztof, on the day after she had first met Jan in the pools. A bolt of electricity shot up her back as she marveled at how much had changed since then.

"Is it one of those fancy cafés with gold fixtures everywhere and tiny china cups that I'll probably break when I pick up?" Jan asked, making a droll face at her.

"Yes."

"Okay, why not?" He sighed. "I'm ready for another adventure with you. Just don't ask me to crook my pinkie while I drink my espresso."

She rolled her eyes at him and they entered the massive double doors of the Café Gerbeaud. Blinking, her eyes adjusted to the marble and gold-leafed interior which trumped the pharmacy they had just left. A large, regal Christmas tree stood in the center, decorated with red and gold foil-wrapped *szalon cukor,* Hungarian marzipan parlor candy.

"I hope no children try to give me their Christmas lists in here," Jan joked as the hostess led them to a green marble topped bistro table. They ordered two espressos then studied the tourist guide. He had already visited all of Budapest's largest museums, so they continued flipping pages for something else.

"What's that?" She pointed to a photo of a large art deco building topped with a gold dome.

"It says here it's the Iparmuveseti Museum—the Museum of Applied Arts." He read from the guide. "A magnificent domed building created by Odon Lechner, major architect of the Art Nouveau movement and nicknamed 'The Hungarian Gaudi.' If there is only one art nouveau building you have time to see in Budapest, this is the one to visit."

"I love Gaudi," she enthused. The Catalan architect from whose name the word "gaudy" was derived, was anything but. Futuristic and nature-inspired was more like it in her book. "Does your son like Art Nouveau?"

"I'm not sure if he knows what Art Nouveau is yet. Let's go see it and get him something that will introduce him to the style."

They finished their coffees, which were served with small glasses of water with no ice, in the style of Viennese cafés.

Time spent with her father had taught Kati that one of Béla Dunai's favorite activities had been engaging in hours-long conversations over coffee and a small pastry in one of many cafés that dotted his German-Hungarian neighborhood in Manhattan. Her father had understood the pleasure of taking his time and focusing his attention. Jan here with her now reminded her of him.

The tourist guide indicated that the number 4/6 tram would take them the Museum of Applied Arts located at Ferenc Körút Plaza. They walked several blocks, asking their way from young people on the street, all of whom spoke some English. Soon the tram arrived and they hopped on. Standing close to each other, they observed the passengers around them. With Jan, she found it more fun to take public transportation than a taxi. She could get a feel for what the real Budapesters were like, going about their everyday lives.

Krisztof had always taken cabs whenever they went some-where together. It may have been the privilege of wealth, but she didn't want to be shielded from this vibrant, exotic city. She wanted to explore it safely; in Jan she had found a perfect partner. Would he prove a perfect partner in other ways too? She moved closer, inhaling his fresh scent.

It seemed to Kati that people were more physically interac-tive in Hungary than in the U.S. They jostled and bumped each other. Schoolmates held onto each other's shoulders, or held hands walking down the street. Older couples embraced and kissed far more frequently than they did back in New York. She only rarely saw couples of any age embracing and kissing in Manhattan. Busy professionals rushed alone somewhere most of the time, picking up their dry cleaning or going to the gym on weekends.

She watched as an old man toward the back of the tram teased his wife of similar years. He stole a kiss, to which his wife smacked him in the chest while hoarsely reprimanding him in Hungarian. He laughed at her and kissed her again. She batted him again, also laughing. Kati nudged Jan, who looked in the same direction, enjoying the scene. It was refreshing to see two elderly Budapesters horsing around like teenagers. Was it because of the spicy paprika used to season so many of Hungary's dishes? Perhaps it was something in the water. If so, Jan and she had spent enough time in Budapest's waters to be immersed in whatever it was that drove Hungarians' robust physicality with each other.

Their stop arrived and they jumped off. Jan bent down to steal a kiss similar to the old man's from his wife. Kati playfully shoved him away. They laughed and set off for the enormous gold-domed building looming in front of them, its distinctive roof made of intricately designed green and gold tiles. Paying a small admission charge, they entered a huge white room with vaulted ceilings reminiscent of an Indian palace or a Turkish mosque. There was no resemblance here to Gaudi, but a vast and original architectural style that made it clear why Odon Lechner's name was included in history books.

Climbing the stairs to the exhibits on the upper floor, they wandered through room after room of everyday household items. Chinaware, clocks, clothes, shoes and jewelry were on display, all made with exceptional artistry. Finally, they made their way to the museum gift shop where Kati asked if a model of the building itself was available. The clerk showed them a small architectural replica, and then a do-it-yourself model kit for children. They chose the kit, and Jan thanked Kati for having led him to exactly the right gift for his son.

Over the next few hours they toured Budapest, taking the funicular to the top of Castle Hill, the city's most ancient and royal neighborhood. They visited Budapest Castle. From its ramparts they admired the enormous complex of Parliament buildings that stretched alongside the Danube. Now and again they stopped for a glass of hot mulled wine from the street vendors. The cold and damp didn't bother Kati in the least, with the wine warming her stomach and Jan's proximity warming deeper parts.

Around three in the afternoon it began to snow.

"Let's go back to the hotel and soak in the pool," she suggested, exhilarated by the soft snowflakes dropping onto her face.

"Good idea," Jan agreed. He looked in his element, his shaggy blond hair dotted with white flakes.

They trudged slowly down Castle Hill and wended their way across the Margit Bridge, passing the spot where Jan had come to the aid of the struggling man the night before.

"How do you think Kovach Lazar is doing today?" She shivered to think of the man writhing on the ground.

"He's probably fine and doesn't remember too much of what happened last night," Jan reassured her.

"Do you think he has any idea who saved him?"

"No, And it doesn't matter. I just did what needed to be done at the right moment." He squeezed her hand in his.

"You did what others might hesitate to do. I wouldn't have had the faintest idea."

"Well, now you do. If someone's having a seizure, turn them over on their side so the tongue will dangle down and make sure nothing is blocking their airway," Jan instructed her.

"How's your hand?" she asked.

"I forgot about it until you asked. It's fine. I just wish I could use it to get to know you better." With his good hand he flipped a strand of hair from her face.

"We are getting to know each other better, and believe me—it's better for both of us that we really get to know each other instead of just thinking we know each other because we had sex." She surprised herself with the direct words that had just fallen from her mouth, but it was what she truly felt. She didn't regret saying it, even if she had been blunt.

"It wouldn't be just having sex with you, Kati." Jan's voice was low, his face serious.

"What would it be?"

"It would be what you'd call 'making love,'" he replied, looking into her eyes as he took her hand again.

"I like you," she said softly. "Very much."

"I like you, Kati. Very much." He didn't blink.

That's all they had for the moment. It was enough. Their restraint satisfied Kati far more than making love with someone she could only say for sure that she liked a lot. It didn't make sense to venture farther until both her heart and mind were as ready as her body was. She thanked God that Jan had wanted to get to know her enough to stick around even if he wasn't getting laid. Instead, they were discovering things in common aside from the obvious physical attraction they felt for each other.

They arrived back at the hotel just as snow began to accumulate on the ground, and hurried inside. The warmth encompassed them like a blanket. A huge fire blazed in the lounge off the lobby.

"Let's come here and enjoy the fireplace after we go to the pools," she suggested.

"Good idea. I don't think we'll be going anywhere for the rest of the day, the way the snow's coming down."

They went up to their respective rooms, changed into their bathing suits and met a few minutes later at the entrance to the pools. After hours of walking, they chose the Jacuzzi first to ease their tired bodies into.

Kati leaned her head back against the tile wall. Warm, strong jets massaged her back like experienced fingers. She closed her eyes in pleasure. Would she have been as receptive to Jan if it hadn't been for the thermal baths where they'd met? After days of sulfured water polishing and massaging her skin, her body had been reduced to silly putty and her brain to mush. Looking over at him, she caught him looking at her with that focused, blue green gaze that energized her every time.

Suddenly, the answer to her question was clear. She would have fallen for Jan anywhere at any time. Now the question was whether her life back in New York would fully recapture her attention, swallowing her up in its busy maw. She doubted it.

"What are you thinking?" Jan asked, his fingers closing around the back of her neck.

She shivered. "I was thinking I'm not going to be the same person when I get back to New York as I was when I left."

"How've you changed?"

"I've slowed down." She stretched her legs under the bubbling water. "And I like it."

"What's your life like back in New York?"

"Busy. I'll be traveling a lot for my new job."

"Tell me about it."

"I'm going to put together programs for international conferences. The first one I'll be working on is in Barcelona in February."

"Tough life," he joked.

"I'm looking forward to it. But what is tough is that I'll be traveling all the time. It's hard to have a life at home, when you're not there most of the time."

"How do you know?"

"I know because my friends who do this kind of work have been telling me about it for years," she replied. "I got my new job through a friend of mine who's on the road about sixty percent of the time. She's the most glamorous person I know…"

"And?" He lifted a brow at her.

"And she has no life."

"What do you mean?" he asked, his brows knitting together.

"I mean she's smart and gorgeous, but she doesn't have time to find a boyfriend or get married or even spend time with her friends. We get together as much as we can when she's in town, but we don't really get a chance to see each other a lot. I admire her, but I don't want my new job to put me in her shoes."

"What if it does?" Jan asked.

"I might re-evaluate my priorities and find something else to do."

"Would you like to work in Europe?" His voice was low, steady.

"I—I never thought about it," she stammered. "I love Europe. But I think it's hard getting papers to work in Europe." Why was he asking?

"Europe is slower than America," he observed.

"So I see."

"You don't rush around so much. There are cafés, thermal baths, lots of holidays…"

"Wow. Why was I not born in Europe?"

"It doesn't matter where you were born, Kati. It matters what you choose. Find out who you are and choose the lifestyle that fits you."

"Who are you, Jan?" His questions were making her nervous. It was time to turn the tables and get the focus off of her.

He splashed her playfully, then looked away, silent for a moment.

"I thought I knew who I was, and then something happened that changed everything."

No doubt he referred to the motorcycle accident.

"So you no longer ride your motorcycle. What else has changed?"

"The way my son and I spend time together. If it hadn't happened, we would have played sports together all the time. I would have coached him in football, or what you call 'soccer.' I would have taught him to dribble and kick, defend the goal. We would have gone camping, fishing and hiking together. It's all different now."

She remained silent, absorbing what he'd said. She didn't want to answer lightly, because the moment had turned serious.

"You told me a few days ago that your son and you spend time remodeling your house," she finally said. "You read design books and build things together. That doesn't sound a lot worse than kicking a soccer ball around. It sounds more interesting."

"Yeah. It is interesting. It's just different. We have a quieter kind of life, living more in our heads and less with our bodies."

"What's wrong with living in your head?"

"Nothing. It's just not what I did when I was a boy, and it's not what I was expecting to do with my own son." His voice was dry, pat. Reality was taking a deep bite out of him at that moment.

She gazed at him, studying the lines of his broad, open face. This wasn't a conversation to take lightly.

"Jan, you had plans for your life as an adult and then something happened to change those plans. You could call it fate or maybe divine intervention. I'd say that God changed your life so that He could show you something new that you would never have seen if this hadn't happened to you."

"That's what the minister of the church I sometimes go to said to me. It's just that I don't know what the new thing is this God is supposed to be showing me." He shook his head sadly, looking puzzled.

"He's showing you a new side of yourself you'd never have discovered if this hadn't happened."

"Like what?"

"Like one of the things I like most about you."

"You think I'm that good looking?" He looked at her slyly; he was back on firm ground.

"Noo." She laughed. "I mean yes, sort of, but that's not it. You have the ability to look directly at me and not let anything around you distract you. I love that quality." She caught herself quickly. She didn't want to throw around such a significant four letter word lightly, especially with Jan.

"That's because I'm attracted to you. I can't help it. I don't notice anything else when you're near me," he said.

"I'm flattered, but I don't think that's entirely it. I'm glad you're attracted to me, but as you may realize, there've been men here and there since I became a woman who've also been attracted to me. None of them ever gave me the attention you do. They just weren't able to be all here, completely present in the moment the way you are. Actually, there was one…"

"Who was that, Kati?" His brows furrowed.

She pushed him backwards, catching him off guard, then dunked his head underwater. He came up for breath sputtering and gasping.

"Don't try to change the subject. Who was the other man who gave you his attention the way I do?"

She looked down, thinking about that other man for a lingering moment. Then she lifted her head and met Jan's gaze.

"It was my father."

"Your father..." Relief flooded his face. He hugged her to him. "Later this evening we'll drink to your father."

"Thank you, I'd like that. But let's get back to you. You don't get distracted the way a lot of guys do. Believe me—I know from sad experience. I'll bet that's something you do with your son, too. Am I right?" She was going out on a limb, but her instincts told her she was on the right track.

"Uhh—well—yes, maybe. Ever since the accident, I feel as if I'm a little closer to death. I could have lost my son. I could have died myself. When he was in the hospital, he got infections after some of the surgeries they did and almost died several times. Now each time I'm with him, I think maybe this is the last time we'll spend together. I guess the accident made me a little less cocky about life."

"That's right, Jan. It did. You don't take life for granted. You really absorb whatever captures your attention and you don't let less important things get in the way. I'll bet you learned how to be that way from spending time with your son *after* his accident. If he hadn't had the accident, you'd still be dribbling soccer balls together and taking time with each other for granted."

"Your words sound like what my minister says to me back home. I'm not sure if I really believe in God, but I started going to the church near my home after I began living alone, and the minister and me got in the habit of taking a walk on Sunday afternoons. We usually end up going for a beer somewhere. He's the only person who talks to me about such things. It's funny that what you and he said are so alike."

"You have a good friend in your minister," she replied. "Sometimes it takes a really tragic event for God to get our attention. I don't know why that accident had the consequences it did, and I'm sorry it was your son who paid the price for it."

She paused. "But don't you see that you and Dirk have a deeper relationship than you might have had if this hadn't happened?"

"All I can say is that I would give anything for this not to have happened. Anything." His face folded into a mask of grief.

Her heart panged. "Well, it did happen and there's nothing you can do about it. You can wake up and realize that because of what happened you've become a more attractive human being and keep moving in that direction, or you can sit around and feel bad about yourself for the rest of your life. Which are you going to do?"

She didn't mean to be so blunt, but she wanted to open his eyes to what he had gained as a result of misfortune. She may have been wrong in her assessment, but her intuition was leading her strongly. It was as if a source outside of herself had given her the words that had tumbled out of her mouth over the past few minutes.

"What am I going to do?" He closed his eyes and leaned back against the side of the pool.

"What are you doing right now?" she asked.

"I'm thanking the God I'm not sure I believe in that you came into my life." He opened his eyes and studied her with a calm, serious expression. "I have no idea what you mean, but I won't forget what you said. Thank you for finding out about me, Kati. You're helping me find out about myself."

He turned away and when he turned back, his face had changed. In a flash, he pulled her legs out from under her, and dunked her into the water.

When she emerged, the serious part of their conversation was over. But she was glad they had had it. She wanted Jan to make lemonade out of the lemons life had handed him. She wanted his son Dirk to become an expert lemonade maker as well. She hoped he was not a bitter boy. Perhaps she'd get to meet him one day.

They moved over to the lap pool and swam side by side for the next ten minutes. Then Jan suggested a drink by the roaring fireplace in the lounge. It sounded heavenly to Kati.

They got out and toweled off. As they retrieved their robes, Jan was more silent than usual. Was he reflecting on what she had said to him?

Ten minutes later they got off the elevator at different floors, not before kissing each other silently and passionately, agreeing to meet in twenty minutes in the lounge.

When she entered her room the light on her phone was blinking. It was as if she'd been away for a week instead of just most of the day.

Krisztof had called. "Kati, I'm still in Vienna. I'm going to be tied up here through early next week. I won't be able to get back before you leave. I'm so sorry. Call me and leave a message to let me know if you were able to complete your business. I'll be in New York sometime next year and will let you know the dates as soon as they're confirmed. We'll see each other then. Thank you for coming with me to the party last Wednesday. You helped me make friends with my inner demons. I hug you. Bye."

Elated, she hung up the phone. Serendipity had smiled on her once again. She and Jan would now be able to spend every minute together until she went through the departure gate at the airport on Monday. If Krisztof had been back, she would have been obligated to spend some time with him. Now she and Jan could burrow deeper into the cocoon they had created together; they would shut out the outside world until the last moment. Even the weather was cooperating, trapping them in their hotel this final weekend, with the heavy, silent snow falling outside.

Trying not to think of how sad she would feel on her flight home or what awaited her back in New York, she changed back into the periwinkle blue scoop sweater. This time she matched it with a deep azure knit skirt and high heeled black suede boots she had brought from New York.

She couldn't help but want to charm Jan with her sartorial selections. She chuckled to herself. They had spent a good deal of their time together wearing only black bathing suits. This week had shown her the truth of her father's observation on how special black was when worn by a blond. Especially the right blond.

When she entered the lounge downstairs, Jan stood by the fireplace, talking to a man and a woman. They were a couple, in town for a medical conference, up from the countryside. They spoke excellent English, and introduced themselves as Nori and Andrasz Parcsami, from Eger, a town about two hours northeast of Budapest. Appearing to be in their late forties, they sat close together on the leather couch, with the man's hand protectively over the woman's shoulder.

"Have you seen much of Budapest?" the woman asked.

"We've seen a lot," Kati replied. "Not everything, but we've spent days walking around."

"You're not here in the busy season. It's unusual for foreigners to visit at this time of year. You're seeing the city as it really is, not all dressed up for tourists."

"I'm enjoying seeing the city all dressed up for Christmas. And it's fun to visit someplace in the off season. You don't see the usual sights but you get to see the real thing, as you said," Kati agreed.

"We like exploring places tourists don't usually know about," Jan added.

She didn't miss that he referred to them as a couple, using the present tense. The couple across from them most likely assumed they were on holiday together.

"If that's the case, have you been to the top of Gellért Hill?" the man asked.

"What's up there? We walked around Castle Hill today. Is it near there?"

"Right next to it. It's where people go sledding in the wintertime. I thought I'd mention it because the snow should stop by tomorrow morning, and Gellért Hill will be covered with hundreds of people racing down it by noon tomorrow."

Kati laughed. "What fun."

Jan echoed her. "We'll go take a look. Can we rent a sled?"

"Just ask the concierge at the Gellért Hotel at the bottom of the hill to lend you one. They have them available for guests at the hotel. I'm sure he'll lend you one if you tip him."

"That sounds like just our style, thank you." Kati said, surprising herself.

One week earlier she wouldn't have thought of sledding as her style at all. Spending time with Jan had brought out the adventurous, physical side of her. She enjoyed all the walking, soaking and exploring they'd done over the past week—especially the exploring part, thinking of his discovery of how sensitive her earlobes and neck were. Jan wasn't a champagne and caviar kind of man, which was proving to be surprisingly fine with her.

Thinking of food, she glanced at her watch. It was time for Jan to take his medication. "Do you have your pills with you?" she whispered to him.

"I forgot all about them. They're up in my room. I'll go take them now."

"You need to take them with food."

"Why don't you order some appetizers while I'm gone? I'll be right back." He excused himself and went upstairs.

She got a menu, but had no idea what to order. The couple steered her to a smoked salmon plate and recommended a wine to accompany it. They then left to go take a walk before the snow accumulated.

In a few minutes, Jan returned. He sat, a pensive look on his face.

"I'm glad I went upstairs. There was a message from Dirk on my phone."

"Is he okay?" Kati asked.

"He's fine, but it turns out his mother and stepfather have been invited to go skiing in Austria next week. He's got his end of semester exams coming up and he can't go with them."

"Does he want to come stay with you?"

"Yes. I'd be glad for the company too. I'm supposed to leave here Wednesday, but they want to leave for Austria on Tuesday.

"Can you change your plans?" Kati struggled to keep her expression neutral.

"I can change my airline ticket. I'll go give the concierge my flight plans and have him check flight availability for Amsterdam over the next few days."

Kati shivered. Now Jan might leave before she did. Their week-long idyll was drawing to a close even sooner than they'd anticipated.

"Let's enjoy ourselves this evening." Jan reached across the fireplace, taking her hand. "We both know we're leaving soon. I want to savor the time we still have together."

She tried not to be sad. "Tell me something to cheer me up," she said, fighting her feelings. Disappointment took a back seat to the needs of a special boy.

"Dirk's not ill. He hasn't taken a fall. There's nothing wrong with his health," Jan reassured her. "This is just the usual schedule changes that sometimes happen when a child's parents are divorced and both look after him."

"You're right." She smiled. "As soon as you said he'd called, I worried something had happened to him."

"I was worried too. Then I heard his message. Now every time I hear about a little problem like a schedule or plan change, I thank God it's nothing more serious than that. He's just got the same set of problems as any other kid with divorced parents."

"I think your accident ended up changing your perspective on a lot of things. For the better. You don't sweat the small stuff."

"Anything less than life or death I can manage."

"What about goodbye?" She couldn't help herself. The question had just slipped out.

"Let's not say goodbye." His voice was low. With his fore-finger, he caressed the underside of her chin.

"What do you mean?" She leaned into his hand.

I mean, why do we have to say goodbye when you or I get on a plane in the next couple of days? What do you think about saying 'see you again?'"

"I hardly know what to say, Jan." She sucked in her breath. "Are we going to stay in touch?"

"Yes," he told her simply, squeezing her hand.

"Yes," she whispered echoing him, rejoicing in his reply.

"Are you okay on all the nonsense that goes with dating a divorced man?" he asked.

"I don't know, but there's only one way to find out."

"Weren't some of the men you dated in New York divorced with children?"

"Jan." She looked at him with amusement. "Most of the men I've met in New York are too busy working on their careers to have even thought about getting married yet."

"When do they get married over there?"

"I think they finally break down and let a woman talk them into it sometime around forty. The minute it happens, they disappear from Manhattan. All I know about dating divorced men with children is that my aunt and uncle once told me dating someone who's divorced with children is like asking for a lifetime of feeling like a second class citizen."

"How do they know that?" Jan asked.

"Because they met each other when they were both divorced with kids."

"How long have they been married to each other?"

"Twenty-six years, I think."

"Do they still love each other?"

"They're mad about each other." She loved the banter between her aunt and uncle. They were constantly reconnecting, checking in with each other in the company of others. Kati longed for a life partner like that.

"That tells me it was worth it, even if sometimes they both felt like second class citizens. Let me tell you a secret." He leaned in closer until his breath caressed her face. "Once you have children, you *are* a second class citizen. You'll be second class to their first class until the day you die. And you won't even mind." He sat back, looking completely content with second class citizenship.

"Here's to becoming a second class citizen." Kati raised her glass. "I guess."

"Here's to us," Jan refrained his toast of the night before.

The evening passed gaily, despite their impending separation. Joy filled Kati's heart at the thought of Jan's words.

They were going to continue their relationship, despite living on separate continents. What was one small ocean, anyways?

Soon Jan had shifted from the armchair to the couch next to her. They laughed and told each other funny stories about their respective hometowns, in between playful kisses. Her head rested on his arm behind her on the couch as he fed her crackers and blinis filled with smoked salmon and caviar in between sips of wine. They basked in the warmth of the fire before them and each other's company. She didn't feel afraid to face the next day, now that they had talked about seeing each other again.

If they had found each other in Budapest, they could find each other in other places too. The bigger question was would each of them find a permanent home in the other's heart? She was glad she didn't have to answer that at that moment or even worry about it. What they had here, right now was enough. She closed her eyes and a vision of her father applauding her filled her mind. *Well done, Kati. Let tomorrow worry about tomorrow's worries. Eat drink and be merry tonight while the snow falls. Let it cloak you in love.*

After they had feasted on appetizers to their hearts' content, they rose to go upstairs. "We can always call room service if we get hungry later," Jan told her, his hand pressing against the small of her back to steer her out of the room.

The Hungarian couple had come back in and were sitting at the bar as they passed by on their way out of the lounge. Jan stopped to thank them for their sightseeing tips and wish them well. The man pulled out a business card, handing it to him. Kati noted he was a medical doctor.

"Please call on us whenever you're traveling in Hungary outside of Budapest. We live about 140 kilometers east. In wine country. We'd be happy to show you around."

Kati looked at his wife. In her experience, it was usually the woman who did ninety percent of the work when visitors arrive, so she studied the woman's face as her husband extended his invitation. It was beaming.

"Yes, yes, we'd be delighted," Nori agreed. "I get lonely sometimes because Andrasz works so much. I would like to show you around our town. It's different from Budapest. Our children are at university, so I like having company. Call us," she encouraged them.

"We're leaving Hungary in the next few days." Jan bent to kiss the woman's hand. "But we would like to come visit you on our next trip back, perhaps at a warmer time of year. Thank you for your invitation."

Kati too thanked the couple, and scribbling Jan's name next to hers, gave them one of her new business cards which had just been made up for her by her new company. They bade them goodbye in a flurry of good wishes and good will.

As they passed the concierge desk in the lobby, the clerk motioned Jan over. There was a direct flight to Amsterdam daily at twelve noon. Monday's was fully booked, but one last seat was available on the next day's flight.

Jan looked at Kati. She scrunched up her chin, searching for courage.

"Do the right thing," she said to him softly, nodding her head.

"Book it," he told the clerk. Then his hand found the small of her back again and stroked discreetly.

Kati moved toward the elevator bank, as if in a dream. In a minute they were upstairs on their way to the room where they would spend their final night in Budapest together.

# CHAPTER NINE

# LAST NIGHT TOGETHER

THAT NIGHT LYING beside Jan, Kati wrestled with physical desire. It would be so easy to fall in love with him, to throw caution to the wind. But if love was what she wanted, and she was yet to make such a commitment even in her mind, then she had to keep her wits about her.

It was another tough test of Jan's ability to observe her guidelines, but his bandaged hand helped to keep them both in check. The night passed blissfully, seasoned with moments of frustration and sweetened by the short, satisfying conversation they had had in the lounge earlier.

They were not saying goodbye, but only "see you again." The melody of their parting was in a major key, not a minor one. Although separation would be difficult, Kati didn't feel sad. They were about to embark upon a transatlantic romance, one they hadn't even consummated yet. Yet precisely because they hadn't consummated it, she could trust the soundness of the foundation they had built.

She was torn. She wanted to know this man, in every possible way and give herself to him before time and distance joined forces to erode their feelings for each other.

But what would that prove? That she was a hypocrite? That she couldn't follow the limitations that she herself had imposed? And as too true as that might be, she wanted to make a lasting impression on this man who had spoken to her of the future. Perhaps it would be their future together. It would change the course of her life, if it was.

Gypsy Kati was hoisted on her own petard. She wanted him and she wanted to forget about any guidelines she had previously mentioned. That was then, and this was now.

But New England Kati steered her back to her senses. She and Jan were about to part on the morrow. Back in her Manhattan studio apartment she'd be lonely and longing for him. Which was the better feeling? Longing and lonely for a man she hadn't slept with or longing and lonely for a man she had slept with? Make that longing, lonely and feeling desperately insecure, wondering whether the man she had slept with was going to stay in the picture?

She didn't need to feel anxiety on top of loneliness and longing. Right now, Jan had put an incredibly sweet feeling in her heart. He had more or less given her the upper hand in their relationship by letting her know he wanted to continue getting to know her at her own pace, whether she was ready to sleep with him or not.

If their feelings continued to deepen, in time they would both surrender to the other. Wouldn't it be best to wait for the time when hearts and minds succumbed as well as bodies? What was the life of her body outside the trajectory of her heart or mind? It was just a vessel. Sometimes the vessel could be made to feel incredibly good, but good feelings evaporated quickly unless the heart and mind were involved too. She wanted to guide her vessel into safe harbor. She would wait.

As HE WALKED into her room, Jan sensed that battles raged beneath the calm surface of Kati's beautiful exotic face. Without turning on the light switch, he led her to the door to her balcony and escorted her outside to watch the snowstorm from under shelter of the balcony above.

Her hotel room balcony had proven a godsend to him. Every time he heated up to the point of no return with Kati, he stepped out on the balcony into the chill of a Budapest December night to help him remember her guidelines.

Having spent his life in one of the most liberal countries on Earth, even meeting a woman near his age with guidelines was something new and unexpectedly stimulating for him. He didn't quite understand where the guidelines were coming from—he gathered she was from a conservative background; but everything about her, beginning with bringing her father's ashes back to Transylvania, told him she was a woman who made up her own mind. What else was it that made her put on the brakes?

Sure, they both went to church. That didn't mean too much, since he wasn't even certain if he believed in God. But when Kati had talked about God working in his life through the accident, he could tell she was talking about someone or something real to her. Come to think of it, he should be angry to think God might have allowed the accident to happen so He could show him something new about himself. What a devastating way to get someone's attention.

Yet Jan wasn't angry; neither was he frustrated. He was extremely interested in all that Kati had said to him in the pool earlier that day. He would spend his time on the flight home thinking about what she'd said, like a boy picking up polished pebbles from the seashore and turning them over, one by one, to examine every detail.

Kati turned up her face toward him and a snowflake landed on her nose. He kissed the spot.

"Jan, I have an idea."

"You have a lot of ideas." He couldn't help but love the idea of her having another idea. She was imaginative, a quality he was certain he'd never tire of.

"Want to play a game?" she asked, reaching up to brush the snow from Jan's hair.

"Sure." He groaned. "I'd love to play another game with you. What else is there to do in a snowstorm?" *With my bandaged hand and your guidelines.*

Would you like to go first, or shall I?" Her eyes twinkled.

"Good question, considering you haven't told me what kind of game we're playing."

"Okay, I'll let you go first."

"Thanks for your sensitive response." He rolled his eyes, pinning her arm behind her back.

"Here we go. Close your eyes and imagine that just one section of your body is the entire universe. It's the entire world. Nothing exists outside of that one spot. Got it?"

"Any restrictions on which spot I can choose?" he asked devilishly.

"Yes. One obvious one." She kicked him lightly. "Other than that, choose any part of your body you like."

"How big an area are we talking about?"

"Umm, something that could be identified as one particular part of your body. For example, your back, your right arm, your left foot, your stomach—no maybe not your stomach, that's too close to restricted areas...."

This time it was he who kicked her.

"Okay, I've got it."

"Fine. Now before you tell me where it is, let me explain what's going to happen. You're going to keep your eyes shut and I'm going to explore that area of your body for a full five minutes. Your end of the bargain is to relax completely. My end of the bargain is to promise I won't do anything that makes you uncomfortable or uptight. In fact, I'll do the exact opposite."

"Whew. This sounds like a challenge. Can I change my choice now that you've explained the game to me?"

"No, you may not. What part of your body did you choose?"

He sighed. "I wish I could change it."

"You can't. Now tell me."

"Okay, my left arm." If only he'd chosen his thigh instead of his arm. But this vixen would probably have told him it was off limits or something.

"Great. Now keep your eyes closed while I lead you back inside," she ordered. "You're one hundred percent in my power, understand? You're mine for the next five minutes."

He nodded as she led him carefully back inside her hotel room. She sat him down in one of the two armchairs and took the other for herself.

He leaned into the chair, every fiber of his body anticipating her touch.

Kati began to stroke his arm with the feather light touch of just one finger. Soon she found a small, sensitive spot on the outside of his upper arm.

He groaned as pleasure shot through him. She turned over his arm and stroked the inside of his forearm from the crook of the elbow to the palm of his hand. The effect left him breathless.

By the time five minutes were up, he had been reduced to Jell-o. He lay back in his chair imagining he was the Earth and Kati's finger a small astronaut who'd landed on the surface and was exploring one small area. *One small step for man, one giant thrill for mankind or at least this kind of man.*

Kati leaned over and kissed the inside of his forearm, invoking yet another shiver from him.

"Time's up," she said softly.

He opened his eyes. He could just make her out staring at him like a cat in a dark alleyway. Who was she? An alley cat or a saint sent from Heaven to rescue him?

He leaned over and lit the candle from their room service dinner. As the flame flared, he fixed his eyes on hers.

So this was what it was like to have a spell cast over him. He didn't know how she'd done it, but he gathered it had something to do with moving at her much slower pace rather than his. She was showing him how to slow down and smell the roses in a way he had never taken the time to do before with a woman. Perhaps she was the true European in her heart of hearts, more so than him.

"So where do I touch?" he asked, filled with desire to know each one of her details without rushing to the next one. It was a new sort of feeling for him.

"Umm, my throat. But don't take any liberties. My throat ends above the chest. Don't travel below my shoulders," she instructed him.

"Are you sure? What about right here?" Jan lightly made a circular motion on Kati's sternum with two fingers.

"Ahhh—umm, okay, but that's it. No lower." Her eyes widened.

The sight of her eyes widening delighted him. She was showing him how to exercise a new kind of power. "Just drift now. Think of nothing," he breathed.

"Every time I try to think of nothing, something comes into my head. That's why yoga never worked for me."

"I know what you mean. Yoga never worked for me either. Probably because I never tried it," Jan joked. Who needed yoga with Kati in his life? Wasn't learning how to achieve pleasure through restraint a sort of yoga in itself?

"Okay, I'll think about how silly that statement just sounded. Did you know you're lighter than air sometimes, Jan?"

"Yeah, I've always thought of myself as a regular butterfly. Now be quiet and relax."

He began to explore the area of her throat from shoulder to shoulder. His left index finger was Lawrence of Arabia marching across the Sahara desert. He couldn't believe how vast the expanse of her smooth golden skin was from one shoulder to the other. He could feel every delicate bone under her skin. With his index finger he traced circular motions on his way from one side to the other. Why not? There was no rush to get anywhere with Kati's guidelines in place. He watched as her breathing deepened and slowed. Had she fallen asleep? No, her throat convulsed and she trembled. She was far from being asleep.

He liked the idea of not being in a rush. It was new to him with regards to women. He knew he would never have figured this out on his own, although he was well aware that it took women about twenty times longer to get to their moment of ecstasy than it did men.

And that was when two people were actually in the heat of things.

For the first time in his life, he wasn't trying to lead a woman down a certain path. Instead, he was wandering in unexpected places, letting a woman lead him wherever she felt like. He hadn't known pleasure with no particular end point could feel this good.

Jan's explorer was joined by the four other digits on his left hand. He rested his palm on her sternum, squeezing and releasing her throat with his five fingers. Her entire body quivered in response. It was a good thing she trusted him, because she was completely in his hands. Literally.

His fingers stroked under her chin.

She purred.

The time was up. It was her turn again.

After several more rounds of their slow motion game, Jan couldn't hold back anymore and took Kati into his arms, kissing her until stars flashed in front of his eyes. He would never forget this night, nor the extraordinary woman in his arms. She had enchanted him; she was his Scheherazade.

THE NEXT MORNING they awoke and greeted each other like big, lazy cats.

Why did it feel so good to wake up next to a woman he hadn't had sex with? Whatever he did with Kati ended up making him feel great. Maybe because she was the right woman for him. Yet he had thought that once before in his life and he'd been wrong. Now he didn't know if he could trust his own judgment.

"What are you thinking?" she asked, stretching like a minx.

"I'm thinking I smell coffee outside your door. Good that you put the security latch on last night. What would the waiter have thought if he'd found a giant bear in bed with Goldilocks?"

"He would have thought this must be the adult version of the story he heard when he was a boy." She belted her robe around her then cautiously opened the door. "I'm glad we weren't discovered, because you're leaving today and I've got to spend tonight here all by myself. I don't want any room service clerks getting the wrong idea."

"I have a feeling they get plenty of ideas from working in a hotel." He chuckled. "Their future wives will probably thank them for all the ideas they've gotten over the years."

Kati liked the way Jan was so comfortable using the term "wives." She'd thought everyone in Europe just lived together and never married. But Jan had been married and had no problem talking about husbands and wives. Smiling to herself, she readjusted her thinking. Was this the first of many readjustments to come?

They finished their coffee and she ordered Jan back to his room. The time had come for him to pack and check out.

"Knock on my door on your way downstairs, Jan. I'll come with you to the airport," she told him as she pushed him out her door.

How was she going to explain the large glossy black shopping bag with his gift in it she needed to bring to the airport with her? She'd figure out something. Meanwhile, she pulled it out of the closet and rearranged the tissue paper on top so the leather jacket couldn't be seen.

She put on the black knit T-shirt with the gold Székely design and then some jeans. She needed to keep busy, so she packed her suitcase with the gifts she'd bought for people back home. In about forty-five minutes, a knock came at the door.

Jan was in his travel clothes. He had had the porter take his bags downstairs. They embraced a final time inside Kati's room; it was time to go. Everything was happening too fast, as if a curtain had descended upon their idyll and the next act was entitled "Real Life."

They descended to the lobby and the porter stowed Jan's luggage in the back of the cab.

The day was bright and cloudless, the stunning cerulean blue of a day after a snowstorm. The cab sped past the Széchenyi Baths where they had first kissed three days earlier. Jan turned to her.

"Let's come back here one day," he whispered.

"Will it be snowing the day we come back?" she whispered back. She couldn't imagine any place on Earth more romantic for a first kiss.

"Yes, it will be. We'll order it to snow just like the first time."

Kati felt like Lara in the film *Dr. Zhivago*. Thank God there was no Mrs. Zhivago in this picture. Yet.

They were at the airport in less than twenty minutes. Jan paid and tipped the driver, telling him to wait curbside to bring Kati back to the hotel.

They entered the terminal, looking for the KLM counter. Spotting the logo of the Dutch airline, Jan led the way to the desk. He picked up his ticket and the agent said something to him in his native tongue. Kati couldn't help but notice how attractive the Dutch woman was, with her gold and pink coloring set off by a royal blue uniform.

"There's a huge tour group on its way here now. She said I should clear passport control before they arrive if I want to make my flight," Jan said. "We'd better get over there now."

They walked quickly to the entrance to the international departures area. The maze of the passport control zone was before them, beyond which non-travelers were not permitted to pass. It was time.

Jan set down his bags and took Kati into his arms. "See you again, Kati." He pulled her chin up to look straight into her eyes.

"See you again, Jan." She willed her face not to crumple.

"Do me a favor," he whispered in her ear, bending down. "Don't wear black until the next time we see each other."

She laughed, then realized there was something about black she was supposed to remember—Jan's gift in the black shopping bag. She picked up the large bag and handed it to him.

"What's this?" He eyeballed the fancy shopping bag suspiciously. "Do I look like a designer kind of guy to you?"

"It's for you." She laughed. "Don't open it now."

"I thought that was some sort of handbag you were carrying."

"It's a designer shopping bag for my favorite non-designer kind of man."

"You're my favorite kind of woman, period." He bent down to kiss her one last time.

Then he was gone.

On automatic pilot, she went out to the curb where the cabdriver waited for her. Jan had paid the fare back to the hotel. She got in and shut the partition between herself and the driver. For the next twenty-four hours she wanted to be alone with her thoughts.

By the time she got back to the hotel, the day had warmed up and the sun beckoned to her. She decided to take a long walk. There was much to think about. First, there was Jan Klassen. Then there was her father. She berated herself for having her priorities all mixed up. She should have thought of her father first, so soon after losing him, and only then the man she had met just six days earlier. Feeling guilty, she went up to her room to change into thick-soled walking boots and take off the sexy black T-shirt that Jan had asked her to wear only with him. How dare he ask her not to wear black until they next met? She was in mourning after all. She had just forgotten for a brief couple of days.

Kati's father was laughing at her again. *Little daughter, don't beat yourself up on my behalf. So you left death behind in the dirt when love offered you a ride. Do you think I wouldn't have done the same when I was your age? I love you for your imperfections as much as for everything else. May the man of your dreams love you the same way.*

She thought about her imperfections. Impulsive, pleasure-loving, sometimes rash—could a man like Jan love a woman like that? It didn't take her long to figure out that those qualities were probably at the top of the list of why he did find her interesting.

Strolling around the city, she held imaginary conversations with her father in her head. He was like a boyfriend she had dumped last Monday evening the moment Jan Klassen had introduced himself to her. She rolled her eyes at the thought. Her father would have forgiven her and been delighted she had let someone into her heart during this time of wrapping up his affairs. What more appropriate way to close a season of mourning than with the birth of new love?

The afternoon passed quickly, and she found herself back at the hotel. She thought she might indulge herself in a massage that evening, before one final dip in the thermal pools. That would kill another hour as well as some cellulite cells too. She called down to the spa reception area to see if there were any massage times available. One was, so she booked it and changing into her robe, descended to the spa level.

There she met her masseuse, a solid-looking, middle-aged Hungarian woman with a kindly manner. Kati was relieved. She needed to be treated with kid gloves this evening. Mentally, she was no longer in either Budapest or New York, but drifting among the stars looking for Jan Klassen's constellation.

The masseuse began to work on her shoulders and neck. Soon Kati was melting into butter. She was going to have a hard time adjusting to American corporate life after these past two weeks. Had it been Budapest or simply meeting Jan that had turned her into a sybarite? She wasn't sure how well she was going to handle spending eight hours a day in front of a computer monitor in an airless office in midtown Manhattan. Luckily, she would be able to travel from time to time, attending the conferences she'd put together.

"Are you enjoying Budapest?" the masseuse asked.

"Yes, it's been wonderful. But I have to fly back to New York tomorrow."

"What did you like best about it?" The masseuse continued her attack on one of her shoulder blades, causing Kati to groan with pleasure.

"Uhhh ..." She was glad her face was staring down at the floor through the massage table cut-out, so the woman couldn't see her blush. "I liked the way people aren't afraid of pleasure here."

"Why would anyone be afraid of pleasure?" The masseuse laughed heartily as if this was the most ridiculous thing she'd ever heard.

"Have you ever heard of the Pilgrims?" Kati asked.

"You mean the ones who sailed on ships to America and wore those ugly gray outfits?"

"Yes. That's them. Well, many people in America are descended from the Pilgrims. And for some reason, the Pilgrims were afraid of pleasure. They thought God would punish them for feeling too much pleasure."

"Huh. They were not Magyars," the masseuse said, referring to the tribe after which the country of Hungary, called *Magyarorszag* in Hungarian, was named.

"No, clearly not," Kati agreed.

"Are you from these Pilgrims?" the masseuse asked.

"Not entirely. My mother's family was."

"And your father?"

"My father was a Székely Hungarian."

"*Yo.* I thought so. When I saw your face I knew you were Hungarian." The woman shot out a stream of Hungarian until Kati interrupted her.

"I don't speak Hungarian. I was born in America."

"Your father didn't teach you?" The masseuse's smile turned upside down.

"I didn't meet him until I was grown up. We didn't live together."

"I see, I see, yes. The Magyars scattered all over the world after 1956."

"That's it. My father came to America in 1957. And met my mother."

"The pilgrim."

"Yes, sort of."

"Darling, let me tell you something." The woman leaned over her, putting all her weight on the other shoulder blade. "You're no pilgrim. You're a Hungarian girl with your face and body. Don't let anyone tell you pleasure is bad. Hungarian women know how to enjoy pleasure. That's why men all over the world like the Hungarian women."

"I've noticed."

"I noticed your man in the pools last week. Is he also a pilgrim?"

"No. Definitely not." Kati thought she would crack up over the image of Jan in gray and white pilgrim clothes on his way to shoot a turkey. "He's—uh—Dutch."

"He's a *Hollandi*?"

"Yes. Not an American."

"You're not entirely an American either, your face is too Hungarian." The masseuse gave the back of Kati's neck a strong squeeze that made her entire body tingle. Your man likes both the American and the Hungarian in you."

"How do you know that?" Her interest perked sharply.

"I saw him with you. He likes to look at you, but he likes to talk with you too. He's not just interested in one or the other part of you, but both."

"Maybe that's just the way he is around women."

"No. I saw him here last year at this time. He was alone then. He looked at many women then. There are so many beautiful women in Budapest."

Kati's blood began to boil; she told herself she was being silly. "Did you see him with anyone in particular?"

"No one. I saw him talk to women here and there, but only for a short time and then he would be by himself. When he talks to you, he looks completely interested. I almost didn't recognize him when I first saw him with you. You changed him into a handsome man."

"I thought he was handsome when I first met him."

"Maybe, but he was lost. You found him. Now he looks better. Where is he tonight?"

Kati sighed. "On a plane to Amsterdam."

"Don't worry, darling. I've been watching that one for a long time. He's yours. Just make sure you don't spend a lot of time apart."

*If only you knew.* "In English, they say 'absence makes the heart grow fonder,'" Kati said out loud.

"It doesn't," the masseuse responded flatly, giving Kati's shoulder blade a smart slap. "The English know a lot about many things, but not about love and pleasure. Don't spend too much time apart from him, darling. Now that you've brought a glow to his face, other women are going to notice. Make sure it's only you that keeps his fires burning."

Kati had just received quite a bit of information from the masseuse. It was like a history lesson combined with a gossip session and psychic reading all rolled into one. She turned over onto her back and closed her eyes. The masseuse followed her cue, lapsing into silence.

She tipped the masseuse well after the massage was over.

The woman's remarks had given her a lot to think about. With her mind preoccupied but her body blissfully relaxed, she decided to swim some laps.

Methodically emptying her head of every thought, the image of Jan Klassen swam again and again into her mental viewfinder as she stroked the warm water. Then she soaked in the Jacuzzi. Remembering every detail from the moment she had first spotted him across the steamy room, she closed her eyes and replayed the last week of her life.

Nothing that had ever happened to her before had even come close.

Not wanting anyone or anything to interrupt her reverie, she slipped out of the pool, into her robe, and hurried upstairs to her room. There she poured herself a drink and went out on the balcony to commune with the stars.

The night was gorgeous, biting and black. But without Jan at her side it didn't seem right to be enjoying it. She went back into her room. The light was blinking on her phone; she hadn't noticed it before.

Retrieving the message, she heard the deep voice she had grown accustomed to over the past six days. "Kati, I'm in Amsterdam, at the airport, wearing this great leather jacket. I'll call you in the next few days. I hope you get this message before you go to bed tonight. Safe journey home. Don't forget me."

She stared at the phone. He'd left no number. He hadn't wanted her to call him back, but only to reassure her he was thinking of her. He'd said he would call in the next few days and she believed him. Nothing he'd done thus far led her to believe otherwise.

Slipping into bed, she let the memory of a thousand caresses play over her. Within minutes, she was asleep, where her dreams delivered a thousand more.

# CHAPTER TEN

# BACK IN NEW YORK

KATI'S FLIGHT BACK to New York the next day proved uneventful.

Malev, Hungary's national airline, served fresh, delicious food with real cutlery. Kati bought a mini-bottle of Bulls Blood wine on the plane to take home in remembrance of Jan. She could barely bring herself to make eye contact with anyone. Her brain wandered in a deep, private space, engaged in sifting over every minute of the past seven days.

She couldn't remember any other time in her life when so much had happened in such a short period. She wanted to write down every detail, but first she needed to prepare herself for the new job she would begin on the morrow. When she walked into her new office, she would not be the same person her new boss had hired the month before. She was someone different now, with her senses sharpened to a deeper understanding of pleasure; one that the Budapest lifestyle had shown her. How would this affect her job performance? Only time would tell. There was no chance her job would become her life, not after Budapest. And not with Jan Klassen in the picture.

Back in her Upper East Side studio apartment, she unpacked her suitcases, setting aside the gifts from Hungary and Transylvania she had brought back for family and friends. She was happy she had thought to snap a shot of Jan the day they visited the Market Hall. Readying her brown striped suit with a velveteen riding collar for work the next day, she shined her high heeled brown loafers then settled onto the couch to call her mother and a few friends. She would update them on some, but not all the details of her trip.

The following day she was ushered into her new private office overlooking St. Patrick's Cathedral in midtown Manhattan. The office manager asked her for a list of supplies she would need to outfit her new surroundings. Then the business of conference planning began. Attending a 10 A.M. meeting, she was introduced to the other directors and an enormous three year calendar at one end of the conference room, outlining every upcoming event with the initials of the director who would be working on it.

She studied the sheaf of papers that had been handed to her. Each director was given a budget for each of the events he or she worked on. It was up to them to attract sponsors or forego their bonus if a shortfall occurred. Kati shifted uncomfortably in her seat. It sounded like a lot of responsibility.

Glancing down at her own list of events for which she was responsible in the coming year, she checked dates and locations. She already knew about Barcelona in February. Then there was Dublin in May, Lisbon at the end of September and a November conference in Europe with location to be determined.

For the rest of the day, she tried to focus on settling into her office, meeting her team and reviewing what needed to be done for the upcoming Barcelona conference. Instead, her mind wandered to when she would see Jan again. Could he join her at the end of any of these conferences?

As much as she was delighted to find herself in such an executive position, the level of responsibility she was being given left her in awe. What if one of these events didn't meet targeted revenue projections? What if she wanted a break between meetings to go visit Jan for a week or have him visit her in New York? How was she going to weave a personal life into such a busy work schedule?

At the end of the day, she rushed through her errands then hurried home. She had laundry to do and presents to wrap for a long list of people. It would be a wonderful holiday season this year with her family.

Her mind wandered to Jan and his son. What did they do for Christmas? Were they together or did Dirk stay with his mom and Jan spend the day alone? She giggled at the thought of Jan looking a bit like Santa Claus, hanging out at his local watering hole on Christmas day knocking back a few Dutch beers.

Her friend Crystal called and they chatted for over an hour about the differences between Budapest and New York, as well as Crystal's break up with the latest investment banker she'd been dating. Kati decided not to mention Jan to her. Was she really his girlfriend? What had seemed so real in Budapest could so quickly fade to just a beautiful memory in New York.

She finished her conversation with Crystal and hung up. Immediately the phone rang again and she picked it up with a sigh.

"Thanks for getting off the phone," said a deep, warm voice. "Who were you talking to—one of your boyfriends?"

"Jan!" Her heart leapt. "I was talking to my girlfriend. How are you? Is Dirk there with you? Are those Dutch girls still as good looking as when you left?"

"No, they're not, as a matter of fact. But this leather jacket is really good looking. I'm living in it. Why did you get me something so nice? Didn't you spend enough time with me to figure out I'm not a fashionable guy?" His voice spilled over her like bubbling warm water from Budapest's spas.

"Didn't you spend enough time with me to realize I'm casting a spell over you?"

"I did. Otherwise why would I be calling you transatlantic?"

Her heart danced. Men didn't call women across the ocean unless they were their girlfriends or wives, did they?

They bantered on, then he had to go. Before he got off, he gave her his phone number in Beekbergen, as well as his cell phone number. Elated by his call, she completely forgot to tell him about her conference schedule for the year, including at least two trips to Europe.

The rest of the week passed in a flurry of planning and activity at her office. The holiday season swung into full gear in New York; she attended party after party with various girlfriends. At her own office party, she danced up a storm with female colleagues and gay male junior staff. Amongst the entire division there was only a smattering of straight men, all of whom were married and commuting into the city from their homes in New Jersey or on Long Island. She had never attended a more attractive gathering of smart, sophisticated women—all dancing with each other or their gay male assistants. Wasn't there something wrong with this picture?

Jan would be surprised to discover what her life was really like in Manhattan. He probably thought she had men pursuing her right and left. His accidental meeting with Krisztof at their hotel in Budapest had most likely fanned the flame of jealousy. She wouldn't rush to fill him in on the real situation here; better if he worried a bit about possible competition for her favors.

The day after the holiday party, she returned home to find a Fed Ex envelope at her door. When she ripped it open, a Christmas card with Santa Claus on it fell out with a large packet. Inside the card was written, "How'd you like to spend Christmas with Santa Claus this year?" She picked up the packet. A round trip plane ticket to Amsterdam was inside.

She shrieked. She wanted to call someone. A girlfriend. But she hadn't told any of them about Jan. She called her mother and sister instead. She'd planned to spend Christmas Eve and day with them, but she knew they'd forgive her. Both of them were incurable romantics, just like Kati.

"Mom—I—I—I've been invited to Holland for a week for Christmas."

"You have? By who??" Her mother squealed like a teenage girl.

"Uh—h-h-h, by someone I didn't tell you about yet. I met him in Budapest. I wanted to tell you about him, but we got so caught up in Dad's stuff, I didn't get around to it."

"Let me guess. Is this that blond guy who looks a bit like Santa Claus in one of the photos you showed me last week?"

"Yes. How did you know? His name is Jan."

Her sister was shrieking in the background, thrilled to hear her big sister's news over the shoulder of their mother.

"I knew because you turned the page so quickly the minute I got to his photo. You can't hide anything from your mother, you know. What's his last name?"

"Klassen. K-L-A-S-S-E-N."

"Does he live in Amsterdam?"

"No. He lives in a small town about an hour away."

Her sister got on the phone. "Oh my God, you're going to spend a week in Holland with a guy you hardly know?" Danielle's excited tone belied her skeptical words.

"Danielle, I know him pretty well. It's just that we haven't known each other for that long."

"Yeah, like several minutes. You'd better give us all his details, so we can contact INTERPOL in case you don't come back after a week."

"I will. I definitely think I can trust him. He was wonderful in Budapest. I'm not worried at all, just excited, and—a bit nervous."

"Why are you nervous?"

"Well—he has a son. So I guess I'll be meeting him."

"How old is the son?"

"Eleven. His name's Dirk. He lives with his mother."

"Does he also have divorce papers with the ink dried on them?" her sister followed up.

"His ex-wife remarried," Kati huffed. "She lives with her husband in some other town not far from his."

"Right. I sure hope so. In any case—there's only one way to find out," Danielle advised. "Just bring enough money and credit cards so you can leave if something isn't the way you thought it was going to be."

There promised to be many things about the week that might not be the way she thought they would be. For example, she had never spent time with anyone in a wheelchair before, other than doing volunteer work for a few hours at a hospital when she'd been a Girl Scout. She had no idea how to handle spending time with Jan's son. Would the boy be resentful of her staying in the house where he and his mother had once lived together with his father? Would she sleep in the guest bedroom? What was she going to do about her romantic guidelines at this point?

"I've got to get off the phone. I've got a million things to do. Can we celebrate Christmas on Christmas Eve this year? I'm flying out on Christmas day. Let me know what you want me to bring back from Holland for you."

"You can bring back a nice Dutch guy for me. I need a date for New Years' Eve," Danielle told her.

"I'll see what I can do." They hung up and Kati quickly dialed Jan's number. She got his answering machine. Letting him know she'd be delighted to spend Christmas with Santa Claus this year, she got off the phone and rushed around her apartment like a happy madwoman.

# CHAPTER ELEVEN

# TRIP TO HOLLAND

THE NEXT WEEK passed quickly. She'd asked for four days' vacation between Christmas and New Years, telling her office she had some family obligations out of town. Her boss had raised an eyebrow, but given her the time. She wasn't sure if she was making the best possible impression asking for time off the first month of her new job, but this was important.

Both her mother and her father had prioritized love over careers and both had ended up poor, not to mention divorced. At least they'd always said nice things about each other. Was she following in their footsteps? All Kati knew was she was following her heart. Its drumbeat was much louder than any other music playing inside her.

Jan had found a reasonably priced ticket because it was for Christmas day, the flight departing just after midnight on Christmas Eve. Kati had never flown anywhere on Christmas day before. It turned out to be a great idea. There were no lines, travelers and airport personnel smiled and gave each other season's greetings, and the airline served free drinks on the flight over. Her Dutch seatmate was pleasant and taught her to say *vrolijk Kerstfeest,* Merry Christmas in Dutch.

The flight arrived on time at Shiphol International Airport in Amsterdam and she hurried to get through passport control.

Sailing through the automatic doors after clearing customs and passport control, she straightened her shoulders and tried to look regal. The women around her were, for the most part, extremely attractive. How was she ever going to compete with these tall, blonde, athletic looking Dutch women? She scanned the crowd for Jan. There he was, wearing the chocolate brown leather jacket she'd given him and sporting a new reddish-blond goatee.

They flew into each other's arms.

"Welcome to Holland." Jan's smile stretched across his face.

"Thank you for inviting me. Is it really you, Santa Claus?" She stroked his new facial hair, surprisingly soft beneath her touch.

"It's me. Let's get your bag and get out of here. My sleigh's right outside," he joked.

They retrieved her black suitcase and exited the terminal into a pale, robin's egg blue winter sky. Jan's car was parked a block away, so he wheeled her suitcase behind him as she held onto his arm. Quickly, they reached his car—a gray van. On the license plate, she recognized the international symbol for disabled parking. So that was the reason he'd been able to park so close to the terminal.

In the car, he gave her a long, lingering kiss. She felt playful, as well as excited to see him. Now she would see his home. She steeled herself, preparing for the messiness of a bachelor pad. Meanwhile, they drove onto the freeway which didn't seem particularly Dutch. She knew she was in Europe, only because the cars were going much faster than in the U.S.

Within an hour they'd turned off the freeway onto a quiet road framed by tall, stately plane trees that led through one country village after another. Jan pointed out occasional rows of white, wind-powered windmills on the horizon. Finally, it was beginning to look like Holland. The streets had whimsical names like Wipselbergweg and Schalterdalweg.

Entering Beekbergen, tidy, red-roofed houses and neatly landscaped yards greeted them. They passed a large, white church that said Geereformeerde Kerk in BeekBergen. Jan told her this was the church he sometimes attended. She remembered his friendship with the minister. Would she meet him on this visit?

In a minute, Jan turned down a small dirt lane. At the end of the road was a two-story stone house with a red tile roof. He pulled into the driveway and up to a wide backdoor. She was charmed to see it was a traditional Dutch door, with an upper half that swung open independently of the lower half. A large, shaggy dog bounded up to the car to greet them.

"Snorry! *Word beneden, schlechte hond*! Behave yourself for our guest." Jan reprimanded the dog, who'd jumped up to greet Kati, planting his front paws on her shoulders.

"Don't worry, he's fine. What a friendly boy you are," she said to Snorry, scratching and pulling his ears. Within seconds, the dog calmed down, then licked her hand.

"How'd you do that so fast?" Jan exclaimed. "Usually he goes crazy for at least ten minutes when a stranger arrives.

"I grew up with neighbors who had a golden retriever. He used to jump on me like this, and I'd scratch his ears until he purred like a cat."

"You have a way of confusing the male of the species."

She giggled and followed him inside. His kitchen was spacious, simple and neat with a high, wood-beamed ceiling and a huge picture window over the double sink. It looked out onto the winter remains of a very large vegetable garden.

"Is this your garden? It's huge," Kati marveled.

"That's it. In the summer we eat whatever's in season. In June it's asparagus, then tomatoes and cucumbers in July. In August, we pick berries."

"Thank God it's winter. I don't know how to pick anything," she joked. "Show me your home."

He smiled, and with Snorry almost knocking her over with each wag of his excited tail, Jan showed her the downstairs rooms. There were four in all.

"This was my grandparents' house. My grandfather built it in 1927, the year before my father was born," he explained. "He ran his business here, so we changed his office on the ground floor into Dirk's bedroom."

There were fireplaces in three of the four downstairs rooms.

"Do you use your fireplaces?"

"I do. Shall we make one tonight?"

"Yes," she said delightedly. "We'll have our own Christmas celebration."

"Yes, and a visitor in the morning. Dirk will spend the day with us tomorrow, if that's okay with you." He looked at her closely.

"It's fine," Kati said, more surely than she felt. She hoped Dirk and she would click. "I got something for him from the Museum of Architecture near my office. I hope he'll like it."

"Don't worry, Kati. Just be yourself. He's very interested in American culture, especially the music."

She beamed while examining the photos on the mantel-piece of the living room fireplace, as well as on the heavy, dark wooden tables. In one photo, a brunette woman with an infant boy played in the sand on the beach.

"Is that Dirk's mother?" she asked quietly.

"That's her. We were in Spain at the beach. I liked the photo, so I kept it there. She didn't take it, because she said it made her look fat."

The woman in the photo didn't look fat, but she didn't look like Anita Ekberg either. Kati breathed a sigh of relief. Jan had married one of the few brunettes she'd seen thus far in Holland. Even Snorry the dog was a big, golden blond.

They went through the dining room to the front hall. Both were paneled in dark wood, with high, wood-beamed ceilings. On the other side was Dirk's bedroom. It was a large room, painted sky blue, with a picture window looking out onto the woods beyond Jan's property. A wide desk stood next to the window with rows of books on it. Adjoining the bedroom was a bathroom custom fitted for wheelchair use.

"We knocked out the hall closet to expand the bathroom that was already here."

"Jan, this bathroom is almost as big as my apartment in New York," Kati said.

"I doubt it!" He laughed.

"You haven't seen it."

"I'm waiting for you to invite me." His gaze was direct, intense. Nothing had changed since Budapest.

Upstairs were two rooms on one side with a bathroom between them. Jan had made one into an office. Next to it was a charming guest room with a view of the vegetable garden out back. It was decorated simply with lemon yellow walls and white trim. Immediately Kati felt at home. She put her bag down on the chair.

They crossed the hall and entered Jan's large bedroom with sliding glass doors at one end, opening onto a balcony. His bed was neatly made, with a white goose down comforter on top.

The rest of the room looked as if it could use a little work. Books, newspapers, magazines and odd articles of clothing were piled everywhere—unquestionably a single man's room. Massive mahogany bureaus stood to either side of the bed. A rocking chair and a dog bed with a plaid blanket on it stood at the foot of the bed.

Jan was still carrying her suitcase. He looked at her questioningly.

"Your room is charming. But put my suitcase in the yellow room. If you don't mind, I'll keep my things in there. It's the same color as my childhood bedroom. And a woman needs her privacy, you know."

"I know, I know—especially a woman with guidelines," he grumbled laughingly. Bringing her suitcase back to the yellow room he set it up on the table in the corner.

Relieved, she smiled at him. Other people could leap into relationships. Apparently her sister thought she was leaping into this one. But she was most comfortable taking baby steps forward with frequent pauses, when it came to getting to know a member of the opposite sex.

Jan had thus far respected her desire to proceed slowly. Once again, he showed sensitivity by allowing her to stake out her own space during her first visit to his home. She needed to get the lay of the land she was about to explore.

They went back downstairs and sat close together on the couch. Snorry jumped up and tried to get into her lap.

"Does your dog like to chaperone you when you have girls over?" she joked.

"My dog's thrilled that I've finally *brought* a girl over. He's been after me for years to bring a nice smelling woman back here so he can slobber all over her and try to climb into her lap."

"Your dog's a true boy." She launched into a stream of high-pitched baby talk to Snorry, all the while tugging and stroking his ears and head.

The dog looked as if he'd found nirvana. Within seconds he was on his back, his belly fully exposed and tail wagging furiously.

Jan looked wistful. She shot him a curious look. What was he thinking? It was almost as if he was jealous of the dog.

"What do you want to do for the rest of Christmas Day?" he asked.

"There's something I really need to do, but I don't know if it's too late."

"What's that? Do you want to call home?"

"No. I need to sing some Christmas carols. What about that church you sometimes attend? Is your minister friend giving any Christmas services today?"

"I'm sure he is. I don't know what time they are, but he's probably got something going on. How about if I change my shirt and we'll drive down to the church, check the schedule, then I'll show you around town before the service?"

They both changed into casually festive clothes for church. Jan wore a red vest, and Kati put on a forest green Angora sweater. As much as they were going to church, she couldn't help but think of Jan's hands on her back, feeling its curves underneath the sweater's soft fabric. God knew all about her contradictions, and whatever He was thinking, He'd be pleased she'd gone to church on Christmas Day.

They set off with Snorry looking woefully through the living room window at them, a study in sorrow. She mentally promised to bring him back a Christmas treat.

The sign at the front of the church said there'd be a four P.M. children's service followed by a candlelight one at five.

They had some time, so Jan showed her around. He drove her past the youth center, next to which his office was located. There was a large playground in back, with adjoining basketball and tennis courts.

Next, they drove down the main street of Beekbergen, gaily decorated for the Christmas season, but now deserted.

"Is everyone at home today?" she asked.

"Mostly. We give each other gifts here on December 5th, *Sinter Klaas* Day. Christmas Day itself is a religious day when people go to church, then spend time with their families. Tomorrow's a holiday too but everyone will be back on the streets. We typically go out to eat the day after Christmas. I'll show you my office and you can help me figure out what we're going to do with the kids this Friday evening."

"What do you mean? What kids?" Kati asked, alarmed. She knew about Dirk. Did Jan have more than one child?

"My kids. I mean the kids in town who are off from school this week and didn't go away. A lot of families have gone skiing in the mountains, but some children are still here. One of my jobs as town youth director is to make sure kids who're still here on school holidays have something to do and aren't just left alone to get into trouble."

"That'll be fun," she said, relief flooding through her. "Will Dirk join us?"

"I'll ask him tomorrow. Maybe you can be the entertainment. We'll have the kids test their English skills on you, and you can give out prizes."

She laughed. This week wasn't going to be suspended in vacation unreality. Jan was introducing her to his real life. She couldn't imagine having him come to visit her in New York and taking him to work with her. His job appeared to have fun aspects that hers didn't.

It was time for church to begin, so they circled back to the large, white building with a steeple. The bells were ringing out *Oh Come All Ye Faithful* as they parked the van. Boys and girls were streaming out of the children's service, clutching white cardboard angels along with their parents' hands. She had never seen such rosy cheeks in her life. The children looked as if they could be from the cast of the Pied Piper from her childhood fairytale books.

They entered the church as the majority of its occupants appeared to be leaving. Apparently church was largely for children and old people here, just as it was in many parts of America. She didn't mind. She wanted God all to herself in this service. He worked in mysterious ways, and with a smaller percentage of young adult and middle-aged churchgoers, the minister was probably lonely and had sought out Jan as much as Jan had unconsciously sought him out.

The service began. There were only about two dozen people there, mostly elderly. The minister was younger, closer to forty. He made eye contact with Jan, then smiled at Kati.

She hoped she wouldn't start crying when they sang Christmas carols. It was something that sometimes happened to her as an adult. Frequently when she sang a hymn in church that reminded her of her childhood, warm, salty tears sprang to her eyes. Soon the introductory chords of *Angels We Have Heard on High* began. The congregation stood and she began to sing in English. She knew the words by heart.

When the chorus began, she saw Jan's eyes close as he joined in. As she knew they would, her eyes welled with tears, good, heaven sent ones.

The carol ended leaving her refreshed. No matter whether it was Holland or New York, she was in church celebrating Jesus' birthday. She knew she was in exactly the right place with the right person, whatever Jan's views might be on Jesus, Christmas, or churches.

The minister told the Christmas story. Then they sang *Hark the Herald Angels Sing.* She loved the hymn. Admittedly, part of the reason she loved it was it gave her a chance to show off the top range of her soprano singing voice. She also knew God would forgive her her hubris as well as a few other less than virtuous motives. Wasn't that the point of sending Jesus to Earth anyways? He forgave her again and again for her sinful nature. The point was to keep asking His forgiveness so they could remain in dialogue. With only a small number of people in the church, she tried to keep her voice low key this time.

It didn't work. Her voice soared to every nook and cranny of the large, acoustically live building.

After the carol ended, they prayed. As she talked to God, the thought of Jan's touch seeped into her thoughts. She sensed God was used to this sort of thing. Like a father with small children, He probably had to put up with a lot of nonsense.

She prayed that God would show Jan how to forgive himself for Dirk's accident. She also prayed God would help her get along with Dirk the next day. She asked Him about the guidelines. Wasn't it time to stop following them? Now that she'd asked Him, He would let her know when the time came for decision-making. She had a feeling God liked being included in her plans, even if she was thinking about doing something that might not be the best thing for her at the time. Peace filled her as she shared the good and the bad inside her with the One who'd put them both there.

The service ended with *Silent Night*. Jan pointed out the Dutch words in the hymnal and Kati tried singing it in the unfamiliar language, following his lead. He had a surprisingly full, bass voice. She sang softly, to better hear him, as well as savor his nearness, standing next to her in the pew.

By the third verse, he had gained confidence and his rich bass was vibrating deep in her heart. She looked up at him. How nice it would be to sing duets with him. Would they enjoy such a hobby together one day?

After the service, the minister greeted his parishioners at the front of the church. Jan embraced the man in a bear hug, then turned to Kati.

"Reverende de Blij, this is Kati Dunai from New York. She arrived today and the first thing she did is drag me to church," he joked.

"Hello, Kati. Merry Christmas. I'm Reverende Hans de Blij in this building, but outside of here call me Hans. Jan is my good friend although he's a lousy churchgoer." He laughed heartily, slapping Jan's back.

"He told me about you," Kati replied. "I hope we'll see you again sometime this week."

"I hope you'll stay longer than a week so I can invite you to be in our church choir," Hans said.

"Thank you for giving me the chance to sing Christmas carols today." She smiled. "Your choices were some of my favorites."

"The Holy Spirit must have known you were coming when He helped me choose the hymns for the service this evening."

She liked Hans de Blij. She could tell he was a good friend to Jan.

Outside, the village was dark, except for the lights on the enormous Christmas tree in front of the church. They strolled over to admire it before getting into Jan's car. It had been a beautiful Christmas day, and now it was time to go home and light a fire. Or two. Remembering her father's observation that it was all right to be a bit confused at times, she asked God to forgive her her dual impulses.

Snorry was happy to see them. Kati had a sugar cookie in her pocket she'd snagged from the reception after the children's service. She instructed the dog to sit before giving it to him.

Jan took a few minutes to bring in firewood from outside, while Kati ripped up newspapers to put beneath the kindling. Soon they had a roaring fire going.

Jan took out some crystal wineglasses and went down to his cellar, returning with a good bottle of wine. Meanwhile, she had looked in his refrigerator and found several cheeses as well as grapes and paté.

She cut some bread from the loaf on the counter, then put everything on a large tray and brought it into the living room.

Soon they were eating, drinking and joking in the warm, dark living room while the shadows of the fire's flames leapt on the walls around them. Their conversation turned to caresses, and they quickly caught up on the weeks that had separated them. Oblivious to time, they were surprised when the grand-father clock in the hallway struck midnight.

"Time for bed," Kati said, softly.

"Are we going together?" Jan asked, a look of questioning hope in his eyes.

She took both of his hands and looked at him boldly. "Let's not sleep in the same bed tonight."

"Why not?" he countered, a sly smile on his lips.

"Because I'm a bit nervous."

"Because Dirk is coming tomorrow?"

"I think so. It's hard to explain. Sometimes I feel like something is leading me. And it's telling me now that I should sleep in your yellow guest room and you should sleep in your own room."

"Is this thing leading you going to keep telling you this the whole time you're here?" he pressed, a mischievous glint in his eyes.

"I don't know." She laughed. "I don't think so. But tomorrow will be the first time your son lays eyes on me. I don't want to have secrets I'm hiding from him from the night before. I want to meet him as your friend, because that's what I am right now."

"You're more than my friend." He stroked her cheek with a gentle finger.

"You're more than my friend too," she responded. "But we don't really know yet what we are to each other, so let's not confuse your boy. Life has already been pretty confusing for him."

"You drive me crazy, Kati. I see you love to confuse *me* day and night, but I can handle it. You're right about my boy—let's not confuse him. He'll like you better for introducing yourself as my friend, although I'll like you less." He nudged her foot with his.

"That's okay." She kicked him playfully. You need to cool down a bit anyway. You make me like you more when you let me take my time. I can't explain why I need you to do that, but I do."

"I know you do. It's probably that same thing inside you that makes your voice as beautiful as a bell ringing when you sing. You sounded like an angel in church."

"Thanks. And we both know I'm not. That's why I need to sleep in my own room tonight." She reached up and gave him one last, lingering kiss. "Merry Christmas, darling."

"Merry Christmas, angel." Jan released her and they went upstairs, turning into their respective bedrooms.

A few minutes later, as her head hit the pillow, she realized she hadn't remembered to get Jan a Christmas present. She had been so wrapped up in finding the right gift for Dirk, she'd forgotten about getting anything for his father.

But Jan had already given her something of great value. His present to her of respecting her need for time and space was the best gift he could have given her on this Christmas night. Feeling loved and cherished, she fell into a deep sleep.

# CHAPTER TWELVE

# BOY IN A WHEELCHAIR

THE NEXT MORNING Snorry woke Kati with a friendly lick of her hand that dangled over the side of the bed. Then Jan came in and greeted her with a kiss. The sun flooded the pale yellow room, setting it on fire. Sunlight, lemon walls, and Jan and Snorry's golden heads all mixed together to create a gilded morning glow. Why hadn't she noticed what an exceptional color yellow was until that moment?

Downstairs, she asked Jan to show her how to make coffee. It was a skill she wanted to learn so she would feel at ease in his home. Then if she awoke first, during the week, Jan would wake to the delicious aroma of freshly brewing coffee. She was in full agreement with the saying that the way to a man's heart was through his stomach; it was largely the way to a woman's heart too, as far as she was concerned. Not having too many cooking skills herself, she could at least make a great cup of coffee.

Wearing woolen bathrobes and socks, they put on clogs and took their coffee mugs out into the backyard, sitting side by side on a plain wooden bench. The day was chilly but not freezing, with wispy cumulus clouds overhead.

Kati was feeling as delicate as the pale blue winter sky. What would this meeting with Dirk be like? She shivered and drew up the plaid woolen bathrobe Jan had lent her.

"Nervous?" he asked, putting his hand on the back of her neck and squeezing slightly.

"Yes," she admitted. "When's he coming?"

"His stepfather's bringing him over around ten." It was less than an hour away.

"I'll go upstairs when we spot them, okay?" Kati suggested.

"That's fine. Dirk and I will spend a minute together, then we'll give you a shout to come down."

"What does he like to do?" she asked.

"He likes to play games."

"He does? So do I."

"You're telling me." Jan's eyes crinkled. "You just like to play different games. His usually involve balls or cards."

"Like what?"

"You'll find out when he gets here." Jan reached out and caressed her knee through her robe. Then he rose.

They puttered around the yard with Snorry following them. Finally ten o'clock neared. Kati headed upstairs to take a shower. Fifteen minutes later she heard the sound of a car pulling into the driveway.

They were here. She dressed carefully, putting on a petal pink turtleneck and jeans. She was feeling pretty petal pink herself today.

In a minute Jan came to the foot of the stairs. "Kati! Come on downstairs. Someone here would like to meet you."

In the living room, a young boy shyly looked up from the sports magazine he was reading. His face was more delicate than Jan's; pale freckles scattered across the bridge of his nose. His hair was the color of spun flax, even lighter and finer than his father's. His eyes were the color of the sky in Saint Tropez on a clear summer day. Dirk was a looker.

"Hello, Dirk," she said softly, walking slowly toward him then extending her hand.

"Hello." The boy ignored her hand and looked down at his magazine again. He wore jeans and sneakers, his legs strapped to the sides of his wheelchair, but she could make out the shape and size of his knees and calves. They were thin and less developed than the rest of him.

She looked at Jan, who smiled encouragingly at her. They sat down on either side of Dirk. Jan said something to his son in Dutch, and Dirk looked up and gave Kati the faintest flicker of a smile. She matched him, telling herself to go slowly. Rome wasn't won in one day, and the son was not the father.

"Do you speak some English, Dirk?" she asked slowly.

He nodded his head without looking at her.

This was going to take some work. She reached inside herself and asked her intuition to guide her. She always felt peaceful after consulting with her intuition. She had the faith to believe there really was something there that was ready to lead her if only she asked. No inner voice spoke up, so she took this to mean she should follow her instincts. She went upstairs to get Dirk's present.

Back down again, she held the gift behind her back. The boy ignored her, immersed in his magazine. She knelt by his wheelchair. He continued to ignore her.

Taking a crazy chance, she snatched his magazine from him.

Dirk shouted something in Dutch and tried to grab it back. She held it behind her back and smiled at him teasingly.

"What did you say?" She cocked her eyebrows at him.

"Give back," he demanded in halting English. His azure blue eyes blazed at her.

Instead of handing him the magazine, she produced the hidden bag from the Museum of Architecture.

"Do you mean this?" she asked.

"What's that?" The boy's eyes widened as he looked at the colorful shopping bag with words printed in English on the side.

"*Vrolijk Kerstfeest,* Dirk." She hoped she was pronouncing Merry Christmas correctly in Dutch. Ever since her seatmate on the flight over had taught her the phrase, she had practiced it, beginning with the airport personnel on her way through customs.

"Hey, you didn't say that to me yesterday," Jan complained. "Where'd you learn that?"

Dirk had grabbed the bag. He was busy unwrapping Kati's gift, while she asked Jan to say the phrase again in Dutch to hear it pronounced correctly.

"You said it perfectly. *Vrolijk Kerstfeest,* Kati."

She silently thanked God that Dutch wasn't anything like Hungarian. Many Dutch words sounded similar to English or German. She could more or less make out a lot of the signs she'd seen along the roads on the way from the airport the day before. Maybe she and Dirk would be able to stumble along in their communication with each other if he'd give her a chance. Right now, that looked like a big 'if.'

Dirk finished unwrapping the present and turned to the booklet which accompanied the model kit. Fortunately, the instructions were printed in eight languages, including Dutch. She had checked before buying it. It was a do-it-yourself model of the Plaza Hotel, one of New York City's oldest and most historical buildings.

Dirk said something excitedly to his father in Dutch. Then he turned to Kati. "Thank you." This time his smile lasted a nanosecond longer. Had she seen a glimmer of impishness in his eyes? Maybe he'd liked the way she'd grabbed the magazine from him. It had been her own way to take the bull by the horns, so to speak.

Jan cleared his throat. "Let's take a drive. The weather's supposed to get bad later, so we can put your model together then."

Dirk appeared to understand his father's English. The boy nodded his head.

Jan turned to Kati. "I want to show you our town now that the holiday's over and people will be out."

They all three proceeded to the kitchen door where Snorry tried to prevent them from leaving.

"Can we take him?" Kati asked.

"Sure, why not?" Jan replied.

Snorry joyfully leapt into the back of the SUV. Then Jan activated the hydraulic lift attached to the side door of the van. Dirk wheeled his chair onto the platform, which raised him into the back of the car, wheelchair and all. She'd seen this many times on public buses all over New York, but had never paid much attention. What a wonderful invention.

Before Jan could shut the door, she tossed Dirk's sports magazine onto the boy's lap.

Grabbing the magazine, Dirk swatted her arm. A good sign.

They set off for the main street of Beekbergen.

Dirk wasn't very talkative in the car; perhaps spending time with someone who couldn't speak Dutch was making him less so. Most of the time they communicated with short glances and the merest of smiles.

Jan showed her around his office, which was stuffed from floor to ceiling with toys, sports equipment, party decorations and cases of soft drinks and beer. His walls were covered with photos of children and older people having fun—in many cases having fun together working on building or landscaping projects. His work looked a lot more exciting than sitting at a computer monitor eight hours a day, the way Kati usually did when she wasn't traveling on business.

They went out to the basketball court and threw some hoops. She couldn't believe Dirk's upper body strength. He could make baskets just by thrusting the ball from his chest, using only his arm and chest muscles.

After about twenty minutes, she hadn't made a single basket. Finally, Dirk said something to Jan in Dutch that made his father laugh uproariously. She knew it had something to do with her subpar athletic abilities.

Without thinking, she got steamed. Marching over to Dirk, she sat on his wheelchair, trapping his arms. Then she tickled him.

He began to scream with laughter. He head butted her in the shoulder and knocked her off his lap. She rolled onto the basketball court, her body splayed out like a fallen angel. Dirk wheeled his chair over as if to run her over. She grabbed one of his legs to stop him.

Then she realized he couldn't feel a thing.

Jan came over to pick her up and physically carried her over to the basketball net. Turning to Dirk, the boy threw the basketball to Kati. Finally, inches away from the hoop, she made a basket. Jan dropped her, and both he and his son roared with laughter.

Dirk mumbled something to his father.

Kati demanded a translation.

"He said you play like a four-year-old girl."

"Tell him it wasn't my best sport in high school."

Dirk and Jan exchanged a few more comments, sailing off again into loud guffaws.

"What did you say?" she demanded again.

"My father say our dog play better basketball than you," Dirk blurted out in surprisingly good English.

"Thanks, friend." She tried to shove Jan but he grabbed her hand and wrestled her onto his back. All of a sudden she found herself being carried like a sack of potatoes across the basketball court. Snorry ran behind them barking. Dirk wheeled his chair behind him and they all proceeded to the car, laughing and hurling insults at each other.

By the time they returned to Jan's house, they had also tried some tennis and stopped by the town pool hall. Kati was now aware that this eleven-year-old Dutch boy in a wheelchair could whup her sorry self in just about any sport they might play. Maybe she would prove a better cards man.

"How about a game of rummy?" she suggested as they traipsed into the house, Snorry trying to trip her and Jan helping Dirk over the kitchen threshold.

"You mean rummy for dummy?" Dirk asked. "Sounds like you could win that game."

She picked up Dirk's sports magazine, smacking him on the arm. The ice had been broken, albeit at her expense. It was clear that Dirk was not worshiping the ground she walked on, the way Snorry and Jan appeared to. She would have to redeem herself through intellectual competition.

After four rounds of rummy, three of which Dirk won, and
Jan winning the last, she was determined to prove to the men
she was a member of the superior sex.

"I have an idea," she announced.

Jan said something to Dirk in Dutch.

"What was that?" she demanded.

"My father say when you have an idea, usually it's fun,"
Dirk piped up.

She smiled. "This will be fun for your stomachs."

"Good," they both chimed, proving her right in her theory
that all men everywhere like to be fed—regularly.

Snorry wagged his tail.

"I need some information from both of you, first," she
continued.

They looked at her expectantly. For the first time, the look
in Dirk's eyes matched the one she frequently saw in Jan's when
she came up with a game for them to play.

"What's your favorite kind of jam?" she asked.

"All jam," Dirk shouted.

"Raspberry," Jan said at the same moment.

Snorry barked.

"Okay, good. What else do you like to put on your bread in
the morning?"

"Nutella," Dirk yelled, referring to the chocolate hazelnut
spread that many European children eat daily.

"Lemon curd," Jan's voice rang out.

"Okay, now final round—what's your third most favorite
jam or spread?"

"*De braambes,*" Dirk shouted.

"Blackberry," Jan said at the same moment, then explained
that Dirk had just said the same thing in Dutch.

"Fine. Now I need to go to the supermarket. Is there one still open near here?"

"Yes, madam. We'll be happy to take you there," Jan replied enthusiastically, with Dirk looking interested. They trooped out to the van one more time, and this time Kati asked Jan to show her how to operate the hydraulic lift for Dirk.

It was fun shopping in a Dutch supermarket. She was thrilled that at last she had a chance to redeem herself with the men by cooking something. She only hoped Jan's pans and stove would behave the same way her equipment did back home. She was going to prepare the one Hungarian dish her father had taught her to make. It was guaranteed to warm the heart and satisfy the stomach of any human or canine anywhere.

# Chapter Thirteen

# Palacsinta for Dinner

Arriving back at Jan's house, Kati ordered the men out of the kitchen, then clinked and clunked around in his cabinets until she found what she needed. She was about to make a very big mess.

After fifteen minutes of mixing, stirring, and melting butter in three different frying pans on the stove, she called them back into the kitchen. They came in, looking full of anticipation.

Jan's kitchen was perfectly set up for serving *palacsinta*, which were very thin Hungarian pancakes or crêpes filled with delicious fillings. She had opened all the jars of jam and Nutella spread she had bought and lined them up along the bar counter separating the cooking space from the eating area. She motioned to the men to sit down on the barstools at the counter. Then she turned to her task.

If she knew how to cook one dish well, it was this one. It wasn't just a dish. It was a performance. Taking the mixing bowl, she poured a thin stream of batter into each of the frying pans. Then she tilted each pan in quick succession, causing the batter to thinly cover the entire bottom. She put the pans back on the burners and waited, not long. As soon as the edges of the batter began to bubble in the first pan, she picked it up and shook it, loosening the crepe. Then she flipped it.

"Cool," Dirk cried. *Koel* in Dutch was pronounced exactly like "cool" in English, so Kati didn't need a translation to know she was being complimented.

She flipped the crêpe in the second pan.

"Wow," Jan said.

She flipped the crêpe in the third pan. This one fell on the floor, for which Snorry was instantly grateful. He gobbled it down then stared up at her, his tail wagging furiously.

She now had the total attention of three adoring males.

Sliding the first crêpe onto Dirk's plate, she told him to spread a thin layer of jam on it then fold it in half, then half again, and eat it with a knife and fork.

She slid the next one onto Jan's plate, and told him that those with less refined table manners could roll theirs up like a cigar and eat with their fingers. He was happy to comply.

Cooking *palacsinta* was a delicate art. Timing was everything. Using lots of butter to keep the batter from sticking to the pan was important. If the batter stuck, she wouldn't be able to flip the crêpe.

She casually turned back to the stove and flipped three more crêpes. Three sets of eyes admired her from behind. She suspected Jan wasn't just admiring her cooking skills.

Twenty crêpes later, Kati had worn out her flipping wrist. She sat down at the counter with the men and spread one for herself with Nutella.

Dirk said something to Jan in Dutch. She cocked her head, waiting for a translation.

"He said, 'at least you can cook.'"

Kati took the knife out of the Nutella jar and spread gooey chocolate on the tip of Dirk's nose. Everyone laughed.

*Palacsinta* was one of her favorite meals. It was like having dessert for dinner. It was a dish guaranteed to turn anyone into a happy five-year-old for a few moments.

After devouring every one of the crêpes, Jan and Dirk cleaned up while Kati pretended to read a Dutch newspaper. She decided to read out loud, for the fun of hearing Dirk laugh at her some more. Pretty soon the handsome boy was holding his stomach in pain from laughing so much at her mangled pronunciation of his native tongue.

In another hour it was time to bring Dirk back to his home in Arnhem. Everyone trooped out to the car again, including Snorry. Kati operated the hydraulic lift for Dirk, who pinched her on the arm as he wheeled himself into the van.

"Your son is starting to get fresh," she told Jan.

"He takes after his father," Jan joked, giving Kati his own pinch.

*Great. Now I'm an object of torture as well as ridicule to these two.*

Only Snorry remained worshipful.

They drove to Arnhem as dusk spread. By the time they arrived, it was dark. Dirk's town was substantially larger, and more affluent-looking than Beekbergen. Pulling into the driveway of a large house, she noted that Dirk seemed more withdrawn. She reached back and tweaked his kneecap. It seemed to flex just the tiniest bit under her touch. But that was impossible. It must have been her imagination.

Dirk caught her hand and twisted it behind her front passenger seat, until she felt something warm, wet and slimy. She jumped. The mischievous boy had slid her hand across Snorry's impressive jowls. No question about it. Dirk was warming up to her.

Meanwhile, a man came out of the house and spoke to Jan, apparently Dirk's stepfather. The form of a woman was outlined in the light spilling from the kitchen, bustling back and forth. Kati hoped Dirk's mother didn't know how to cook *palacsinta.*

Dirk wheeled his chair out of the van, but not before giving Kati a final, playful punch on the shoulder. She'd made a friend that day. The cost was only in a few black and blue marks here and there and her bruised ego. She sensed her prowess as a cook had made up for her lack of other skills.

Jan and she drove off and for the first time that day, her thoughts turned from Dirk to his father.

"Today I met you all over again," Jan said, as if reading her mind. His hand reached for her knee and found her thigh instead.

"So what do you think?" Kati asked, still in a playful mood from Dirk's final swipe at her shoulder.

"I think you stink at basketball."

"Thanks."

"You need help at cards. Did you really graduate from Columbia?"

Kati gave him a cuff, then thought for a moment. "How'd you know I went to Columbia?" Had she told him? If she had, she didn't remember it.

"Your friend told me at the hotel bar in Budapest." he explained.

Krisztof. What else had he told Jan about her?

"And?" She wanted to get him off the subject of Krisztof.

"And you're a fantastic cook."

She beamed. She might be an Ivy League grad, but it pleased her that her boyfriend liked her cooking. There was something about feeding someone she loved that satisfied something deep inside her.

"Now I'm taking you to a place I like to go sometimes," Jan said.

"But I'm still wearing my basketball clothes."

"Kati, you're in one of the most casual countries on the planet. It's not a problem."

"Okay. Are we going to have a drink there?"

"Yes. We're going to have a drink and we'll probably bump into a few of my friends. This time you can make fun of me, because they'll tell you a whole lot of bad stuff about me."

"Great. I can hardly wait." It would be fun to get some discreet information about Jan's past romantic history, but she wasn't sure if she'd be able to do this just meeting his friends for the first time. Perhaps after they'd all had a few beers.

Several rounds of good Dutch beer later, she had met a few of Jan's friends and had a great time. She hadn't been able to find out anything about his past romantic history, however. Was it possible there wasn't a big story to tell?

The rest of the week continued in a similar vein. They took Dirk to his physical therapy session the next day, then the boy came over on Wednesday to help plan for the Friday night party at Jan's youth center. After they'd put together some posters and tacked them up around town, they visited the local pool hall, where both Jan and Dirk cleaned her clock. She made a note to practice shooting pool with her girlfriends back in New York when she returned.

In the evenings, she and Jan spent hours snuggled up on his couch with Snorry trying to get in between them. She was happy he'd wanted to introduce her to his life back home in Beekbergen. He wasn't trying to create a fantasy with her. He was showing her his real life.

Without a doubt she was falling in love with Jan. She had a feeling the same thing was happening to him. But she decided to stick with her policy of sleeping in the yellow guestroom for the week. She knew herself well enough to know she would probably lose her head completely once she gave herself to him. She suspected this wouldn't pose a problem for Jan, but it would pose one for her. She had learned from experience that once sex entered the picture, her sensual nature overwhelmed her good sense. She didn't want to be a fool.

She also needed to proceed carefully in the house that Jan's former wife had once shared with him. Frankly, Kati had a fastidious nature. She wasn't going to share Jan's bed if this had once been where his wife had slept. Was Jan's bedroom the place where Dirk had been conceived? She kept her concerns to herself and thanked God He had sent her a man who let her take the time she needed to proceed in his direction.

MEANWHILE, JAN WAS spending time out on the balcony adjoining his bedroom after he bade goodnight to Kati every evening. She was killing him. He felt like a boy back in high school trying to control himself around the girls.

Kati was a complete contradiction that somehow made sense. He didn't think she was afraid of sex. His impression was that her nature was deeply sensual, given her reactions to his touch. Maybe that might be the problem. She was afraid of herself.

But if he pressed her and forced the issue, he was certain he would miss some of the nuances of getting to know her. He'd never felt this way with any woman before, but with Kati he wanted to take his time and linger along every step of the path to... to... what?

It was the path to something serious, but for the moment he wouldn't try to give it a name. Why hurry? Kati's guidelines had given him the luxury of having fun with her without having to wrestle with his conscience over whether he was leading her on or making promises to her with his body he had no intention of keeping. He laughed. His heart felt light and heavy at the same time. Another contradiction that made sense. This woman was getting to him in all the best ways.

FRIDAY'S PARTY WENT well, with Kati conducting a spelling contest in English for the dozen or so teenagers who came. She marveled at how close to bi-lingual the children were at such a young age. After the contest the teenagers danced and took turns trying to shove each other under the mistletoe which Jan had hung up in the recreation hall entryway.

At the end of the evening, she walked to the door to see off some of the kids and Jan grabbed her as she passed beneath the mistletoe. He kissed her and the young people cheered. Apparently they weren't used to seeing their director kiss a woman. That made her smile.

On New Year's Eve, they went to Jan's friend Hans de Blij's party. Shortly before midnight, they slipped out and drove home to usher in the new year alone together, with Snorry on the couch.

The next day she flew back to New York. She was sad to leave Jan, but elated that their time together had passed so perfectly. She was in an ongoing relationship with a man she loved.

Now all she needed to do was figure out where the rest of her life fit in.

# CHAPTER FOURTEEN

# PRIORITIES

THE NEXT FEW months flew by quickly. The conference in Barcelona in February was successful but hectic. Barcelona itself had been gorgeous for the ten minutes of free time Kati had had to explore it. She wished Jan could have been with her to explore Gaudi's stamp on the city, the way they had explored Budapest together.

By the time the Dublin conference at the end of May was over, she realized she wasn't going to be able to incorporate Jan into her daily life the way he had done so well with her the week after Christmas. She couldn't drag him along to an international conference and then disappear for the next three days, while she ran from moderating a panel to hosting a cocktail party, then evaluating the keynote dinner speaker she'd booked. At the end of each day all she wanted to do was go upstairs to her hotel room and fall into bed. The conference business was exhausting.

Her passport was beginning to fill up with stamps, but she hadn't really seen any of the places she'd visited. She'd typically fly in to a large city, taxi to the four-star hotel where she would spend the next three days, then taxi back to the airport. If she was lucky she had time to pick up some perfume in the duty free shops for herself or her mother or sister. It wasn't difficult to figure out why almost all of her colleagues were single. They were mostly on the road and when back in New York, running around like madwomen doing errands which hadn't gotten done while they were traveling.

In June the location of the November conference needed to be decided. Kati had enough successes under her belt to have a say in the decision-making. The conference was to be in a major European city, but had been allotted a lower budget than the previous ones she had worked on, as they were nearing the end of their fiscal year. As usual, they were running out of money until next year's budget began.

Her director asked her to submit a budget for three European cities to her. Kati decided she wanted to give Jan a big surprise on the anniversary of when they had first met.

The cities of Central and Eastern Europe were a far sight less expensive than the usual European conference destinations of London, Paris, Amsterdam, Barcelona or Milan. And November was an off season, well after the summer tourists had gone home, and before the holiday season swung into full gear. Asking her logistics director to get hotel rates from four-star hotels in Berlin, Prague and Budapest, she decided to secretly stack the deck in favor of the latter.

Berlin and Prague were cheaper than the European cities farther west, but not by much. Budapest was a bit less expensive even than Berlin and Prague. She contacted her friend Krisztof, asking for help. The next day he called back to say the head of corporate conferences at the Budapest Hilton had agreed to offer her company a special rate in exchange for Krisztof's guarantee that he'd book his out of town clients exclusively in his hotel.

Krisztof's name was well known in Budapest business circles, so when the bids were returned to Kati's office, the Budapest Hilton had given them a room rate offer well under any of the Berlin or Prague hotels. Her boss was delighted.

"I've never seen a hotel rate like this for a Hilton. How'd you do it, Kati? Did you pull some of your Hungarian strings?

Kati smiled her Cheshire cat smile. She had her reasons, as well as her connections.

"We'll go with Budapest," her director continued. "If the conference goes well, you've earned yourself a nice Christmas bonus," she enthused.

Kati ran back to her office, slammed the door shut and called Jan.

He wasn't there. She left a message on his machine, letting him know they could be together in Budapest in November.

She would be sure to take a few days' vacation at the end of the conference so that she and Jan could celebrate the first anniversary of their meeting. Right away, she put in for the time off.

That evening, Jan called her at home; they spoke excitedly of Budapest in November. She couldn't believe it had already been eight months since they'd met. He'd visited her in New York in April for a long weekend, during which time they'd jogged in Central Park almost every day, visited the Metropolitan Museum, gone to her church together, and roamed the bars and restaurants of her Upper East Side neighborhood.

Jan had relished trying different foods every evening; they'd dined on Thai, Vietnamese, French and Ethiopian cuisine over his four-day visit. Her mother and sister had joined them at the Ethiopian restaurant, where they'd broken the ice while struggling to eat dinner with their hands. It had been messy and fun.

That summer Kati threw herself into planning both the Lisbon and Budapest conferences. The theme for the Budapest conference was on sports-related injuries and rehabilitative therapies. She wondered if Dirk could benefit from the expertise of some of the speakers she would engage.

Weeks turned into months and soon it was the end of September. Kati flew to her Lisbon conference. It was a success, yet she wasn't able to visit Jan in Holland on her way home, as planned, because the Budapest conference was less than six weeks away and she still needed to book some key speakers. Then there was Coral Gables in December. It had turned into a busy end of the year.

Two days after returning to her New York office from Lisbon, she received an unexpected call from Budapest. It was Krisztof.

"Kati, something has come up for me with some American investors and I've got a meeting in New York next Tuesday. This fell on me out of the blue, but I've got a favor to ask you."

She couldn't deny Krisztof any reasonable favor he might ask of her. He had just assisted her in pulling off a coup at her own job as well as making it possible to be together with Jan on their first anniversary.

"Name it, you've got it," she told him.

"My secretary has called around to all the usual hotels. They're booked solid. She can't find anything for under a thousand a night in midtown Manhattan."

"Fall is New York's most popular season. You won't be able to find anything. If you need to stay at my apartment while you're in town, it's yours," she said without hesitation. "It's a very small studio, so I'll go stay with my mother while you're here."

"I know this is an inconvenience."

"Don't say another word. This is my chance to thank you for all the help you've given me this past year," she insisted.

"Are you sure? I may need to stay until Friday."

"It's yours for as long as you need it. What day are you coming?" She was pleased she could offer her place to her friend. Krisztof was on his way to becoming a wealthy man, but he wasn't there yet.

"I'll plan to come in Monday afternoon. I'll have to talk with my contact who's introducing me to the investor on Tuesday. Would that work?"

"Yes. I'll leave the key for you with my downstairs neighbor when I go to work Monday morning," she said on the spur of the moment. Meredith was an attractive, single freelance writer in her early thirties who worked from home. Kati had never seen her with a boyfriend. She smiled. What would her neighbor think of Krisztof?

"You're great, Kati. Choose any restaurant you like. I'm taking you there next week. Invite your mother too. Would Monday evening work for you?"

"Sure, Krisztof. I'll ask my mother to choose a place she really likes."

They ended their conversation and she called her mother to let her know she'd be crashing at home for a few days the following week and to pick a restaurant for Krisztof to take them to the following Monday evening.

THE NEXT DAY, Jan's phone rang at home in the evening.

"I'm booking speakers now to talk on rehabilitative therapies for athletic injuries," Kati told him. "Do you think there's anyone I can find who could help Dirk?"

"Thank you for wanting to help him." He was warmed by the way Kati cared so much about his son. No other woman he'd dated had taken such an interest. The few he had spent time with had seemed ill at ease at the mention of Dirk's handicap. "He's seen a lot of specialists already," he said. "How about if you let me sit in on a few sessions and take notes if anyone says anything that might apply to him?"

"You've got it. I'll arrange for one of my staff members to give you a guest pass. Then you can see for yourself just what I do when I'm at a conference," she laughed.

"Will you be tied up in the evenings too?" he asked, wondering how much time they'd be able to spend alone together in Budapest. He'd been sharing Kati with her job ever since she'd returned to New York.

"I'll be tied up until the conference ends," Kati told him. "Then I'm all yours. I've already put in for four days off, after it's over."

"Good. We've got a lot of catching up to do."

"Speaking of catching up," she said, "My Hungarian friend is coming into town on business next week and needs a place to stay. I've offered him my apartment, so I'll go downtown and stay with my mom."

"Which Hungarian friend?" Jan didn't like the sound of the pronoun he'd just heard.

"Krisztof. You remember—you met him in Budapest the night he dropped by our hotel."

"He couldn't find a hotel room?" he asked, his hand tightening around the phone. Why did this guy need to stay at Kati's place instead of booking a hotel like any other businessman on a business trip?

"He had something come up at the last minute. He tried to get a hotel room, but everything was booked," Kati explained. "He's done me so many favors, Jan, including helping me negotiate a great hotel rate for my Budapest conference. I really couldn't say no."

"Uh-huh." Why had the Hungarian businessman done so many favors for Kati? Was he interested in her? Thinking back to the conversation he'd had with Krisztof in the hotel bar in Budapest, he wondered if he'd made himself clear to the man that he wanted him to keep his hands off her. Even if he had, would that have stopped Krisztof from moving in on her if he chose to? He had to admit, it wouldn't stop him if he was in Krisztof's place.

"Kati, does he know you and I are together?" He tried to keep his voice neutral.

"Of course." She paused. "I mean—I think so. You're the reason I begged him to help me get a great hotel room rate in Budapest so I could hold the conference there."

"All right, Kati. I appreciate you telling me upfront. Just know I care and will be thinking of you constantly while he's there ... I hope you'll be thinking of me too." He got off, his stomach tied up in knots.

ON SUNDAY KATI buzzed her downstairs neighbor to ask her if she'd give the key to Krisztof when he arrived the next day. Meredith happily agreed to let him in; she promised to help him out if he needed anything or didn't know how something worked while Kati was downtown at her mother's. Kati managed to work into the short conversation the fact that her friend from Budapest was a newly divorced venture capitalist with a business degree from Columbia University.

She laughed inside to see Meredith's eyebrows move upwards in the midst of her description. It would be fun to hear about their interaction the following weekend after Krisztof had left.

On Monday morning, Kati set off for work with her overnight bag. That evening she fetched her mother at her place and together they taxi'd over to her apartment to pick up Krisztof for dinner. Her mother had decided on the Red Tulip on the Upper East Side. It was the finest Hungarian restaurant in New York and the site of her wedding reception with Kati's father. It had also been the place where they'd gathered with family and friends after Kati's father's funeral.

"Mom, are you sure you don't want to go with Krisztof to some place that's not Hungarian? It might not be so interesting for him. Maybe it's not as good as Hungarian restaurants he's used to back home."

"Honey, didn't you ask me to choose the restaurant? If it's my choice, I'd like to go there with him so he can help me talk to the manager. He remembers your father, but his English isn't so good. Maybe Krisztof can help me to ask him a few questions."

"Okay," Kati conceded to her mother's wishes. She remembered how limited the manager's English had been when he'd spoken to them at her father's funeral reception. Hungarians who lived in Yorkville, the former German-Hungarian enclave on the Upper East Side, managed to go about their lives speaking their native tongue most of the time, despite being in the middle of New York City. "It will be interesting to see what he says about the food compared to Budapest restaurants," she said, giving her mom a hug.

IN BEEKBERGEN, KATI was on Jan's mind. It was almost midnight and he couldn't sleep. Their last phone conversation had left him less than satisfied. He couldn't help it. He didn't like the idea of Krisztof staying at Kati's apartment, even if she was staying elsewhere. They'd missed each other's calls over the past few days and only left short messages. Although they would see each other in Budapest in November, it was only September.

He found the demands of Kati's job on her free time disconcerting. He wasn't used to the American corporate world. She had told him she had only two weeks' vacation annually, which shocked him. In Holland workers typically took six weeks. When did Americans find time to relax? She had said she typically worked from 8:30 A.M. to 6 P.M. every day and when she went on conferences, she worked late into the evening until she fell into bed.

Finding time to visit each other was proving to be challenging. He was proud of his busy, professional American girlfriend, but he was still lonely in the evenings and on weekends in his small town. Maybe he could hop over to New York for just a few days, depending on Kati's availability. Although he usually called her in her office in the early evening his time, it was now past midnight and five hours earlier should find her at her mother's place. He called her there, but got an answering machine, so he left a message. Then he called her on the first number he had in his phone for her.

A man's voice answered.

"Hello, is this Kati Dunai's number?" Jan tried to keep his voice neutral.

"Yes. She'll be home in a minute. Who's calling please?"

At the sound of Krisztof's voice, Jan's blood began to boil. He was well aware that Kati's apartment was a studio, with only one room. Why was she not at her mother's place, as she'd told him she would be? Had she lied to him?

"I'll call back." Jan hung up abruptly without identifying himself. Inadvertently, he had called Kati's home number instead of her cell. It was late and his low mood had colored his ability to think straight.

What kind of "friend" was this guy to her, anyways? There appeared to be more to their "friendship" than he had been aware of. He was furious. Was this the real reason Kati had been hesitant to become lovers? Was she already sleeping with this big shot businessman?

He had already been dumped once for a wealthier man. His former wife was now married to a doctor. He had thought that had more to do with her disappointment in him from allowing their son on his motorcycle the day of the accident, but had there been other factors? His ex-wife had married her old school chum, but it hadn't hurt that he also happened to be a successful physician, had it?

He steamed and stewed and grew more uncertain as the day went by.

He tried not to paint Kati with the same brush as his ex, but he was hurt. His girlfriend had a man staying at her studio apartment. Instead of being at her mother's place, as she'd told him, apparently she was still at her own place. He thought about the well-dressed, prosperous-looking businessman with whom he'd had a drink in the Budapest hotel lobby bar while waiting for Kati to come downstairs to go out for the evening. After she'd spent the day with him.

Unable to sleep, he got out of bed then paced the floor of his bedroom. Snorry looked worried and began to bark.

*"Zwijg,* Snorry," he snapped at the dog. Unable to control his frustration any longer, he punched his hand into his bedroom wall. A largish hole appeared, the size of a deflated volleyball—or his own deflated ego.

He had some serious thinking to do. There was something not right with this picture. He'd thought about flying to New York over the coming weekend, but he'd be damned if he was going to show up on Kati's doorstep on the coattails of her businessman "friend."

The next evening, he went out for a few drinks with his friends. He needed diversion. Getting home late, he called Kati at her mother's place. Once again, he got the answering machine.

He wasn't sure if he'd put her home or cell number on his home phone's speed dial function, so he hit it regardless, frustrated at not having kept better track of which number was which. He hadn't paid close attention because he usually called her in her office when it was early evening in Holland and early afternoon in New York. Now it was hours later.

After two rings, a male voice answered. "Hello? Hello?"

After a burning moment, Jan spoke.

"Hello," he said tersely. "May I speak with Kati please?"

"She's not here right now, could I take a message?"

"Do you know when she'll be back?" Jan asked.

"She'll be back soon. Who's calling please?" Krisztof asked rather sharply.

"I'll call back," Jan replied just as sharply, slamming down the phone.

Two days and two more calls to her apartment, Jan had had it. Had Krisztof been the reason all along why Kati had suggested he call her in her office rather than at home or on her cell phone? He'd thought it was because of the time difference or the cost of calling between the Netherlands and New York, but perhaps not. Had there been something more to it? Maybe Krisztof came to visit her on a regular basis. He was an international businessman after all.

Work didn't give Jan too much time to dwell on his personal problem. Holland was in the midst of a heat wave that first week of October. The kids in his youth group were supposed to go camping that weekend with two of his junior staff members, including a newly hired worker who had joined the office one month earlier.

But Wit, his male colleague who was supposed to go on the trip, appeared to be coming down with a cold. He coughed and hacked around the office, and by Thursday afternoon he asked Jan if he could take his place.

Jan agreed. He needed some time away—to think and maybe to forget. He and the newest staff member Skyla packed up the van after lunch on Friday and rode off with six teenagers in back in the early afternoon, before rush hour traffic began. As they drove down Beekbergen's main street, Jan's minister and friend, Hans de Blij, spotted them and waved. Jan gave a half-hearted wave back, wondering if Hans had ever had women troubles of his own.

MEANWHILE, KATI HAD spent the week at her mother's place, regaling her with stories from her workplace and describing her upcoming Budapest conference. She hoped to sneak in a few days of pleasure with Jan, celebrating the first anniversary of when they had met.

"Have you thought about whether your conference topic might be helpful to Jan's son in any way?" her mother asked, after listening carefully.

"It was in the back of my mind. I just don't know enough about sports-related injuries to know if a specialist in that area could do anything for Dirk," Kati told her.

"Some sports injuries result in paralysis. Why don't you research doctors who've treated athletes who've suffered paralysis and find out if there are any cases in which a partial or full recovery has been made?"

"Mom—you're so smart. Why don't you go into conference planning?"

"Honey, it's all I can do to keep up with your stories of gallivanting around the world. I'm exhausted just listening to you tell me about your job... speaking of which, do you know any doctors in Hungary you could call?" her mother asked.

"Uhh no, not really. Let me think about it."

They watched TV in companionable silence while Kati flipped through a mental rolodex of all the people she'd met in Budapest the previous November. Her mind circled back to thoughts of Jan in the thermal pool, at the Market Hall, at the Széchenyi and Gellért Baths, in the lounge with the fireplace back at their hotel. There, she paused.

What about the couple they had bumped into in the hotel lounge the night before Jan had left? Andrasz Parcsami had handed her his card, which had indicated he was a doctor. He had told them he was in town for a medical conference.

"Mom, I do know a doctor in Budapest," she burst out. "Not very well, but Jan and I bumped into him and his wife at our hotel. They were really friendly and invited us to visit them in their hometown, outside of Budapest."

"Do you have his phone number?"

"I've got his business card back at my apartment."

"Call your friend, Krisztof, and have him look for the business card. He might know who the top sports injury doctors are in Hungary. I'll bet they're all based in Budapest."

"You're a genius, Mom." She picked up the phone and called her apartment. Krisztof answered after a few rings.

"Kati, it's gone really well," he told her. "My investor's on board and I owe you an enormous favor. I've got one final meeting tomorrow, then I'm free. Can I take you out for dinner tomorrow evening?"

"Krisztof, I—uh—already have some plans tomorrow with Meredith. The woman you got the key from. Do you want to join us?" Even though Jan was thousands of miles away, her conscience told her he wouldn't be happy to know she'd spent an evening alone with Krisztof. This was her chance to introduce him to Meredith as well as to let him know about Jan.

"Why not?" he agreed. "Was there a reason why you called?"

"Of course, I almost forgot. I need a phone number," She laughed. "Could you look for a business card in the top middle drawer of my desk?"

"Sure. What's the name on the card?"

"It's Parcsami—Dr. Andrasz Parcsami from Eger, Hungary." In the background she heard the ring of Krisztof's cell phone. He picked up and spoke to someone in Hungarian, then came back on the line.

"Kati ?"

"Yes?"

"Could you call back in a minute? I've got to take this call. It's international."

"Of course. I'll call you again in ten minutes. Bye."

She hung up, chuckling to herself. Her friend was once again multi-tasking. Some things never changed. She hoped he wouldn't take calls on his cell phone while they spent the evening with Meredith. Her girlfriend wouldn't be impressed.

MEANWHILE, KRISZTOF HAD a crisis of conscience. When Kati called back, he would let her know a man had been calling for her all week long. She rang again and he gave her the phone number she was looking for. Just as he was about to tell her about the man's calls, his cell phone rang again.

"Gotta go, Kati." He made a mental note to tell her the next evening when they met.

THE NEXT DAY Kati called Dr. Parcsami in Budapest. He remembered her and was delighted to be asked for a recommendation for a top specialist in sports injuries. Taking down the dates of her conference, he promised he'd get back to her with the names of one or two of Hungary's leading experts in this area.

Two hours later, he called back. He'd spoken to a few professional colleagues in Budapest and had the name of Hungary's leading sports injuries specialist. He'd spoken to the man personally and learned he would be in Budapest on the dates of Kati's conference. Now it was up to her to work out the details of engaging him to speak.

She spent the rest of the day in a whirlwind of work, hunting down Dr. Parcsami's contact, convincing him to speak, then finding colleagues who would offer different viewpoints to join him on a panel.

Planning to surprise Meredith, she decided not to tell her that Krisztof would be joining them that evening. This was fortuitous, as Krisztof rang her in the office at four that afternoon with news. His investor's plans had fallen through for the evening and he would now have to take him out.

"Kati, darling, I'm so sorry. I really wanted to spend my final evening here with you and I would have liked to get to know your friend, Meredith."

"Krisztof, it's not a problem." Kati breathed a sigh of relief. She counted herself lucky that she definitely was not this man's "darling." She could only imagine what his wife had put up with when they'd been together. It was clear Krisztof's business interests were his overriding priority.

Jan's face came into her mind. Happily, the man she had given her heart to was fully capable of giving her his total undivided attention.

As soon as she got off the phone she called Jan. His answering machine picked up, with an outgoing message saying he'd gone out of town for the weekend. Dialing his cell phone number, she got his voicemail; she left a short message.

Her heart felt lighter now that her evening plans with Krisztof had been cancelled. Even though she'd planned to take Meredith along, she knew Jan wouldn't have been happy about it.

On her way to meet Meredith she thought back to Monday evening at the Red Tulip where she and her mother had dined with Krisztof. They had been regaled by gypsy music played by a violinist who came to their table. Her mother had closed her eyes and smiled. Had she been thinking of her early days of courtship with her father? Images of the evening Kati had spent with Jan at the Hungarian restaurant across the street from their hotel in Budapest made her smile. It had been the evening of the afternoon of their first kiss. She sighed to herself, hoping she and Jan would revisit the Széchenyi Baths again in November after her conference was over.

She looked forward to telling her girlfriend about Jan. Although she was lonely, she felt deeply satisfied. She had had the good judgment to fall in love with a man who knew how to make a plan and keep it. Her heart tugged at her as she thought of the sound of Jan's deep voice. She needed to hear it again as soon as possible. She'd try calling him at the end of the evening on her way back to her mother's place.

THAT WEEKEND OUTSIDE of Beekbergen Jan found himself in a dilemma. He owed it to Kati to at least talk to her about where she'd stayed over the past week. But why hadn't she called all week long? He burned to think of the day they'd visited the Market Hall together. Krisztof had shown up at the hotel at the end of the day they had spent together and whisked her off for a glamorous evening out.

Feelings of insecurity continued to gnaw at Jan. He couldn't offer Kati glamour. He was a man who wore plaid shirts and jeans to work, and took kids on camping trips. Who was he kidding, dating a woman from the Upper East Side of Manhattan who traveled all over the world for her job? The bloody Hungarian guy was a much better match for her. They could both spend their time jetsetting around and bumping into each other every few months. It wasn't what he wanted with a woman. He wanted a woman who was—there.

Sitting on a log across from him in their campfire circle, Skyla, his new office colleague, smiled shyly at him. When she suggested a dip in the river near their campsite, he agreed and called to their charges to join them. The weather was unseasonably warm, so everyone had brought their bathing suits. He went into his tent, grabbing a towel to wrap around his waist.

They made their way down to the river, where he peeled off his tee shirt. Skyla dropped her jeans and unbuttoned her shirt, casually tossing it behind her. Slowly, she walked into the river, her long, lean body sinuously beckoning him to follow.

He tried not to watch. It was hard.

He wanted Kati, but she was so busy. And now it appeared she was busy entertaining her Hungarian businessman "friend" in her home in the evenings, while he sat at home with Snorry night after night. His thoughts on Kati, he followed Skyla into the water.

Their teenage charges made cannonball jumps from a high ledge above, noisily splashing and dunking each other. Then Skyla climbed to the high ledge and dove gracefully straight down. She stayed underwater for a long time, ten seconds, then twenty. Frowning, he stood.

"Skyla," he called frantically.

Nothing.

He dove under the surface to find her. He discovered her thrashing about but when he got close she wrapped her arms around his shoulders and clung to him.

They emerged with all six teenagers staring at them.

"Nice couple," one of them teasingly said.

"Do you think so?" Skyla laughed, her voice sparkling in a way Jan hadn't noticed before. She splashed water into his face.

He splashed her back. Had she really been in distress or just trying to get his attention? His instincts told him the latter. For the first time, it occurred to him that the shy Dutch girl liked him. And that she wasn't so shy.

He wasn't prepared to do anything about it, no matter how mad he was at Kati. He needed to have a serious talk with her. However, he couldn't help but notice his Dutch colleague's graceful curves and pretty face. He would keep her at arm's length, but there was nothing wrong with enjoying the view, was there?

KATI'S VIEW BACK in New York was becoming increasingly dismal. After a pleasant evening out with Meredith, she had spent the weekend alone and miserable, wondering why Jan had not called the entire week before and where he had gone for the weekend without telling her. She'd called him on his cell phone numerous times, but always got his voicemail. She didn't want to appear to be hunting him down, so she didn't leave messages after the first one. Little did she know that Jan's cell phone wasn't working, deep in the woods far from any transmission towers.

On Sunday afternoon she phoned again and got his voicemail. She couldn't take it any longer. It was time for action, even if it meant embarrassing herself.

She'd saved the program from the Christmas day service at his church. The telephone number was listed on the cover page, so she called his friend Hans de Blij, the minister there. She guessed his evening service must have just ended and he would be around straightening up the church.

Hans picked up after three rings.

*Goedenavond*, he answered. She knew it meant 'good evening' in Dutch.

"Hans, it's Kati Dunai from New York. I'm trying to find Jan. Have you seen him recently? I don't want to bother you, but I haven't heard from him in a few days and I'm wondering if everything's okay."

"Kati! How are you?" Hans' voice was warm, reassuring.

"Worried."

"Uh—I saw Jan Friday afternoon. It looked like he was driving out of town with a bunch of teenagers and— uh ..." His voice changed, trailing off.

"And what, Hans?"

"And—uh—his colleague from work."

Hans' pauses spoke volumes. She wasn't a woman for nothing.

"Hans, do you mind telling me which colleague was with him?"

"Uh—I didn't recognize her, actually. I think it's a new girl who works in his office."

"Hans—I don't want you to be a rat, and I know you're Jan's friend—but would you please answer one very important question for me? Just one, then I'll let you go."

"Sure, Kati," he said, his voice rising. He sounded uneasy.

"Was his colleague from work good looking?"

"Uh—I—uh—"

"In other words, yes, right?"

"Well, I—uh—ummm..."

"Hans—let me rephrase the question. Was Jan's colleague from work ugly?"

"No. Definitely not."

"Thanks, Hans. You've been a gem and this conversation never happened. Okay?"

"Kati, I think you need to talk to Jan directly when he gets back."

"No, Hans. *He* needs to talk to me. *If* he can find me."

She hung up abruptly. What had Hans meant by saying she needed to talk to Jan when he got back? What was going on over there??

She fumed and steamed, then called Crystal. Without meaning to, she divulged details about her relationship with Jan that she'd kept from her friend up until this point.

"Are you telling me you haven't had sex with this guy yet?" Crystal sounded incredulous.

"I—uh—yes, I mean, no, I haven't. Not yet."

"Are you insane? What are you waiting for—a marriage proposal?" Crystal's viewpoint on sex and relationships differed widely from her own. Their complementary views were among the many reasons they enjoyed each other's company.

"No. I was just waiting for the right moment. I wanted to be sure this was the right guy for me, because once we do make love, I'll be a goner, Crystal. That's the way I am."

"So what's wrong with being a goner? Better a goner than a loner. Do you really think this guy's waiting patiently for you to get your groove thing on month after month? What about him? What about all those cute Dutch girls running around over there? Aren't they all gorgeous or something?"

Kati shuddered. They had been by and large very good looking from what she'd seen on her visit. Maybe he'd succumbed to one. A lump welled in her throat.

"What should I do?" she asked in a tiny voice.

"You should get the hell on a plane and get over there," Crystal roared at her.

"I can't. I'm up to my ears in work and my biggest project right now is less than six weeks away in Budapest. I booked it there on purpose, so Jan and I could spend a few days together after it was over. It's where we met almost a year ago. What do I do now?" she wailed.

"Get a life, Kati. Which is more important to you, your job or your boyfriend?"

"I—uh—my—uh, my... both."

"Okay, question answered. Keep your job, and don't ask your boyfriend questions you don't want to hear the answers to when he lives in another country and on the rare occasions you do get together, you don't have sex. Hello." Crystal's deep disgust resounded through the receiver.

"I get the message. Thanks for being my friend. Let me go now. I'll call you again in a few days." Kati needed to get off the phone before she started to cry.

"Call me anytime. You need to think and then you need to act. Remember—no man is worth crying over. Just move on if this isn't the right one for you. And for God's sake, find one who lives in the same country." Crystal hung up with a decisive click.

Kati began to cry. She wasn't going to be able to find a man who lived in the same country while Jan Klassen inhabited every room in her heart and mind. She needed to find him and find out what was going on between the two of them. Then fix it, if necessary.

# CHAPTER FIFTEEN

# A CHINK IN JAN'S ARMOR

"JAN, I MISS you. I don't know what happened last week but you didn't call. Where were you over the weekend? I'd really like to hear from you soon. Bye."

Jan got the message that evening when he got home. He thought about calling Kati back. He missed her. It had been all he could do to resist the advances of Skyla throughout the weekend.

The Dutch girl had crept into his tent the first night of camping and lain down next to him. Unconsciously he'd turned over and flung his hand over her warm body. Then he'd woken up and realized it wasn't Kati's body he was touching. Leaping out of bed like a mad dervish, he hadn't known what to say. She'd laughed at him and beckoned him back. He'd been gracious, but refused to budge until she left his tent. She was quite something for a shy, Dutch girl.

The next day neither mentioned what had happened, and Jan tried to keep his distance from her for the rest of the weekend. It had been hard. He'd been so flustered by her that he'd practically leapt out of the camp van when it pulled into his driveway, leaving behind one of his bags in his haste to get away.

About to pick up his home phone to call Kati, it rang. Dirk's stepfather was on the line.

Dirk had had an accident, and was on his way to Arnhem Hospital with his mother. The chair of his wheelchair had gotten caught in a loose paving stone and he'd flipped over and out of the chair down a flight of stairs.

All else forgotten, Jan whipped on his leather jacket and ran out the door. He was at Arnhem Hospital within thirty minutes. Dirk had broken his left leg in the same place it had been broken four years before in the motorcycle accident. Jan remembered all too well the infection that had set in at the same hospital the last time Dirk had been hospitalized there. His son had almost died.

He wasn't taking any chances again. Speaking to Dirk's doctors, they agreed it was best to take the boy to a rehabilitative clinic in the suburbs of Amsterdam, where he would be seen by Holland's top specialists. The risk of infection would be lower there, as the clinic was small, with top standards. Dirk's mother couldn't take time off from her new job in Arnhem as an elementary school teacher, as it was the beginning of the school year.

Returning home to pack a bag with clothes and supplies for the next few weeks, he hunted for his cell phone. Where had he left it? He thought back over the last few days, retracing his steps. Had he lost it on the camping trip? He'd tried to call Kati with it that weekend, but there'd been no service deep in the woods where they'd camped.

Combing through his kitchen, living room and bedroom it was nowhere to be found. He needed it badly, not just to make arrangements for Dirk and to stay in touch with his office, but because he was ready to speak to her again. They needed to talk before he concluded anything about where Kati had stayed while Krisztof had been at her apartment the week before. He would call her from home before leaving, but first he needed to find someone to look after Snorry in his absence.

Too bad his friend, Hans de Blij, wasn't answering his phone. He couldn't remember if Hans had told him he was going away this week or the next, but he knew he was going off on a two week mission sometime soon, so Jan needed to find someone else to feed and walk Snorry.

Jan called his office and made arrangements. He would take a leave of absence for however long it took his son's leg to mend. His two junior staff people could handle the flow of work over the next few weeks. Wit was out, but Skyla was there.

"Listen—do you think you or Wit could stop by my place to feed Snorry and give him a walk once or twice a day until I get back? I'll leave the house key in an envelope under the doormat," he instructed, slightly uncomfortable at the thought of her in his home alone. What else could he do? He had no alternative but to depend on his co-workers at this time.

"No problem, Jan," Skyla's voice purred. "I'd be happy to look after your dog. What else can I do for you?"

Get off my back, he silently answered, then remembered the lost cell phone.

"I can't find my cell phone. Could you take a look on my desk and see if I left it there?"

He waited while Skyla rummaged through his desk, opening a few drawers. Would she find the photos of Kati he had in there?

"Sorry, it's not here. Did you bring it on the camping trip?"

"I think so. But I don't think I ever took it out of my back pack." Thanks to feeling upset about Kati's male visitor and nervous over Skyla's advances, he had been off kilter the entire weekend. "Could you take a look around the office?"

"Was your backpack blue? Someone left one behind in the van. Was it yours?"

"That's probably it. Could you take a look in the outside pocket and see if my cell phone is in there?"

"I'll be happy to, but Wit's out in the van now. He's due back this afternoon."

"Great. I'll call you again later to see if it turns up," he said, thinking it wasn't so great. It was extremely inconvenient as he had to get back to Arnhem within the next hour for the final consult with Dirk's doctor, who would be giving him the paperwork to transfer his son to the rehabilitation clinic where they were due later that day. Even worse, it was his own fault that the cell phone was missing. He kicked the leg of his kitchen table, stubbing his toe and startling Snorry, who leapt from his resting place at Jan's feet.

"Just let me know if there's anything else I can do for you, Jan. I'm totally here for you," Skyla said before hanging up.

*I'll bet you are,* he thought as he got off the phone. Calling Kati's office in New York, he remembered she had a ten A.M. staff meeting every Monday morning. He decided to leave a message. But her voice mailbox was completely full, so he wasn't able to. He didn't want to call her cell and have it ring in the middle of her meeting, so instead he picked up his duffle bag, gave Snorry a conciliatory pat, then rushed back to the hospital in Arnhem.

He would never forget the months after the motorcycle accident, when Dirk's leg had become infected not only once but twice. They had thought they might lose him. He wasn't leaving his boy's side for a minute this time.

He thought of Kati fleetingly, but put her out of his mind. She'd clearly prioritized her job over her relationship with him over the past ten months. And now it appeared she had entertained another man in her apartment in New York. She'd made her choices, and now he was making his.

Dirk was his priority. Maybe one day he would understand why Kati hadn't valued her love for him as much as he had for her. Maybe he hadn't been wealthy or successful enough for her. Who knew?

Jan spent the next week at a small clinic outside of Amsterdam playing cards and board games with Dirk, making jokes and watching old movies on TV. Calling into his office he discovered his cell phone had indeed been found in the blue backpack he'd left behind in the van. He asked Wit to hang onto it for him, but didn't give him the details of where Dirk and he were.

Dirk's risk of infection was too high. He didn't want anyone visiting them there, other than Dirk's mother and doctors. Friends were well-meaning, but sometimes showed up with colds or dirty hands. Jan himself would have been one of them if it hadn't been for the months of life and death uncertainty that had followed his son's accident during his eight-month hospital stay in Arnhem four years ago. He knew only too well that all it took was one moment of exposure to someone with the wrong kind of germs to give his son a life-threatening infection. He would take no chances this time.

KATI WAS BESIDE herself with worry. She'd already left several messages on Jan's home phone and cell phone, to which she'd received no reply. This, beside the fact that Jan hadn't contacted her the entire week before told her their relationship was in serious trouble. She didn't know what to do.

By Friday morning, she couldn't stand it any longer. Bringing a weekend bag with her to work, she booked a seat on the overnight KLM flight to Amsterdam using most of her bonus for the year to pay for it. After work, she hopped a cab directly to the airport.

Arriving in Amsterdam early Saturday morning, she took a train to Beekbergen. Then she taxi'd to Jan's house. No one was there. She walked the five blocks to his office, knowing it was sometimes open on Saturdays, as many of the activities at Jan's job took place on weekends. There she found a young, attractive Dutch woman.

"Jan's son had an accident," the woman said, eyeing her with curiosity. "He isn't expected back until further notice. He's in Arnhem as far as I know, with his boy."

"Thank you," Kati told her, wondering if this woman worked closely with Jan. Had she been a fool to have thought a long distance relationship was realistic? This young, beautiful Dutch woman was working next to Jan at close quarters, full-time. Perhaps she was the reason he no longer called her.

"By the way, I didn't meet you when I was here earlier this year. Have you worked with Jan a long time?" Kati continued.

"No. I started as junior youth coordinator last month. We just got back from taking a group camping about ten days ago. It was so much fun. What a shame Jan came home to find out his son had an accident." The woman smoothed a strand of her long silky brown hair behind one ear. "I feel so badly for him. He's such a nice man."

Kati could see exactly how nice a man this woman thought her boyfriend was. She couldn't believe Jan had gone away on a weekend camping trip with the woman without telling her about it. She was furious.

She went back to Jan's home to leave a message on his door. Writing a short note, she told him she'd been there and was now going to Arnhem to find him. She taped it to the side door, and spent a moment baby-talking to Snorry, whose frantic barks echoed from the other side of the door. Recognizing her voice, he calmed down and began whining. She only wished she could calm herself down, but she was a mess.

Bidding Snorry goodbye, she walked to the end of Jan's road, hopped on a local bus and got off at the train station. The next train to Arnhem left in twenty five minutes. She took it.

When she got off in Arnhem, she didn't know where to go. She could go either to the hospital or to Dirk's mother's and stepfather's home.

She tried the hospital first. At the admitting desk she was told Dirk and his father had checked out a few days earlier. Their destination was not available for disclosure to non-family members. The hospital staff was kind, but firm on this restriction.

Steeling herself, she took a taxi to Dirk's mother's and stepfather's home. Fortunately, she had remembered the street address when she and Jan had brought back Dirk on her previous trip there. She knocked on the door and breathed deeply, preparing herself to meet Jan's ex-wife. After a moment, she was greeted by a tall, dark-haired woman who looked tired.

"*Hello, kan ik u helpen?*" she curtly asked Kati.

"Hello, I'm Kati Dunai, Jan Klassen's girlfriend from New York. I'm looking for Jan. Could you tell me where he is?"

The woman responded in Dutch, her face expressionless. She didn't appear to understand English.

"Please, could you tell me where Jan is? I've come from New York to find him," Kati tried again.

*"Ik kan u helpen niet. Ik ben droevig,"* Jan's ex-wife responded, shrugging her shoulders.

Kati was close to bursting into tears from frustration. She stood in front of the only Dutch person she'd ever met who didn't speak a word of English. Kicking herself for her presumptuousness, she realized she should have prepared what she had to say to Jan's ex-wife in Dutch, but she'd assumed the woman would know a few words of English. It was entirely possible that Jan's ex-wife hadn't traveled much and was just as limited in English as Kati was in Dutch. Or perhaps it was something else. Kati sucked in her breath and held her ground before the unyielding look on the woman's face.

Quickly, Kati scribbled a short note, put Jan's name on the envelope, and handed it to Jan's ex-wife. She wasn't sure if it would ever find its way into his hands.

She had no idea what to do next. It was late Saturday afternoon in Arnhem in mid-October. The weather had turned cooler, and the sky was laden with heavy clouds. As she walked away from Dirk's house, she wondered who to ask for help. Maybe Hans de Blij back in Beekbergen? He was the only close friend of Jan's that she'd really spent time with on her visits to his home town.

She took the train back to Beekbergen and walked to Han's house behind the church in the deepening gloom. No one was home.

It had turned into the worst day of her life. She could only hope that wherever Jan and Dirk were, they were having a better day and that Dirk was healing from his accident. She scribbled a note to Hans and left it on his door.

Passing by the church she went around back and sat in the small graveyard for a moment. She prayed that Dirk's accident wouldn't have serious consequences and that he and his father were safe and together. She also prayed that Jan would contact her and let her know why he'd disappeared these past two weeks.

Then she asked God for insights into her own balance of professional and personal life. It was becoming clear to her that she couldn't be there for Jan if she lived in another country and had endless professional commitments and deadlines that got in the way of spending time with him. Perhaps it had become clear to him too in the past few weeks. But why hadn't he called to talk to her about it, then?

She offered up her worries to God, but no voice inside responded. She couldn't think of anything else to do other than go back to Amsterdam and get on the next flight back to New York. She had an important meeting early Monday morning, where the directors would receive their conference assignments for the following year. Just thinking about what would be loaded onto her plate made her tired.

As the train pulled out of Beekbergen station, the skies opened up and a fierce rainstorm began. How lucky she'd been not to have been caught outside in it. Then she thought of the note she'd left on Hans's door. What if the rain ruined it? At this point there was nothing she could do but pray it didn't get soaked and become unreadable.

She made it onto the last flight to New York out of Amsterdam on Sunday and got home exhausted late Sunday evening. There was no message waiting for her on her answering machine. On Sunday night, she took a sleeping pill and fell into a deep, dreamless sleep. It was beginning to look like her dreams of the future with Jan were over.

Sitting silently through the nine A.M. directors' meeting on Monday morning, she felt as if cotton balls had been stuffed inside her head. Why didn't she feel more excited to hear she'd been given responsibility for conferences in the year to come in Singapore, Toronto, Rome, Scottsdale, Arizona, and one additional destination yet to be determined? She'd done such a great job over the past ten months that her director had awarded her two more conferences for the following year. It was a terrific opportunity to make more profit for the company, as well as to double her bonus.

She dragged herself back to her office, an empty pit weighting down the bottom of her stomach. If she ever managed to hear from Jan again and patch things up, he would not be pleased to hear about her work schedule for the coming year. What was the point of having a terrific international career if it interfered with having any sort of personal life? She couldn't believe she felt this way after less than one year in the job of her dreams. Maybe this particular dream wasn't the right one for her anymore.

It was all a moot point, because Jan hadn't called and apparently didn't care. Maybe she had sent him the wrong signals. She hadn't been able to visit him at the end of September as planned. They hadn't seen each other for months, since she'd managed to squeeze in a two-day visit on her return from Dublin in late June. What had she been thinking?

Suddenly, the effect of the sleeping pill from the night before wore off and she felt wide awake. She had been an idiot; she needed to fight to get her boyfriend back. This was the man she loved, and it now looked like she had lost him.

She called Jan's home in Beekbergen, and left a tearful message on his answering machine, begging him to call her.

IN BEEKBERGEN, WIT and Skyla had divided up duties between them to keep the office running smoothly in Jan's absence. Wit had gone over on the weekend and Monday to feed Jan's dog and take him out for a walk. Tuesday through Friday it was Skyla's turn. She walked the five blocks to Jan's home and let herself in the side door. Snorry was overjoyed to have company, even though he didn't know her. Immediately, she fed him and refreshed his water bowl, cementing their friendship. While Snorry ate, Skyla looked around Jan's place.

She picked up the photo of Jan's ex-wife at the beach with his son, noticing how similar her own long brown hair looked to the woman's in the picture. Skyla had heard she was now remarried and living in Arnhem with the boy. Then she wandered over to Jan's answering machine, thinking she'd better check his messages in case he called into his office.

He'd received a few messages from worried friends, including Hans de Blij. Then there was a message in English from the blonde American woman who'd shown up at their office on Saturday. Skyla knew enough English to understand her words. They must have had a falling out, because she was begging his forgiveness for not having had time to see him at the end of September. This woman was not what Jan needed. He needed a girlfriend who had time to be with him. Was there something she could do here to help him? She hummed to herself as she hit the erase button.

Spending another few minutes wandering around the upstairs of Jan's home, she went into his bedroom and noticed the balcony adjoining the room. She shivered, thinking of what it would be like to be out on that balcony, breathing in the night sky with his powerful arms wrapped around her from behind.

On her way out, she picked up a shirt thrown over the back of a chair. Burying her face in it, she breathed in his scent. She'd do a great job for him while he was out of the office, taking care of his son. On his return, he would realize what an invaluable assistant she had been for him. Then she would prove herself invaluable in other ways. She hugged the shirt to her chest then carefully draped it back over the chair.

Floating downstairs, she found Snorry's leash and took him out for a nice, long walk. When she returned, she left some dried autumnal flowers on the counter, with a note apologizing for her forward behavior on the camping trip and letting him know she was thinking about him and his son. Finding the note Kati had left for him, which Wit had put inside the door, she picked it up and read it. With a shrug, she placed it in her pocket and left.

Again on Wednesday, Thursday and Friday, Skyla went to Jan's house and listened to his messages, writing down the important ones and erasing the ones from the American woman. There was no point for Jan to have a girlfriend in another country. He needed one here. And if she had anything to say about it, she knew exactly who it was going to be. Someone with long silky brown hair like Jan's ex-wife and herself. If Jan had a type, she guessed she was it. If she wasn't, she would find a way to become it.

On Friday she told Wit she might as well cover the weekend and Monday too, as she'd grown fond of Snorry and enjoyed walking him. Wit shrugged and readily agreed.

KATI WAS JUST days away from the Budapest conference. The planning for Coral Gables in December was piling up on her too. She tried not to think about Jan every second of the day, but every afternoon before leaving her office, she called his home and left another message on his machine, telling him she missed him and asking how Dirk was.

She'd had a chance to tell the sports injury specialist a bit about Dirk during their calls to prepare the doctor's remarks for the conference. He promised her he would speak to Jan personally in Budapest, and introduce him to one of his colleagues in particular who'd had some success in helping accident victims regain use of their limbs. Kati could hardly wait.

She dropped by a church on her way home from her office almost every evening to pray for Dirk's recovery and to ask God to tell Jan to call her. If he called, she would tell him she was ready to make some changes in her life so they could be together more frequently. Maybe the international conference business wasn't for her. It was time to think about a more settled life-style, so that she could accommodate her personal needs. She hoped Jan would give her another chance, wherever he was.

JAN CALLED HIS office almost every day to retrieve his messages. He didn't entirely trust Skyla to give him all his messages, so he also called home and using his remote access number, retrieved the messages on his home answering machine. Kati hadn't called. Not once. Apparently she hadn't called on his cell phone either, because he'd asked Wit to retrieve those messages and he hadn't reported any from Kati. Wit hadn't mentioned to Jan that he'd delegated this duty to Skyla who had been more than helpful in looking after Jan's affairs in his absence.

He was surprised. As much as he'd been angry at Kati, he'd expected her to call. Is this how American women broke up with their boyfriends? They just took up with the next one and disappeared? It must have been convenient that he lived across an ocean. It was so easy to dispose of him, when someone wealthier and more successful came along.

He was ready to cancel his trip to Budapest this year. He'd already spent two weeks unexpectedly out of work, and he wanted to be near Dirk while his leg was still healing. He called his travel agent and got the bad news that the trip was non-refundable. He talked with his son about what he should do.

"Take me to Budapest with you, Dad," Dirk pleaded. "Come on! We'll have fun."

"You've missed most of the fall semester of school already," Jan argued. "I can't just keep you out for another two weeks."

"Dad, what about the doctor you told me Kati booked to speak at her conference? The one who knows someone in Budapest who's helped paralyzed accident victims?"

"It'll have to wait." Jan didn't want to see Kati in any case, even if it was only about business. Or so he told himself.

"Why should it wait, Dad? My semester is completely messed up now. I'm not going to get back on track if I go back next week. Why don't you take me to Budapest so we can meet this doctor? Don't you want to see your girlfriend again?"

"She's not my girlfriend anymore," he snapped at his son.

"She's not? When did you break it off with her?" Dirk looked up surprised. Then his expression turned to disappointment.

Had his son come to care for Kati too?

"I didn't. She broke it off with me," Jan barked. "Okay? Don't ask me any more questions."

"When did she break it off with you?" Dirk demanded. "I thought she was coming here at the end of September. Tell me what happened, Dad. I'm eleven. I can understand."

"Right. You're eleven and you can't understand. End of story."

"It's not the end until you tell me what happened."

The boy stared him down, until Jan had to look away.

"Alright, I'll tell you. I don't know what happened. She just disappeared. She couldn't come over at the end of September after all, so I thought I'd go over to New York for the weekend. I called her to let her know and a man answered the phone."

"And?"

"And he said she wasn't there at the moment, could he take a message? I called her the next night and the next. The same man answered the phone. Every night he said she'd be back soon. What was I supposed to think? I finally heard from her the Sunday you broke your leg. She called and I was about to call her back when your stepfather rang to let me know what happened. I ran out the door without my cell phone and didn't get around to calling her back."

"Dad, how could you not call her back? Don't you like her?"

"What about that man in her apartment night after night?"

"What about him? How do you know she was there too? Maybe he was staying there and she was staying somewhere else. How could you not even give her a chance to explain?"

"The man who answered her phone was someone she knew from Budapest. I met him there right after I first met her. He was some sort of friend of hers. He took her out one night when we were just getting to know each other. Now I know he was more than a friend."

"How can you know that, Dad? Did she tell you herself?" Dirk frowned.

"How can you keep coming up with all these questions? What are you—an investigative reporter?" Gruffly, Jan ruffled his son's hair. "Let's watch some TV."

Perhaps the boy was right. He needed to at least have a conversation with Kati. But why hadn't she called all these weeks?

The next day, he called the principal of Dirk's school in Arnhem. The principal was relieved to hear Dirk's leg was healing well and happy to either let Dirk come back to class the following week or to take another few weeks off, in which case he would give Jan Dirk's course books and homework assignments to help the boy keep up with his class until he returned.

Jan thanked him and said he'd get back in touch with his decision.

Then he called his office.

"How are things going, Wit?"

"Things are going okay here," his colleague told him. "Skyla's been great, looking after your dog and taking care of your house. We've got our hands full with the programs, but we're following the same format we used last year for the fall season."

"Can I afford to take those two weeks off that I was going to take to go to Budapest? I'm thinking of taking Dirk with me to see a doctor there."

"Man, you can do it. Everyone understands your situation here," Wit reassured him. "Do what you need to do. Just get back in time for the Christmas party. We'll need your help then."

"You got it. We'll be back before the first of December. You're my right hand man."

"I can't take total credit. Skyla's been knocking herself out for you, just to let you know," Wit said.

"Yeah. Well thank her for me." Jan felt sick at the thought. She was a knockout alright. She just didn't knock him out. Instead, the woman who did no longer seemed interested in the job.

He got off the phone and thought. Dirk was still in his physical therapy session, so this was his opportunity to call Kati. At three in the afternoon in Holland, she would be in her office in the morning in New York. Getting her voicemail, he remembered she had a ten A.M. meeting a few times each week.

"Kati, it's Jan. We need to talk. I don't have my cell phone here with me, but you can find me at 31-23-531-9091, room 314. Goodbye."

Kati still had a hold on his heart. It was time to clear the air and find out once and for all if she'd really moved on. If she had, it would be a long time before he gave his heart again to any woman.

# CHAPTER SIXTEEN

# BUDAPEST ONE YEAR LATER

THE NEXT WEEK, Jan and Dirk flew to Budapest. Jan stared out the window of the cab into the city at the drizzly, gray sky. It matched his mood exactly. Kati had called back the evening of the day he'd left a message for her, but their conversation had been strained. It had sounded like she was drowning in work. Someone had come into her office within the first minute of their exchange and she had had to get off abruptly. He had called her again the next day to find her out, then when she'd called back, he'd been with Dirk in a consultation with his doctor.

Was a long distance relationship realistic? Especially with a woman who offered her apartment to a male friend? He didn't care how many favors Krisztof had done for her, he didn't feel comfortable with Kati's friendship with this man. How could he be sure of what was really going on?

He couldn't even remember what hotel Kati had said she was holding her conference at. Come to think of it, she hadn't mentioned the hotel, she'd been so busy telling him about the doctor she'd engaged to speak who might have some ideas on new therapies for Dirk. If so, nothing would stop him from meeting with this doctor to see what he could do for Dirk. He would just keep things between himself and Kati on a business level. That was—if he could find her at all. She was always so busy behind the scenes during these conferences.

They checked into their hotel, then went down to the thermal pools to soak. Dirk loved the atmosphere.

"Dad, the girls here are really cute," the eleven-year-old commented, looking as if he was wondering how he could start up a conversation with one of them. It was hard enough to talk to girls in his own language, never mind Hungarian.

Jan didn't have eyes for any Hungarian girls. All he could think about were the conversations he'd had with Kati almost one year earlier in the same pool he was floating in now with his son. What had happened? He'd never trust a woman again.

After a few hours, they went upstairs to their room, ordered room service and watched some TV. Pretty soon Dirk was nodding out. Jan switched off the TV, but couldn't sleep. How was he going to locate Kati? He'd tried calling her on her cell phone, but kept getting her voicemail. Either she was on an airplane to Budapest and inaccessible or already on stage at the conference moderating a panel, with her cell phone shut off.

He decided to go down to the lobby to call Kati's mother in New York. It was too late to call Kati's office, as it would be after five there. He didn't know any of her office colleagues anyways, so who would he ask to speak with? But he had her mother's number, which she'd given him the evening they'd all gone out for Ethiopian food the April before. He remembered her name was Elizabeth, the same name in English as his own mother's, Lijsbeth.

In the lobby, he bought an international calling card and dialed the number in New York.

"Hello?" Kati's mother answered.

"Hello, is this Elizabeth?"

"Yes. Is that you, Jan?" The woman's voice was friendly.

"Yes. It's me. I'm in Budapest trying to find Kati and I can't remember the name of the hotel where she's having her conference."

"The Hilton. The Budapest Hilton, I think. Kati told me she'd gotten a great room rate there when she stayed with me in September."

"She—when she stayed with you in September?" Had he heard Kati's mother correctly?

"Yes. Her friend Krisztof Nagy came into town and couldn't find a hotel room anywhere. Kati gave him her place for a week and came down and stayed with me. She told me all about her plans for the conference. Did she mention the doctor to you she booked who might be able to help your son?"

"Uh—yes, she did mention him. We've had some trouble reaching each other recently, so that's why I didn't have the name of her hotel."

"I'm sorry. Well, by all means find her at the Budapest Hilton. She talked about you and Dirk non-stop while she stayed with me and we both thought this doctor might have some ideas on special treatments for him. I think his name was Csordás."

Jan got off the phone. Had it been possible that Kati had really been at her mother's place after all, the week that Krisztof had stayed at her apartment? Then why had Krisztof said she'd be there in a minute the first time he'd called? The following night the man had said she'd be back soon when he had asked for her. Where had she actually been?

He needed to find Kati and get an explanation from her as soon as possible. If she confirmed what her mother had just told him, he was going to have some major apologizing to do. Maybe she hadn't slept with that rich, Hungarian jerk. Jan's face flamed as he thought of Skyla sneaking into his tent on the camping trip. Thank God he hadn't succumbed to her.

He ran upstairs to his room, filled with confusion, guilt, anger and a tiny glimmer of hope. He wished he could hop in a cab and go over to the Hilton that very moment, but he couldn't leave Dirk alone in a hotel room for more than a few minutes. What if he fell out of bed and broke his leg again? Jan's heart contracted at the thought.

The following morning, Jan took a cab with Dirk to meet his Dutch-speaking Hungarian friend Sandor Toklas at the Gellért Baths. Sandor was eager to try some of the massage techniques on the boy that Jan, Kati and he had worked on together the previous December.

As soon as Jan dropped Dirk off, he rushed to the Budapest Hilton, where he was told that the conference on Rehabilitative Treatments for Sports Injuries was going on in the Grand Ballroom on the second level of the hotel. Taking the stairs two at a time, he bounded up to the foyer and introduced himself to one of Kati's colleagues at the registration desk outside the thick double doors of the Grand Ballroom.

"Excuse me. I'm Jan Klassen, a friend of Kati Dunai's. Could you tell me where I might find her now?"

"She's on stage at the moment." The assistant eyeballed him curiously. "The morning session will end in about thirty minutes. Why don't you wait here until then?"

"Thank you, but Ms. Dunai mentioned to me that a Hungarian doctor will be speaking today whom I should meet. Do you know if he's on stage now?"

The conference assistant looked at the agenda then up at Jan. "Yes, Dr. Csordás is speaking now."

"That's him. Would you mind if I slipped in and stood in back so I can hear him?"

"Did you say you were Jan Klassen from Holland?" The assistant asked, peering at him more closely.

"Yes. I am." He hadn't said where he was from, but apparently Kati's colleague had heard about him already.

"Kati mentioned you to me." She smiled. "Let me see if I can find a guest pass for you so you can pass through security."

He felt elated, then confused. Her office colleague knew who he was. Had Kati told her he was her boyfriend? If he still was, then why hadn't she called him when Dirk had been in the hospital? Or had she, and someone had intercepted the messages?

For the first time it dawned on him that Skyla had had access to both his cell phone and his home phone while he'd been at the rehabilitation clinic.

"The session is almost over, so you're only going to catch Dr. Csordás's finishing remarks," the attendant mentioned.

"That's fine. Thank you." He clipped on the guest pass, then slipped through the double doors to the ballroom.

The room was packed with what looked to be hundreds of people. Far away onstage, a man stood at a podium speaking into a microphone, while two people sat on either side of him. One was another man and the other was Kati.

Jan's heart leaped. Flattening himself against the back wall of the ballroom, he glued his eyes to her. His Kati was on stage conducting a panel in front of a huge crowd. He couldn't tear his eyes from her. She wore a crisp dark suit and high-heeled shoes. Her legs were crossed and what fine legs they were. But her face wore a distracted expression. He willed her to look at him. Instead, she stared off into space, looking as if she had lost something.

KATI'S THOUGHTS WERE far from what was taking place on stage. She couldn't get Jan out of her mind. Here she was, in Budapest, the result of months' worth of planning and hard work, and the whole point of coming here had been to spend time with the man she had met and fallen in love with one year ago in the same spot.

Instead, here she was, Kati Dunai—international business-woman, lucky in work and unlucky in love. She would throw it all in for a chance to be with Jan Klassen again. But apparently he'd moved on, judging by his silence and the insinuations of his office colleague, the good looking Dutch girl she'd met at his office. She couldn't believe he hadn't even had the decency to call to let her know it was all over. Looking up, she decided to put him out of her mind, and focus on what she might ask the speaker in the question and answer period following his remarks.

Idly, she scanned the room. A tall man had come in and was standing against the back wall. He was dressed oddly, the only man in the room without a suit jacket on. Instead he wore a plaid shirt. He looked a lot like—like—

Jan.

Kati gasped. Then she remembered where she was. What was he doing here? She looked at him, frowning. Was he smiling at her? What audacity. That bastard had the nerve to show up in the middle of her conference just to completely unsettle her and throw her off her professional duties. Then he had the cheek to smile at her.

Why hadn't he returned her calls for five weeks, then finally called to say they had to talk? Couldn't he at least have had the decency to let her know he was dumping her? Most likely for that Dutch chick in his office, too.

Her face grew warmer. She looked down at the stage floor to compose herself. She couldn't let herself get thrown off course now. This was the panel she'd put together to gain some insights that might help Dirk. She struggled to put aside her personal feelings for Jan at the moment. He was not the man she had hoped him to be, but his son was a sweet boy who needed help. Silently, she formulated a few questions to ask Dr. Csordás, who was concluding his remarks at that moment.

The audience applauded and she rose, willing herself not to look in Jan's direction. She would kill him if she ever got her hands on him. The fact that he'd just smiled at her really made her sick. Was he insane? How did he think she felt at this moment?

She carefully scanned the audience for questions. There were one or two. Then no further hands were raised, so she turned to Dr. Csordás herself.

"Doctor, can you tell me if your therapies for injured athletes could have application for people who've been injured in other ways—for example in car or motorcycle accidents?" Why had she mentioned motorcycle accidents? The words had just popped out.

"I suppose so. In the case of someone who's been in a car accident, if the same group of muscles and nerves that were damaged were those that might be damaged on the playing field, we would apply similar therapies," the doctor replied.

"I see. Can you tell me if there might be any particular profile for a patient most likely to have a successful response to your treatments?"

"It's hard to generalize, as it completely depends on the severity of the injury. But one could say, in general, the younger the patient, the more likely a successful outcome can be achieved. When a person is still growing, their bones, muscles and nerves are still in a dynamic state. We can effect a positive outcome more frequently with children than with adults." The doctor paused. "But as I said, one cannot generalize. It all depends on the specific case."

"Thank you, Dr. Csordás." She turned to the audience, unable to keep herself from looking in Jan's direction. "Let's give our panel a final round of applause for sharing their expertise with us today." She ignored the thunderous applause as her eyes locked with Jan's.

He looked sorrowful, almost ready to cry.

He deserved to cry. She'd knocked herself out for this moment, and now that it had come, all they had left between them was a shared concern over his son's condition.

Dr. Csordás's panel had been the final one before lunch. Conference attendees began to stream out of the room, except for a lone man in a plaid shirt fighting his way through the crowd toward the stage.

Kati wanted to run. This wasn't a good place to break down and start crying. She needed to get away fast. On her way to the side exit door, Dr. Csordás tapped her arm, thanking her for having him on her program. He reminded her that she'd mentioned a specific case to him involving a young Dutch boy. He wanted to know if the Dutch boy happened to be here in Budapest.

"No, I don't think so. But, his father is here."

"Oh, really? I'd like to have a word with him. Would you give him my business card?" He reached inside his suit jacket to retrieve a card to hand to her.

"Thank you. I'll take it directly. And thank you, Ms. Dunai, for asking those questions on my son's behalf at the end of the panel."

Jan's deep voice sliced into Kati's heart like a knife.

"Dr. Csordás, I'm Jan Klassen from Holland. Ms. Dunai told me you might have some ideas on treating my son Dirk." He bowed to the doctor.

The strangest combination of conflicting emotions Kati had ever experienced battled within her. She wanted to beat Jan Klassen to a pulp. She also wanted to get help for his son. She wanted an explanation, but also something more from the man who stood less than two feet away from her. Much more.

Jan gave her a lingering look as he raised his head after bowing to the doctor. His eyes seemed filled with regret. Something else too. Was it longing?

"Hello, Mr. Klassen," she said, frostily. "I didn't expect to see you here."

"Hello, Ms. Dunai. I remember you mentioning Dr. Csordás to me." He turned to the doctor. "I'm very glad to meet you."

"As I was saying to Ms. Dunai, it's a shame your boy isn't here in Budapest with you," Dr. Csordás replied. "I have a professional colleague who specializes in pediatric paralysis who'd be interested in his case."

"My boy is here with me. I decided to bring him along after our plans changed last month." He stared intently at Kati, who looked back at him dumbfounded.

"Dirk is here?" she asked.

"Yes, he's over with our friend Sandor at the Gellért Baths right now."

*Our* friend? The man standing before her hadn't returned a single one of her phone calls for five weeks, then had finally called to say they needed to talk. He hadn't even bothered to acknowledge her trip to Beekbergen to find him. What did he mean by *our* friend?

Completely at a loss, she couldn't speak.

"Call Dr. Kovacs this afternoon after three." Dr. Csordás jotted down the name and telephone number of his colleague and handed it to Jan. "I'm going back to my office now, and I'll call him immediately to tell him you're in town and your son is with you. I've already spoken to him about the case."

"Thank you," Jan said simply. Then he looked at her. "May I have a word with you?"

She ignored him, turning to Dr. Csordás.

"Thank you for speaking to our group today. We've been honored to have you give us your time. Will you be able to join us for lunch in the Crystal Room?"

"Regretfully no, Ms. Dunai, I've got to get back to my office. It's been a pleasure." He bent over and kissed her hand.

Over his head, Kati glanced at Jan, her eyes filled with hurt and anger.

He met her glance with the same attentive eyes he'd fixed on her almost one year ago; they captured her completely, unfairly.

She hated him. Especially for having that same firm gaze.

The doctor left them, and they stared at each other, motionless. She had no idea what to say or where to start.

"Let's go somewhere we can talk," Jan said, finally. "I need to tell you something."

Her heart fell. This was going to be it, the final scene. Who was the something he needed to tell her about? The Dutch girl back in his office? Someone else? She had only herself to blame, not having given enough of her time to the man she'd wanted to be part of her life.

They exited the ballroom from a side door and found themselves in a corridor. Walking down it, Jan put his hand on the small of her back.

"What do you think you're doing?" She jerked away from him.

Jan answered calmly. "I think I'm getting ready to make an apology."

"Well, let's find a private room. I don't really feel like crying right out here in the hallway while someone from my conference walks by," she snapped.

They ducked into a small salon with elegant French windows and Louis Quinze gold gilt chairs. It looked a most fitting spot in which to have her heart irrevocably broken.

She sat while Jan closed and bolted the door behind them.

He pulled up a chair and sat directly in front of her.

She hung her head.

He cleared his throat. "Kati, look at me. I made a mistake."

"What mistake, Jan?" She assumed he meant something to do with that girl back in his office. Or some other woman.

"I mistrusted you. I thought you and Krisztof were together in New York in September."

"What do you mean, together?" She tried to keep her voice low, but it rose uncontrollably. "He came to New York on business and I let him stay in my apartment while I went down and stayed with my mother. I told you he was coming and that I'd be at my mom's. You didn't even call me the entire week."

"I did call you. I tried to reach you at your mother's apartment on Monday evening and got her answering machine. So I tried calling you on what I thought was your cell, but I mixed it up with your home number. Your friend said you'd be there in a minute. What was that all about, then?"

"I have no idea, Jan. I was at my mother's place the entire time Krisztof was in town." She hung her head, then looked up, her eyes wide. "Did you say Monday night?"

"Yes."

"Monday evening Krisztof took my mother and I out to dinner. We were probably on our way over to pick him up when you called my apartment. That's why he said I'd be there soon." Kati's brows knit together stormily. "My mom had a power outage at her place that evening. When we got back, the electricity was back on, but the messages on her machine had all been erased. Why didn't you call me on my cell phone anyways?"

"I was going to, but I couldn't remember which was the cell and which was your home number. The next day I called your mother's place again and got the answering machine. So I called the second number I had for you and got your apartment. Your friend said you'd be back soon. He said the same thing the next day too."

Jan looked at Kati sternly then continued. "I got angry. It occurred to me that maybe you hadn't gone down to your mother's place to stay after all."

"Jan, how could you not trust me? Why didn't you call me in my office? Or on my cell?" Kati wondered what game Krisztof had been up to by insinuating that she was about to come back soon when Jan had called her at her place. She would have a word with him very soon.

"Kati, I'm sorry. I didn't like you letting your businessman friend stay at your place. It didn't make me feel too good."

"Jan, he's done me a zillion favors, including helping me hold this conference here in Budapest so you and I could be together..." Her voice trailed off. She hadn't spent a lot of time considering Jan's feelings about her letting Krisztof stay over. She had just overruled his feelings in her desire to do a favor for the friend who had done so many for her. Maybe that hadn't been wise, not to mention insensitive.

"I'm sorry," she said in a small voice.

"I didn't know for sure you were at your mother's until I called her last night to find out which hotel you were at in Budapest. She told me you'd stayed with her the entire week, and you'd talked about the doctor you booked who might be able to help Dirk. I'm sorry, Kati, I just didn't think. I mean— I thought the wrong thing." His blue green eyes cast grayish now; they were beginning to mist over.

"How could you think the wrong thing, Jan? Don't you know I love you?" She hadn't meant to say that. She hated him, right? She—she —

He pulled her into his arms and hugged her fiercely, his chest heaving against her head. She didn't want to succumb, but his scent was all around her, overpowering her defenses. She melted against him. Then she remembered his cruel silence. She pulled back.

"What about my calls? Why didn't you call me back? Couldn't you even bother with one phone conversation to find out where I was when Krisztof was at my apartment?"

"I—I got a message from you the day Dirk broke his leg again. I was about to call you when the phone rang and I found out he'd had an accident. Then I had to rush to the hospital. The day after I took Dirk to the rehab clinic where we spent the next eighteen days. I called in for my messages every day but you never called once. I figured you'd dumped me for that Hungarian guy."

"Never, Jan. No way." She shuddered to think of dropping Jan for anyone, never mind her multi-tasking, permanently distracted friend. "I called you every single day. Both at home and on your cell phone. Are you crazy? I came to Beekbergen looking for you. I left messages everywhere."

"Kati, you flew to Holland to find me? You're kidding." Jan's eyes widened, his face one big question mark.

Had no one told him she had been there looking for him?

"I had no idea you were in Holland trying to find me," he went on. "How many days were you there and when?"

"The worst weekend of my life, Jan, that's when. It was hell. I left a note on your door, a note on your friend Hans' door, gave a note to your wife and dropped by your office, where some bombshell colleague of yours told me what a nice time she had camping with you. What were you doing camping with a woman anyways? And why didn't you ever answer your cell phone?" She shoved him back into his chair. Then she stomped on his foot.

"Ouch. Calm down. I went camping that weekend because I was mad at you. I'd wanted to surprise you and come visit you in New York. But when I called to let you know I was going to jump on a flight, your rich businessman friend answered the phone and told me you'd be back soon. He glared at her, his brows knit together in a single line. "I'm not in the habit of being someone's second helpings, Kati."

"You're not and you never have been," Kati stormed. "And Krisztof's not rich. He's just trying to become rich." She thought to herself how very poor Krisztof was in his ability to give his time and attention to anyone outside of his professional life. "That's why he needed to stay at my place. The only hotel rooms left in Manhattan that week were $1,000 a night suites at the Pierre." She looked daggers at Jan. "Don't try to change the subject. What about that camping trip you went on? What about that Dutch girl working in your office? Wasn't she with you?"

"What about her? Maybe she's got a crush on me, that's all. I could care less, Kati. Okay, I admit I didn't feel like answering my cell phone the weekend I went camping because I was mad. When I got back I found out Dirk had had an accident and I had to get to him right away. But I waited to hear from you week after week, and you never called. I know because I called in for my messages every day while I was with Dirk at the clinic outside Amsterdam. I forgot my cell phone in the van on the way back from the camping trip, so I didn't have it with me. Why didn't you call me?" Jan was getting steamed up again.

"I did call you." Kati punched her thigh with her fist in frustration. "Every night I left a message at your house asking you to call me and apologizing for not coming to visit you on my way back from Lisbon. I called you again and again on your cell phone but you never picked up. After awhile, I got a message saying your voice mailbox was full and I couldn't leave any more messages. I realized I hadn't made enough time for us, Jan. I'm sorry."

"Kati, something happened to those messages. I never got any of them." He looked puzzled for a moment, then nodded slowly, his mouth set in a grim line. "Wit told me that Skyla walked Snorry every morning I was away. I'll bet she also listened to my answering machine every morning and erased your messages for reasons I can only guess."

"Well, I can guess too," Kati said, remembering the smug, sweet air of the attractive brunette in Jan's office.

"She probably erased your messages on my cell phone as well. When I get home I'm going to arrange a transfer for her to another social services office far from Beekbergen."

"You would do that?" Kati asked wide-eyed.

"For you I would do anything. Now what did you intend to do about your discovery that you weren't making enough time for us?" he asked.

"Make more time for us," she said, meaning it with all of her heart.

"What about your job?"

"I hate my job," she blurted out.

"You do? I thought you loved your job."

"I don't. Not anymore. Not since I lost you. I wish I'd lost my job instead."

"Kati?"

"What?"

"You haven't lost me."

"I haven't?"

"No."

"What about what happened with Skyla?" she demanded.

"So I went on a camping trip with her. There were six other people with us too. I didn't sleep with her, Kati." Jan was yelling now.

"You didn't?" she asked in a tiny voice.

"No," he roared. Then, gathering steam, he volleyed back. "What about your rich businessman friend?"

"He's poor, Jan."

"What do you mean, poor? Too poor to be able to afford a hotel room when he comes to New York on business?"

"Jan, I made a mistake too. I didn't realize how upsetting it would be to you for me to let Krisztof stay at my place. I just assumed you knew how uninterested I am and always have been in him."

"Are you sure about that?"

"I'm sure."

"I thought maybe you liked rich men." His face was a study in uncertainty.

Kati paused. Then she gave him a sly smile. "I do."

"So why don't you prefer him to me?"

"I told you already. He's poor. And you're rich."

Jan looked flummoxed. "I am?"

"Yes. You are." She beamed at him. "Jan—you have time for me. You always have. When we're together, I know I'm your total focus. I told you how much I appreciated that in Budapest. That's what I mean by you being rich. You're rich in spirit and in really sharing yourself with me."

"I am?" Jan's eyes widened. He shook his head in confusion.

"Yes, you are. And what you don't know is how special your qualities are. Krisztof has been a great friend to me, but he can't focus on anything for more than a nanosecond."

"A nanosecond?" Jan asked. "What's that supposed to mean?"

"It means he's in three different places every time we have a conversation. He can't keep a plan, he can't even wait to listen to the end of a sentence. He's very busy all the time and it ultimately undid his marriage. I tried to introduce him to my downstairs neighbor and he cancelled the date at the last minute because of some business thing that came up." She snorted derisively.

"Jan, you have no idea how boring some men can be," Kati continued. "If he had all the money in the world, it wouldn't make any difference. Whatever woman he ends up dating, I guarantee you she'll be unhappy no matter how much money he spends on her." She took a deep breath then looked him straight in the eye. "I want to be with someone who gives me his time. And I don't mean taking me to a fancy restaurant then spending the whole time taking business calls on a cell phone."

Her heartfelt words seemed to fall on receptive ears. They stared at each other for a long moment.

Finally, Jan cocked his eyebrows. "Forgiven?"

Kati cocked hers too. "Forgiven?"

They both nodded their heads and smiled at each other.

She went over and stood in front of him, encircling him with her arms. He buried his head against her for a long moment of total surrender.

"Kati ..."

"What?"

"I love you."

"I love you too, Jan."

They melted into each other's arms, at peace with and completed by each other.

# CHAPTER SEVENTEEN

# THE SZÉCHENYI

# BATHS–AGAIN

KATI'S CONFERENCE WAS over at the end of the afternoon. Jan needed to pick up Dirk at the Gellért Baths, then call the doctor whose name he'd been given by Dr. Csordás. They made a plan to meet that evening.

Kati spent the afternoon with a glow on her face and in her heart. Her emotions had been so tossed around over the past month that she couldn't wait to wrap up the conference and run into Jan's arms again before something else happened to come between them. Luckily, she hadn't cancelled the days off she had put in for after the conference. She had been so exhausted and emotionally spent that she'd thought she'd just spend them quietly in Budapest by herself.

Now everything had changed and once again her heart was on fire.

The conference ended promptly at five. Within fifteen minutes, she was in a cab on the way over to the thermal bath hotel where she'd met Jan almost one year earlier. She hurried up to Jan's and Dirk's room, where she found a note on the door for her. It read "Downstairs in the lounge playing ping pong. Join us. J & D."

She ran down to the lounge where Dirk was beating his father at a game of ping pong. Rushing over to the boy, she gave him an enormous hug; the boy tentatively returned it. Then she turned to Jan, who kissed her forcefully, forgetting his son for a moment.

"I called Dr. Kovacs. He wants me to bring Dirk over tomorrow at two. He's going to put him through some tests that'll take a few hours. His office said they prefer if I don't stay, so I'm supposed to go back and get him around five. Will you come with me?"

"Of course I'm coming with you. You're the only reason I'm here in Budapest as of right now." She turned to Dirk. "And you."

"Don't worry, Kati," the boy said. "I know you're here because of Dad. Try not to have any more big fights okay? He was really cranky when you weren't talking to each other." He lobbed a ping pong ball toward her, hitting her neatly on the arm.

She smiled, thrilled to see Dirk's regard for her hadn't changed.

"Dirk, could you hang out here for a minute by yourself?" Jan asked.

"Sure, Dad."

Jan took Kati's arm and walked out into the lobby with her. "Let's see if we can book another room for us."

At the front desk they were told there was nothing available for that night, but on the morrow, a suite would be available for the next three nights.

"We'll take it," he said.

The desk clerk smiled. "It's our honeymoon suite, with a private Jacuzzi bath and very nice decor. Would you like to see it first?"

Jan turned to Kati, smiling. "Sound good to you, darling?"

She blushed. "Sounds perfect." Turning to the desk clerk, she said, "We don't need to see it, we'll take it."

"For the whole three days," Jan added.

The desk clerk nodded. "Very good, sir."

Making their way back to Dirk, Jan pulled Kati into one of the private phone booths lining an out of the way corridor. Pulling her onto his lap, he shut the door.

"Kati …"

"Yes, darling."

"I have an idea about tomorrow—"

"I know what it is," she broke in.

"You do?"

"You want to go to the Széchenyi Baths while Dirk's at his appointment."

"Yes!" Jan's face lit up. "How did you know?"

"We talked about it in the cab on the way to the airport last year the day you left me here," she reminded him as she ran her fingertip down his arm.

"I didn't leave you here. You told me to catch that flight the day before yours."

"I'm just kidding," she laughed. "But don't leave me again, okay?"

"Don't worry." He squeezed her until she couldn't breathe. "Just try and figure out what you're going to do about finding time to be with me."

"I will." She meant it too. She was ready for a change.

That evening they dined with Dirk at the hotel, then she returned for one final night's stay at the Budapest Hilton. Dizzy with desire, she sensed Jan felt the same way, but with Dirk in the picture, they would have to hang onto their emotions for one night longer.

THAT NIGHT, JAN lay in bed thinking about all that had transpired in the past year since he'd met Kati. He thought about his pain of the month before. She'd told him earlier that day that she hated her job. He wasn't sure if he believed her. She'd also told him she loved him. He was sure he believed her on that point. It was time to do something about their feelings for each other.

Closing his eyes, he made a plan for their time together the next day. He would take a chance and see what happened. If Kati really loved him, she would take a chance too.

The following morning, he called his friend Sandor at the Gellért Baths and asked him for a favor. Jan had offered the man a place to stay when he'd been a student in Holland. Now Sandor was only too happy to help him out with his plan. He agreed to meet them at the doctor's office at two, then stay with Dirk for the duration of his appointment, where his bilingual skills in Dutch and Hungarian would come in handy. He would bunk with Dirk for the next few nights over at Dirk's hotel, taking Jan's place as his roommate. Jan could spend time with Kati without worrying about his son and Sandor would be able to continue working on Dirk.

KATI AWOKE THE next morning and packed her bags. She had one final piece of business to take care of before leaving her hotel room. Picking up the phone, she punched in a local number.

"Kati, how nice to hear from you!" Krisztof's voice rang out. "Where are you?"

"Krisztof, I need to know something," she answered, ignoring his question.

"What is it?" Her friend's voice tightened.

"Did a man call for me at my apartment while you were staying there in September?"

"Uh—yes. I think someone did call for you once or twice."

"Or three times?"

"Yes, it might have been."

"How could you have not told me I had calls?"

"I meant to, Kati. I was planning to tell you, but things were hectic and I kept getting interrupted. Plus he never identified himself so I couldn't even tell you who'd called."

"That was my boyfriend calling from Holland, Krisztof. The one you met at my hotel in Budapest last year. You almost cost me my relationship with him."

"You're kidding." He seemed genuinely surprised. "Why didn't he just call you on your cell phone?"

"I told him you would be staying at my place and he wasn't happy about it. He called my apartment the first time by accident. He'd mixed up my home number with my cell phone number. He told me you told him I'd be back soon. What did you mean by that?" Kati demanded. "Why did you mislead him?"

"I—uh—think you may have been arriving soon the first time he called. Then the second and third times I thought it was really none of his business where you were, since if it was, you would have told him directly."

"Krisztof, you should have told me he called and you shouldn't have told him I'd be right back. It was either very thoughtless of you or very calculating. Either way, I don't like what you did."

"Kati, darling, I'm so sorry. I had no idea this man had any importance for you."

"I'm not your darling, I'm his. And I want to be his wife one day, so I'm sorry too, Krisztof. I'm not going to be able to offer you my apartment again when you come to New York."

"Kati, I don't know what to say. I didn't think. There were just too many things going on. Forgive me, please," Krisztof pleaded.

"I forgive you," she told him. "But you need to think about the consequences for you of too many things going on all the time in your life. Isn't all that activity getting in the way of you actually having a life?"

There was a long pause at the other end of the phone followed by something that sounded like a strangled choke.

"Krisztof," she continued more gently. "I think you need to slow down and focus on one thing at a time. Especially when it comes to women."

"Especially when it comes to women," he echoed in a disheartened voice. "Kati, are you in Budapest now? Could I see you? I'd like to make it up to you."

"No, Krisztof. Not this time. I'm busy here with the man I love. One hundred percent totally focused on and happy to be with him. Alone. See you some other time."

"All right, Kati. And once again, I'm sorry." He sounded sincere. She hoped he would absorb the lesson he appeared to have learned and apply it with another woman soon.

"Goodbye, Krisztof." She hung up, grabbed her suitcase, and hurried downstairs to get to the man of her dreams.

Kati arrived at Jan's and Dirk's hotel mid-morning. They breakfasted leisurely, then took a long taxi ride around Budapest, showing Dirk the places they'd visited together the November before.

Finally, it was time for the appointment. They picked up Sandor at the Gellért Hotel, then drove to an attractive stone house in one of Budapest's better neighborhoods. A small gold-lettered sign outside identified the clinic. They entered and Jan was given some paperwork to fill out. Kati idly picked up one of the business cards of the doctors in the practice at the reception desk.

"Jan, this Dr. Kovacs is 'Dr. Lazar Kovacs.' Doesn't that sound like the name of the man you helped on the promenade last November? The man who bit your hand?"

"Wasn't his name 'Kovach?'" Jan asked.

"I think so."

The nurse called them in. "Dr. Kovacs will see you now. Please come this way." She pronounced the doctor's name "Kovach." Jan glanced at Kati as he wheeled his son into the doctor's large private office. Sandor followed behind.

A dignified looking older man rose from behind the desk and greeted them. He shook Dirk's hand and motioned to Jan, Kati, and Sandor to sit.

Kati studied his face as they sat. It had been dark that night one year earlier; she couldn't be sure.

"I understand from my colleague, Dr. Csordás, that you had a motorcycle accident a few years ago in which your legs were crushed," he addressed Dirk directly.

"Yes, sir," the boy replied.

"We're going to spend the next few hours doing some exercises. Will that be okay with you?"

"Will they hurt?" Dirk looked at him anxiously.

"No, they won't. And my staff here is very pretty, so I think you'll be in good hands." The doctor looked up at Jan, signaling for him and Kati to leave.

Kati looked intently at the doctor's face.

"Doctor, could we have a word with you?" she asked.

"Of course." Dr. Kovacs came with them to the door, closing it behind him as they stepped out into the hallway.

"Dr. Kovacs," Kati began, "one year ago we were here in Budapest. Jan helped a man having a seizure on the Pest promenade near the entrance to the Margit Bridge. It was a Thursday night, toward the end of November."

Dr. Kovacs' face became pale. "*Istenem,*" he said quietly, studying Jan.

Kati recognized the word. Her father had used it from time to time, only in serious moments. It meant "My God."

Jan gave the doctor a small smile, saying nothing.

Kati continued. "When the police arrived, we heard the officer say the name of the man."

"You saved my life." Lazar Kovacs turned to Jan. "It was you who saved my life."

"I just managed to clear your airway until help arrived." Jan looked abashed.

"When I thanked the police, they told me that a foreigner had stopped to help me and had gotten his hand cut when I bit him. I tried to get your name from them, but they only knew you were from Holland."

"It's a small world, isn't it?" Jan said quietly.

"I will do everything I can to help your son. Go now and let me get started with him. And thank you, Mr. Klassen. We'll speak more about this later."

They said goodbye and exited the building. The afternoon was now theirs. What a remarkable coincidence to meet Dr. Lazar Kovacs again, only to discover he might be able to help Dirk. It was as if magic was happening all around them since their reconciliation.

Arm in arm, they walked to the Széchenyi Baths. The day was overcast and cold with an early winter chill in the air.

Holding hands, they strolled along the Pest promenade, stopping to kiss at every corner. They talked about the misunderstandings of the past month. Kati told Jan about the note she had left for him on Hans de Blij's door, which Hans hadn't mentioned.

"Do you think it might have blown away or gotten rained on?" Jan asked, his grip tightening on her arm. He looked upset.

"It had to be the rain. A huge storm hit as I was leaving. The rain probably washed away my message and the napkin I wrote it on as well."

His heart swelled when he thought of Kati coming all the way to Holland, then being thwarted in every effort she'd made to find him. What a rotten weekend it must have been for her.

He was irritated with both his ex-wife and his office mate for not having told him about her visit, but he knew they had had their reasons. In particular, he knew his ex-wife would have reason to worry that his relationship with an American woman might cause him to leave Holland and Dirk behind. He would never do that. But he could understand why she might have had reasonable cause not to want the father of her son involved with a woman who lived across the ocean. It was a legitimate concern, which he too shared. In fact, he'd thought about it all night long, the night before.

Arriving at the baths, Jan separated from Kati and headed into the men's locker room to change into his bathing suit. He was beginning to sweat, so he adjusted the shower water to a cooler setting. In a minute he met Kati at the entrance to the first pool, where they slid into the water, then paddled lazily until they reached the outdoor pool.

He slowly directed Kati to the far corner where they had shared their first kiss the year before. There they floated side by side, feeling lighter than air, breathing in the frosty air, while the twilight of early evening crept up on them.

After several minutes of perfect peace and stillness, Jan's heart was as full as the sky above them, where ripe clouds looked ready to burst. He was trying to steel himself for the life-changing chance he was about to take.

Underneath the water, Kati wordlessly took his hand. Just the encouragement he needed. It was as if she knew what he was thinking.

He turned to her and drank in her face for a long moment. Then his heart swelled. It was time.

"I want you to tell me something honestly, Kati. How important is your job to you?"

"I told you yesterday. Nowhere near as important to me as you. I figured that out this past month when I thought I'd lost you."

"Are you sure?" He studied her intently. The day before she'd also told him she loved him. It had made his heart sing. It had also given him a sleepless night.

"I never want to spend a month like last month again. It was horrible."

"Yes it was, and it can't happen again. We can't go on like this," he said.

"What do you mean?" She looked alarmed, her back stiffening.

He released her hand and put both of his around her back, drawing her to him.

"I mean it doesn't work with you in New York and me in Holland," he told her, meaning it with all of his heart.

"What do you mean, Jan? What should we do?" she whispered.

"Marry me, Kati."

Her eyes lit up. "In a heartbeat."

"Was that a yes?" he asked, puzzled.

"Yes. Yes, yes." She flung her arms around his neck, kissing him all over his face.

"And one more question," he continued.

"What is it? Whatever it is, the answer is 'yes.'"

"Good. Because when I get back to my office, I'm making some changes. There's going to be an opening for an assistant to help me put together parties and camping trips for the kids. Maybe even put on a conference or two every year. Are you available?"

"Yes." Her voice rang out joyfully. "I'm all yours, Jan."

"Good. Now kiss me again, then we'll go tell Dirk our news."

She threw herself into his arms, and as they kissed, Budapest's first snow of the season fell from the skies.

❧

Rozsa Gaston writes playful books on serious matters. Women getting what they want out of life is one of them. She studied European intellectual history at Yale, and then received her master's degree in international affairs from Columbia. In between, she worked as a singer/pianist all over the world. She lives in Bronxville, NY with her family.

Other books include *The Ava Series: Paris Adieu, Part I* and *Black is Not a Color, Part II, Running from Love, Dog Sitters* and *Lyric*. Her upcoming novel, *Sense of Touch,* is a fictionalized story of Anne of Brittany and Queen of France. Visit her at www. rozsagaston.com to learn more.